WHERE SHADOWS MEET

WHERE SHADOWS MEET

PATRICE CALDWELL

First published in the UK in 2025 by
HOT KEY BOOKS
an imprint of Bonnier Books UK
5th Floor, HYLO, 103-105 Bunhill Row, London, EC1Y 8LZ
Owned by Bonnier Books, Sveavägen 56, Stockholm, Sweden

Copyright © Patrice Caldwell, 2025

All rights reserved.
No part of this publication may be reproduced, stored or transmitted
in any form or by any means, electronic, mechanical, photocopying or
otherwise, without the prior written permission of the publisher.

The right of Patrice Caldwell to be identified as author of this work
has been asserted by them in accordance with the
Copyright, Designs and Patents Act 1988.

This is a work of fiction. Names, places, events and incidents are either the
products of the author's imagination or used fictitiously. Any resemblance
to actual persons, living or dead, is purely coincidental.

A CIP catalogue record for this book is available from the British Library.

ISBN: 978-1-4714-1186-1
Also available as an ebook and in audio

1

Typeset using Atomik ePublisher
Printed and bound in Great Britain by Clays Ltd, Elcograf S.p.A.

bonnierbooks.co.uk/HotKeyBooks

*To my younger self, who loved vampires and believed
in happily ever afters but doubted if she was deserving
of one—who tried to mold herself into someone
everyone would love. Everyone but herself.*

*You are enough just as you are.
This one's for those like you.*

*And to Sara, Vicki, and Vanessa. This book wouldn't have
become the story I needed it to be without you.*

Author's Note

Thank you for reading *Where Shadows Meet*, the first in a romantic fantasy duology featuring vampires, humans, and the gods that created them both. Fantasy and romance have, at many times, provided me with a much-needed escape as well as validation and catharsis. As such, it was important to me for my characters to reflect the world I've lived in and the things I've lived through—the struggles, joys, and everything in between. For the royal family tree and a guide to the vampire bloodlines, please see the back of the book.

Content Warnings

Please know that this story contains depictions of blood (including the drinking of blood), death (including that of multiple family members), kidnapping, psychological abuse, murder, systems of oppression (pulling from my family's history in the American South and the use of enslaved Black people as disposable labor but, of course, unfortunately relating to many different people across the world), and violence of all sorts. There's also a character who has self-harmed and shows and makes reference to those scars. The actual self-harm occurred years prior and is not depicted.

It's my hope that I've treated all this with care. Enjoy this book of my heart.

Sincerely,
Patrice

"... *He who eats My flesh and drinks My blood has eternal life.*"

—JOHN 6:54

Before

1,201 Years Ago: The Heavenly Realms

Once long ago in the Heavenly Realms, a princess in a gown of sunlight made her way through a floating forest.

Though it was her first visit, she walked with confidence. As if this overgrown forest of the southernmost realm was her home and not the glittering cloud castles of the eastern realms.

No one saw the princess arrive. No one bowed or cleared her path. There, she was treated like all other gods, which was to say, she was mostly ignored.

In the forest, there was usually only one god—*if* she could even be called that. The daughter of a human and a god, she was more outcast than anything else. As if respecting her self-imposed isolation, the forest had spread, consuming everything it touched around her. Except for a stream, a cottage, and a small graveyard the outcast visited each night.

The princess stopped when she happened upon that very same

stream. From behind a tree, she observed the girl who seemed so much a part of this place. The forest's spirit personified, the princess would've thought—if she didn't already know the truth.

The sun, beaming high overhead, kissed the outcast's dark-brown skin in a warm glow. She stood there naked; two giant, majestic wings sprang from her back. Wider than any the princess had ever seen. Stark white and glimmering, the wings dipped into the waters, shrouding the girl, protecting her, ever ready to whisk her away.

The princess watched as the girl parted her hair into four sections and brushed them, one by one. She half expected a song to come from the girl's lips and birds to dance in the air above her, chirping. But there were only the trickling stream, the rustling of the wind, and the girl detangling her thick, long, curly hair.

When the princess finally pulled her gaze away, stars were in the sky and the chill of night had settled. It was as if the girl had woven a spell and the princess had lost all track of time while caught in it.

Soon, the princess would be missed. Soon, her father would realize he hadn't seen his daughter all day. The last thing she needed was for the king of the gods to find out where she was. To suspect what she might be up to. Still, she hesitated to reveal herself. Once she did, there'd be no turning back.

She could easily return to where she came from and forget this girl. But there was nothing easy about forgetting, and the princess did not want to go back to the way things were, had been, and would always be with her father caring more about the next goddess he could lay with and her mother doing nothing to stop him. Soon enough, he'd have what he really wanted ever since her brother's death: a son who could replace her as his heir.

She had to take control of her destiny.

She had to act now.

She took a step forward and snapped a twig, at once breaking the spell.

The girl in the stream gasped, and her wings innocently wrapped around her. The two stared at each other, neither knowing what to say. Finally, the outcast broke the silence.

"Can you hand me my clothes?" she said in a clear voice. She gestured to the branch just above the princess where undergarments, a dress of handspun wool, and a leather belt hung.

The princess grasped the rough wool of the gown—so very different from the silks and satins she and the other royals and nobles wore—and stepped forward, holding the clothing out to the girl. The girl glided forth. Her water-pruned fingers brushed against the princess's soft, slender ones, causing small bumps to appear along the princess's arms and shivers to rush down her spine. The princess quickly withdrew and turned away before the girl could catch sight of the blush creeping up her cheeks. After a few moments, she peeked and found the girl was fully dressed.

Her green gown fit loosely, doing nothing to complement the curves the princess had glimpsed or the girl's skin, which glowed beautiful and blackish blue in the moonlight. The girl's wet curls fell over her shoulders and all the way down her back. She looked at the princess, a hard edge in her eyes. "If you expect me to bow—"

"I don't," said the princess, voice soft as if in a trance.

"You're a long way from home."

"I'm lost."

The girl threw her head back and laughed. The sound echoed throughout the forest, making the hairs on the princess's neck stand straight up. "The princess of the gods, lost in the very kingdom she'll one day rule?" She shook her head. "I'm no fool. Your family has taken enough from me. Let me live and die in peace." The outcast fastened the princess with her stare once more, her eyes dark, empty, and alone.

The girl was right. The princess had come there for a reason, a means to an end, but in the girl's eyes she saw something she wasn't expecting—an instant connection with a person she barely knew. She, too, was often alone. Used by others to get closer to her father, never seen for who she was, who she wanted to be—who she deserved to become.

"You're right. I'm not lost. But I'm also not my father. I—" The princess paused, unsure of how to explain what she was here for. "It's getting dark," she said instead. "I must get back. I'll return again."

"Whatever you say, your highness." The girl shrugged, trying to hide the shift in her eyes, but the princess seized on it: the smallest glimmer of hope.

The princess, Thana, went back every seventh morning. Her wash day, explained Favre, the outcast, the day she did her hair.

Every visit, Favre expected Thana to ask for something—like the gods who'd visited her mother always had. But Thana asked for nothing; she merely offered her company. And soon, Favre looked forward to those days. The ones when she wasn't so alone, when she had someone to speak to, to create dreams with. Still, she tried to hide her truest parts. But slowly, with time, Thana gained her trust. In her, Favre had found a friend, and soon after, a lover—a girl who also longed to be someone else, a girl shunned because she was misunderstood by all the rest.

One evening, Favre headed toward the graveyard she visited each night. She'd been telling her mother about Thana, about how happy Thana made her, about the small yet powerful joys her presence—and acceptance—brought her. She wished to see Thana always, but they had to be careful. Thana's father wouldn't like them seeing each other. And when people did *anything* the king of the gods didn't like, they wound up dead.

The graveyard was marked by a wrought-iron gate that towered over Favre. She held the only key. Just one person, her mother, was buried there. Far away from the gods who had used her mother for her powers; far away from the king who had let her mother die.

But when she approached, the lock was broken off. And standing there, placing roses onto a mound of dirt, was Thana.

Favre's chest tightened.

"What are you doing here?"

Seeing her there, uninvited, felt like a violation. Like Thana had forced herself where she didn't belong. Even the forest hadn't dared to creep there. It was as if Thana was reminding Favre that, no matter what, she was the princess of the gods, and thus owned this land. Nothing here belonged to Favre.

No. Favre took a deep breath, trying to calm herself. She *knew* Thana. Thana wouldn't do that . . . not intentionally. Thana, who had so much, likely hadn't thought twice about breaking the lock, hadn't considered how it would make Favre, who had so little, feel.

The graveyard was her place. Her sanctuary. And now something she had to share.

"I needed to see you." Thana closed the distance between them. She touched Favre's arm. Unlike the other times, she didn't ask first. She leaned in for a kiss.

Favre stumbled back, gripping the broken gate. "You could've met me at the—"

"I didn't have time to wait." Her voice was sharp, a tone she'd never used. A tone that the men who'd seduced her mother had used when they needed something from her and had grown tired of waiting for her to give it. A chill went up Favre's spine.

Favre's gaze raked across Thana. Her gown, usually made of silly, amusing things like starlight or flowers or even the air, was jet-black satin, like she was in mourning. Her hair, usually in neat braids with golden cuffs clipped onto each one, was wild, fanning out across her head. Her baby hairs were curled and damp at her temple. Tiny beads of sweat ran against her brown skin, cheeks flushed a deep shade of pink.

"We can't be together." Thana's voice cracked. "My younger siblings followed me. They spied on us and told my father." After that, Favre only heard snippets. How he gave Thana a choice: Favre or her crown. Kovnu wouldn't have a witch tainting *his* bloodline.

Witch. Thana's words rang through Favre's ears. Of course he'd called her that. Of course he'd spoken of her like that. *Like a disease.* When he was the one who plagued the Heavenly Realms.

Her blood surged; she wanted to scream.

All the hatred she had buried deep rose from within. All the rage she'd tried to tamp down.

Her mother had not been a good one; she'd cared more for powerful men than she had her own daughter. But still, she had been her mother—the only family Favre had ever had. Men like him, men like the king of the gods, had asked her mother for favors she could only grant with the power running through her blood, gifts her mother had thought it was her duty to bestow, magic that had cost her life. Kovnu had promised to save her, but he let her die in the end. *She's just a witch*, he'd said, while Favre begged, not worth the years off his own near-immortal life that resurrecting her would require.

If it weren't for Kovnu and his many broken promises, her mother would still be alive. If it weren't for the king, Favre wouldn't be alone. No one would ever choose her over a crown. She had to give Thana a third option. Quietly, she said, "We'll figure this out. Will you come back tomorrow? Tonight, I'd like to be alone."

After Thana was gone, Favre curled up beside her mother's grave. She looked to the sky, the night bright and clear. She could easily fly away from here. But what use was the freedom her wings gave if to claim it she must do so alone? As long as he was alive, Kovnu would find a way to ruin her life.

And so, she called upon the magic her mother had passed down, and it told her its price.

She dug into the ground beside her mother's grave and found the buried knife. Then, before she could change her mind, she hacked off her wings.

Her screams filled the forest. But no one heard. No one was there to hold her and tell her everything would be all right. No one stopped the pain or the blood streaming down her back and soaking into her mother's grave.

As she cried, her blood forged a weapon that could kill any god. The very wings that had once freed her would now free Thana, too, allowing them to be together for eternity.

The next night, Thana killed her father with the sword Favre had made.

She severed his head in one fatal swoop. But she didn't stop there.

She drank his blood, not wasting a drop. And as the blood filled her, it changed her into something else, into something *other* . . .

Had Favre been there, she would've seen the predatory gleam in Thana's eyes, the meticulous actions of one who'd dreamed of this moment for a *long* time: a princess tired of waiting, a girl determined to have power at any cost.

But Favre did not see that.

She was weeping for her wings.

PART ONE

He refused me his kingdom, though I was his rightful heir. And so, I drank his blood, destroying his flesh, not wanting to wait in the shadows.

Eternal life is mine.

—THANA ADAEZE,
FROM *SHE WHO CROWNED HERSELF QUEEN:
THE RISE AND FALL OF THE FIRST VAMPIRE*, CHAPTER ONE
FIRST EDITION, 901 AD
MERKESH ROYAL ARCHIVES

CHAPTER ONE

Favre

Present Day: Nekros

I place my back flat against the wall of a long corridor outside of the manor house's great hall, watching and waiting for her. The corridor has no light, making it the perfect place to disappear into the shadows.

Souls drift into the hall, one after another, single file, heading to their final resting place. They're translucent. Some have symbols inked on the back of their necks, denoting *what* they once were: *Vampires.* The humans have no such symbols.

I can't see into the hall, yet I know every feature. Long ago, this house was mine—my sanctuary, my home, the last place Thana and I were together. Hands float from the wood-paneled walls, each gripping a rusted candelabra and caked with wax. The wax drips slowly onto the stone floors and the vines snaking through their cracks.

When I first arrived here, I wondered . . . Thieves' hands? The hands of those who'd wronged the gods? I thought of my life growing up in the Heavenly Realms, of the many cautionary tales Mother used to tell me. *The gods punish first and they never forgive*, she'd say. And, for once, she was right.

After the gods trapped me, I learned there is no point in wondering. Things happen how they happen; fate is on your side, or it's not. My mother thought she could change her fate, she thought that she could control it. Instead, she ended up in an early grave, brutally abandoned by the god she served and loved.

The line of souls grows shorter, until the sun dips below the horizon and darkness seeps into the sky, until there are no souls left at all. Finally, the goddess of the dead leaves the judgment hall. Eyes barely open, the goddess stretches her arms out wide and yawns. Moonlight slips in from cracks along the walls, bathing her brown skin in midnight's blue.

Eventually, she makes her way to her chambers.

I wait, and then I follow, wrapped in a cloak of shadows.

Slowly, we climb the spiral staircase to the house's second floor. My bare feet grow cold against the stone stairs, a breeze from an open window slicing through my tattered dress. The stairs are splintered with cracks, and the railing groans as we ascend. Whereas I stumble, trying not to make a sound, adjusting to legs I haven't used in centuries, the goddess glides from stair to stair, her gown fanning out behind her, cutting a stretch of darkness, velvet indigo atop white marble. She holds her head high, as if she is the mistress of this place, not just a tool of the gods. I sneer. Easy to be replaced.

Soon, we reach the top and head down a long corridor. Like the hall, it's dimly lit with candelabras held by floating hands. Wax drips and pools beneath them on the chilly floor.

A shadow flickers before us, and the goddess hesitates, clutching her hands, gripping them until her knuckles pale to yellow. My eyes flit back and forth before they still—there's nothing there. This place has a way of taking root deep within you. Creating images only in your mind. Planting suggestions you know to ignore but don't. That's what happened to the goddess of the dead before this one. And to be honest, the one before that one, too—they lost all sense of what was and what wasn't and had to be replaced.

Finally, we reach her bedchamber. I stop well before and press myself within a nook in the wall. I make myself small, like I did as a little girl. Only, instead of hiding from Mother, lest she drain a pint of my blood for a spell, it's the Reapers I need to avoid. They stand guard on either side of the door, putting themselves between me and my plans. They hover over her, nearly as tall as the corridor's vaulted ceiling is high. Ligaments gnarled like a tree. Nails sharp like a beast's, which I suppose is what they are with their fleshless faces—all bones except for a slender red tongue that flicks out between two *long* fangs.

The goddess says something inaudible to them, closing the door behind her as the Reapers turn back the way we came, walking right past me. I hold my breath until they're gone. Then I walk to the goddess's door and turn the knob.

"Hello?" she calls.

I swing the door open.

The goddess sits, brushing her hair in front of a dressing table. She looks at me and gasps. Her brush clatters to the ground.

A mirror is beside her, but I don't need it to know the truth. I look like some*thing* the swamp spat up. My black lace gown barely fits where it should, my eyes are blood red, and my hair is terribly matted. A far cry from the girl I once was.

I can smell her fear, and it awakens something deep within me: the taste for human blood.

I feel my fangs as they descend, as they hunger with a thirst I haven't been able to quench in centuries.

The goddess falls from her chair. Quickly, she pulls herself up and glances out the window, searching for it: a tree separate from the woods surrounding us and right in front of the house. A peculiar tree, adorned with bottles instead of leaves. Bright blue bottles that gleam under the moonlight and clink together in the wind.

Clink. Clink.

Her heart rate quickens. The bottles sway in the wind.

She gasps. She's seen it. The glass shattered underneath the tree. She looks at me. She stumbles back. A wicked grin spreads across my face.

The color leaves hers as she puts it all together. "H-how? It's impossible."

I step toward her. I once thought the same. A thousand years I hoped and prayed. A thousand years I called upon every ounce of my magic. A thousand years I was trapped there.

How? I'd wondered, as I'd tumbled to the ground. As I was suddenly free. As fate was on my side once more.

I take another step. She grabs her brush and holds it before her like a sword. I throw my head back and laugh. Her knuckles pale.

"Y-you can't open it. They cursed it. Protected it. You seriously think you're the first to try?" Her voice wavers as she references the real reason the gods created her role a thousand years ago, after they locked me and Thana away. The gods told the people of the lands of the living that there is a goddess of the dead. That she lives on an island named Nekros, a place where all souls go at their end. There, she sits atop a gilded throne in a manor house where she judges the dead, ushering them, one by one, to their final resting place. I snort, suppressing a laugh at the thought. The spirits would go wherever they go regardless of her. It's just more lies spun by the gods to keep people from seeking out this island, to keep them from finding out the truth: what's really hidden here.

Her heart rate quickens, and her breath grows shallow. Her veins pulse under her skin, the blood calling to me. I step toward her.

"I know I'm not," I say with a grin. "But unlike the rest, I was there that night—I know how to free *her*."

The goddess picks up the chair and throws it at me. I stumble to the ground, caught off guard, and she jumps over me. She opens her mouth in a scream, making a run for the open door. But I am faster. I grab her leg and pull her down just before she reaches the hall.

On the wall there are four hundred tally marks.

Five hundred years, the gods had promised the goddess of the dead when she was but a human girl and I watched her arrive from my glass prison. *Five hundred years of playing this role and we'll make you a real goddess.*

Like a fairy tale.

Of course, they didn't lay out the logistics of *how* they'd do that: make a human a goddess. A question the girl failed to ask before she took the blood oath that bound her to this lonely, haunted place.

She twists around and scratches my face, but I summon my

strength and throw her across the room. She barrels into the mirror, splintering it into a million pieces.

She tries to push herself up off the ground, but her arms give out. She looks up at me, pleading, but it's too late. The hunger within me has grown into a full-fledged thing, starving and furious. I couldn't stop now if I wanted to. It begs to be fed.

I run my tongue across my fangs and kneel beside her trembling body. "Shh," I whisper, "it'll be over soon." But that only provokes her. Her fists beat upon my chest. Punching and scratching, doing whatever she can to break free. I lean down, hovering over her, over the pulsing of her vein. My fangs graze her, caressing the skin on her neck. I inhale slowly, taking it all in, and bite down.

With a whimper, she quiets. Toxins release into her bloodstream, making her still. I drink and drink. Until her blood becomes my own. Eventually, her whimpers die down. Her kicks soften until she releases the grip on my hand.

Her body, drained of its blood, slumps to the floor.

Moments after killing the false goddess, acid fills my throat, and I try not to hurl. The images of what I've done replay on a loop in my head. Crushing her, silencing her, killing an innocent girl.

No one is innocent, I remind myself. *No one is without their faults.*

Her ring, slick with blood, I slip onto my hand, crowning myself the new goddess.

"You won't get away with this," a voice howls at my ear.

I turn around. A spirit hovers over where her body used to be. Just my luck. She's still here.

She wags her finger at me. "You won't get away with this." But this time it's Mother's voice that I hear. A voice that always reminds me of who I really am: a disappointment, an outcast, a girl who will never be anything more than the bastard, undesired daughter of a sorceress and a god.

I clutch my hands so hard my nails dig into my skin. *You're dead*, I repeat to myself, again and again, even as I slap on a smile and throw my head back and laugh before leaving the room wearing the trappings of another's life, the taste of her blood still on my tongue.

I walk down the same candelabra-lit corridor until I reach its very end. A simple wooden door is there, gold paint peeling off. I sink to the ground.

I want to close my eyes and rest my head there, to touch it, caress it. I yearn to thrust the door open, to pull Thana into my arms. But I can't do any of those things. The door is cursed, just like the dead goddess said. Touching it will kill me. Cursed to hold my beloved Thana in—the queen the gods tried and failed to kill, and so they trapped her in a tomb in a spell-locked room and told everyone alive that she's dead.

I gather myself from the ground and return to the bedroom. Along the way I pass a Reaper, who bows at me. I hold my head high, the mistress of this place. Soon, I will release Thana. Then we will be together again. Together, we will reap vengeance on those who brought us down and tried to lock us away for eternity.

Ignoring the dead goddess's howling spirit, I reenter the room. I sit upon her chair. I pick up her brush and, finally, do my hair. Trying to soften what I see before me, trying to hide the creature I've become. But the brush only snags painfully. It'll take more than its bristles to detangle this. To undo what has been done.

I toss it to the ground. *Focus, Favre. On what you came here to do.*

I stand and walk over to the mirror. Now cracked and stained with the dead goddess's blood. Distorting my image even more. I look away and out the window to the bottle tree where the gods trapped me for a thousand years. Once, when I was a little girl, Mother told me that her own mother had a bottle tree right at the entrance to their home. It was filled with the same bright blue bottles, just like the one that once held me, ready to trap evil beings and stop them from entering the home.

With hope I thought long abandoned, and a wicked grin, I concentrate on what I need, and the mirror shakes and glows. It shows me where the people I wish to destroy and the person I seek are found.

CHAPTER TWO

Najja

Present Day: The Kutmenian Sea

I rush up the tower's stone steps. What does my sister want this time?

She summoned me to the tapestry room, at the tower's very top, pulling me from my duties training the children, teaching them the same old tales of how we yamaja are blessed by the gods. Tales that conveniently leave out how much of a curse our visions are—how heavy a burden they will become. As I've learned, knowing the future doesn't mean you can change it—it only means you'll suffer twice the pain.

I climb the winding staircase, bracing myself for the inevitable. Another lecture. Another argument. Another reminder that I am not as good as she, that of Mama's two daughters, I am the one letting Mama—letting our people—down.

Halfway up the staircase, I pass a large, arched opening in

the stone wall. A breeze rushes in as the sun rises in the sky. I inhale the morning air, laced with salt from the Kutmenian Sea surrounding this tower. When I was a little girl, I used to climb upon this window ledge, legs curled up toward my chest. I'd sit, not once thinking how ancient the tower was, how the very stones that make up the thin ledge could crumble at any time and hurl me toward my death.

I would sit there and take everything in: the only world I ever knew. The tower whose base extends into the sea, as if it was born from it. The rocks encircling this sacred place, waves crashing upon them. The wooden bridges connecting the tower to the shore where our homes, stone cottages with roofs of thatch, beckon in the distance. If I listen, I can hear it all: the rustling wind, the lapping waves, the clucking of chickens and the bleating of goats in their pens not too far from here. Someone telling stories to the children of how our world came to be. Of how we came to be the yamaja—the messengers of fate. Tasked by the goddess of knowledge herself not to control fate, for even we are subject to it, but to ensure that it is carried out. Most of all, though, I hear the sea. The way it speaks to me—living forever in my soul like it does for all of my kind.

Najja, it sings to me, my name a whisper in the air. *Najja*. It tries to entice me, to reassure me that this is where I belong. But I shake it off, ignoring its empty promises. How can a home bring comfort and yet also be a place you cannot leave? Like all yamaja, I am trapped here—thanks to the vampire queen outlawing our kind and banishing us here for the last hundred years, ever since my late grandmother showed the queen a fate that she did not like.

When I was a little girl, I dreamed. I loved living here. I thrived.

Until the day I woke with my sheets soiled in blood and my head splitting with pain. My menses had come, and with it, visions that chased my dreams away.

There are only nightmares now.

A colder breeze rushes by, and the hairs on my arms rise. I wrap my arms around me, suppressing a shiver. I look up to meet her, knowing what I'll find.

"Excuse me, dear." The spirit slips past me, wearing a bright blue robe. The remnant of a yamaja so obsessed with her duties that even after death she couldn't let them go. When her body disintegrated, turning to sea foam—as we all do when we die—some part of her remained, was bound to this land, became a spirit who repeats the same motions day after day, as if she were still alive.

The stone staircase is narrow; only one person can fit at a time. I press myself against the wall, in deference to the spirit, so that she may pass by and not trouble me. She glides past and I watch her go—unseen to all except for me. An ever-present reminder of who I am, of *what* I am, the only one of my kind in eight generations.

I see death. And it sees me. The dead whisper in my ears, tormenting me.

I take the last flight of stairs two steps at a time—trying not to think that I could end up like that spirit, trapped here for eternity—until I reach the wooden double doors that are twice as tall as me. The entrance to the tapestry room.

I push open the doors.

"Took you long enough." My sister stands from her desk and walks over to me, cutting through the sunlight that bursts through the room, as well as the spirit who always lingers beside her desk.

The circular room is lined with oval-shaped glass windows that amplify the sun beaming in from all sides. The room itself is made of stone like the rest of the tower: stone bricks for the walls, stone tiles for the floors, a tower supposedly built by Anae herself—another tale I've been force-fed; another lie disguised as a truth. I seriously doubt the goddess of knowledge had time to build a tower in the middle of the vast Kutmenian Sea.

Simi crosses her arms, lines etched into her forehead, wearing the same high-waisted gown Mama wore. The gown itself is bright blue and parts down the center to reveal a navy chemise embroidered with silver thread. The embroidery tells the story of the first yamaja, me and Simi's ancestress. If it weren't for the sword tied around Simi's hip and the outline of knives barely visible through her flowy, floor-length sleeves, she'd look the part of a Lienne noble lady. But she's not—she's a yamaja through and through, ready at all times to defend the truths hidden within this room and us all. Just like Mama was, back when she was alive and I still believed we were favored by the gods.

Makeshift wooden shelves line the room. Upon first glance, they look straight, but after years of looking upon them, they seem just a little bit slanted. Each is packed with relics. Items found in the sea's depths, lost to time, belonging now to us. The shelves are stacked one atop the other, crowded, competing for space—so close to one another that in some parts the stone walls barely peek through. Simi's driftwood desk is in the center of the room; much like her gown, it's been passed down from one eldest in our family to the next. Candle wax is caked on the desk in spots from when our ancestresses stayed up late reading reports from yamaja at our temples, notating prophecies, and mapping out journeys that needed to be taken to spread such predictions. Papers are strewn across it, and quills and pots of ink. A giant leather-bound book takes up a third of the space—right beside a portrait miniature of Mama and Simi and me. Mama had it commissioned years ago, when I was twelve and Simi was seventeen.

Simi sizes me up. Though she's a few inches shorter than me, it's as if she's six feet tall. Her glare sends shivers down my spine. Her eyes are like mine—ever-changing to match her mood and capturing the sea's hues. Today, they are a cloudy blue gray, like the sky anticipating a hurricane. Before I can utter a word, her brows knit together in concern. "I'm worried about you," she says in the tone elder siblings are well-versed in, as if they think you the child and they the parent.

"Let's not," I say, knowing full well the lecture that comes next.

Simi, like all yamaja, hungers for something more that we cannot have, trapped on this land as we are. Once, we had temples everywhere where humans *and* vampires left us tokens: food, drink, and gold—it was how we fed and maintained ourselves.

But then my grandmother had a vision of the then vampire princess, one that took her to Tssaia, the capital of the vampire nation. What she told the princess, I do not know—she never returned to us; my grandmother was slain by the princess herself. That princess convinced her older sister, who was queen at the time, to banish us from their lands, to label us outlaws and remove any protections we had been afforded. Because of the key trade routes the vampires control, we were forced to stay here even as our temples were looted. If not for a few kind human fishers who taught us their ways, we would've starved.

There is a yearning that grows within us—passed down by our mothers and their mothers, who remember what it was like *before*.

When our people were revered, not feared. When we were more than a story spun to restless children.

But among our people, Simi is still revered. For only our family, descended from the first yamaja, has powers of foresight through visions. Everyone else learns to glean what they may from the tapestry—an ever-growing work that we weave with the threads of fate we find in the sea's depths. I, however, am an outcast even here. No one wants to be friends with the girl who might tell you when you'll die.

"Najja," Simi snaps. "Did you hear what I just said?" Her arms are still crossed and the circles under her eyes are deeper and darker than they were a few days ago. I haven't seen her since then, since she last came into our hut to grab food and left without saying anything. I think to ask her what troubles her, what causes her to lose sleep and spend her nights up here instead, but it's always the same.

She wants to restore us to our former glory. She wants the old ways back.

I nod my head, even though I heard nothing. "You don't need to worry about me," I say, taking a guess at the heart of her words.

"I don't need to worry about my little sister? You're *my* responsibility." She grabs my left arm and pushes up the sleeve to where faded gashes trail my forearm.

I yank back my arm and march away from her, adjusting my sleeves so they cover my scars. "I told you, I stopped doing *that*." I reference the faded cuts, self-inflicted, now months old. Why can't she just mind herself? Maybe if she did, she'd start to live in the now and realize that her life, one full of constant hoping, will be our downfall. Hope doesn't feed the bellies that grow empty every time our people fail to catch enough fish because we're too busy gathering threads for our tapestry.

"And yet, you continue to punish yourself in other ways. Pain is all over you." Simi breaks through my thoughts. "Why haven't you led the morning dives for the threads of fate? You have a duty—to yourself, to your people, to our family. You told me last week you'd take over from me, but here we are. Again."

I look up, unable to meet her gaze. It's always the same with Simi. *Why aren't you doing this or that? Why aren't you more like me?* she might as well say. After Mama's death, Simi moved her things to the tower, leaving me in our hut alone. She took on Mama's duties as high priestess—watching over the tapestry we weave each day that, along with our visions, shows us the fate of the world. She mourned Mama, and her sorrow became part of a higher purpose, a calling, a duty. But every time I try to do the same, all I can think about is how the very gods who gave us this duty, this power, who supposedly watch over us every day, peering down through the clouds, took my mother away. "What happened to Mama was *my* fault. Had I not been out there she would still be—"

"I bear the same burden," Simi interrupts. "She was my mother, too. But with her gone, there's a gap that must be filled. I can't just sit around all day like you. It's been years, Naj."

I scoff. Apparently, six years is enough time to mourn your mother, to simmer your grief and stop it from boiling over. "I thought this was about me? You're making it all about yourself. Do you even worry about me, *or* am I just embarrassing you—letting down the great family name?" Maybe if she stopped worrying about our reputation, she would see that trying to preserve it is futile. She'd realize that what we need to move on from isn't mourning our mother, but being yamaja. That we need to figure out something else. A way of life that's not a relic. I don't say any of that, though. I've tried, but Simi never listens.

She rolls her eyes. "It's always the same with you. I never said you were embarrassing me. I said you have a duty, like we all do. Maybe, instead of putting words in my mouth, you should ask yourself why you feel this way. Maybe you shou——" She balls her hand into a fist but stops herself before she pounds the table. Instead, she tilts her head up to the domed ceiling, likely whispering a silent prayer to Anae, who supposedly created us to help shape the fate of the world. Simi takes a deep breath, and when she speaks again, when she looks at me, her eyes are more blue than gray and her voice is soft. "I'm not asking you to forget her. I'm asking you to stop letting your grief consume you. The hurricane was too strong. Had you stayed, you would've died, too."

I grit my teeth, not wanting to think of that day. If only I could feel nothing; if only I could forget. I drop my head, resigned. "Maybe I should've stayed. It should've taken me, too." I blame my sister for being a single-minded leader, but at least she gives our people hope. It's not like I ever do anything of use. I turn my face away so she won't see the tears forming.

"Najja." Sadness creeps into her voice. She reaches out for me, but I step away from her. I push down my anger and pain like I do every day, lest they seep out and a trickle becomes a flood. Lest they become beasts that I can no longer control, that I no longer *want* to control.

"It feels like yesterday." My lips tremble; my voice cracks. "I saw her struggling to breathe, I saw the water fill her lungs, I saw her head hit that rock. She died bleeding out into the sea, alone and afraid. All because I was trapped in the hurricane's eye. All because I was diving for threads for that stupid tapestry. Why do we even bother? It doesn't matter anymore. What's the purpose of knowing fate, if we haven't been seen in so long that most don't believe we exist at all?" At once, the tears break forth. I double over, shaking as they run down my face. How can I ever hope to move on when the images of her death keep me awake at night?

Simi wraps her arms around me, pulling me toward her. "I'm sorry," she says. "If I could take them away, I would."

"I know." And I do. We argue, sometimes two, three times a day, but we would do anything for each other. With Mama gone, we're the only family we have left. I wipe my tears away, only for more to fall. All while Simi hugs me tight like she did on the day Mama died. Her arms are firm and strong the way Mama's always were. She's more like her than I can ever hope to be.

After a while, my tears dry, and I take in one deep, ragged breath and another, feeling lighter and more centered than I did. I'm just stepping away from Simi when a glimmer catches my eye. I start to dismiss it, but the light pulls me toward it: a heap of silvery-pink threads, peeking out from under a curtain and crumpled on the floor.

I gasp, nearly backing into Simi, who's followed me to where the tapestry usually hangs.

"Is that—" I pause, not wanting to give weight to my fear.

Simi nods slowly, eyes glued to the tattered tapestry. "That's why I summoned you here."

CHAPTER THREE

Favre

1,201 Years Ago: The Heavenly Realms

Don't spill, I tell myself, as I weave through the crowds, carrying a glass filled to the brim with the honeyed drink the nobles love so much. All I need is to give these gods one more thing to whisper about—another reason to believe they are better than me and that Thana should make one of them her queen instead.

Even in the corridors, the castle is aglow with celebration. Stars from the sky drape upon the stone walls and ceilings, illuminating the narrow pathways that are packed with huddled groups of nobles, laughing, toasting . . . gossiping about me.

The gods have been here all week, as part of the ten-day celebration leading up to Thana's coronation. A day barely passed between Kovnu's funeral and the start of the festivities. Not a soul is still dressed in black. No one dares to mourn too much and miss out on celebrating the soon-to-be queen of the gods and on their opportunity to impress her and raise their status at the same time.

A few dip into curtsies for me, but most simply nod their heads in acknowledgment of my soon-to-be status. Just like Thana commanded. I plaster on a smile until my cheeks ache from it, from all the smiles I've forced myself to wear, all the joy I must now show. Joy at being here, at my suddenly altered fortune—at me, having Thana's heart.

A flamethrower maneuvers through the crowd. Fire spouts from her fingertips. She shoots a flame up in the air and catches it in her mouth, and when she smiles wide, the flame is still inside. The nobles clap and cheer. An ember falls, singeing the shoulder of my dress. It's made of yet another impractical thing: violets freshly picked. And though they are my favorite flowers, it's a dress that is only good for one night, not at all like the ones I used to wear. A dress that doesn't have slits for my wings, wings I no longer have.

My breath constricts. I need air. I need to be anywhere but here. Those crowded corridors; the even more packed great hall. This castle is constantly so loud. I can barely hear my own thoughts—a sacrifice I never thought I'd have to make when I accepted Thana's marriage proposal, when she whisked me away.

The nobles blur together as I walk pass. Gold and silver jeweled rings laden on every finger. Luxurious, natural diamonds and pearls draped around their necks. Stars borrowed from constellations their ancestors formed interwoven throughout their hair. Gowns and suits made of anything imaginable: the sea, the desert, the air. Nothing but the best for the nobles—the oldest and most powerful gods of the Heavenly Realms.

They toss their heads back and laugh as they sip their drinks.

Pausing only long enough to look me up and down, before returning to their conversations as if I was never there to begin with, though I am the very subject they talk about.

Her mother was a human.

One of the king's whores.

They say her mother entered into a bargain with the king for power.

But he tricked her. To use the powers, she had to first use her blood.

She drained herself to death, poor thing.

But not before she had a daughter.

A bastard.

Her father was some minor god her mother seduced.

I hold my head high, and I don't dare to let them see me cry. I weave through the castle, blocking them out, until I am finally outside.

I take a deep breath, calming my shaking hands, letting the cool air rush against me. *Get a hold of yourself, Favre.* I inhale slowly then exhale again. Why do their words affect me so much? It's not like I haven't heard it before.

I take another deep breath. Then I reach into my gown's deep pockets and pull out a diary, bound in leather.

I open it and read the dedication inside.

To my daughter, Favre,
  May this help you keep your thoughts close, and your heart locked away. These are the words I wish my mother had told me and so I pass them down to you.
  It is the only way to survive.

It was one of the few things my mother gave to me that wasn't some gift discarded from one lover or another. To be honest, I'd forgotten about it. Like I tried to forget all the things she'd done and said. Until Thana showed up, ready to whisk me away, and I saw it while packing, in a corner underneath my bed. I've carried it on me ever since, waiting for the right words to fill its pages.

~~I am lucky.~~ I start to write.

~~I should be grateful.~~ I try again.

~~My very own fairy tale.~~ I shake my head in frustration. Why do I lie even to myself?

I take a deep breath and stare at the stars around me, each one created by gods who are no longer here. Between these pages, I will carve for myself a sanctuary, like the forest once was.

Here, I will tell the truth.

My mother was the first to remind me of what I lacked. Her words, reiterated over nineteen years, should've thickened my skin, and shored up my defenses. They should have prepared me for this night. Instead, she gave me hope. I came to anticipate her actions. How she was gentle one moment, brutal the next. Her mood ever shifting, dependent on the god she was seeing and the price of the gifts he asked her for. I thought that if I could make it through those years, I could survive anything.

But not even she prepared me for this—to be whisked away from the forest by Thana, her brown eyes now blood red, and brought to this castle—like the knights in the stories Mother used to tell me did, after defeating the monster and saving the princess, who could never save herself. Only I didn't need saving. The forest was not a monster but my home. Overnight, I became the center of attention, the show everyone had admission to see.

How will I survive this?

I still hear their laughter ringing in the distance. But as I write, it fades. As I write, their words cease to exist and I can finally find my own.

The castle here floats upon a cloud. The highest one. Below are the lights of the nobles' estates—each on a cloud of its own. Below these are the homes of the minor gods—the commoners, as the nobles call them, for technically everyone here is a god. Those who are gods, yes, but whose lineages are not as fabled and long, whose powers, in comparison, are mundane: the gods who instead of moving mountains can only shift pebbles; who can grow any flower, but cannot control life itself; who can maybe make something from nothing but cannot create an ocean to wear to a party simply because they wish it so.

Thana told me she is more powerful than them all. And that beside her, I am, too. But I don't feel it. I just feel very small.

Even now my gaze drifts to the easternmost part of the realm, where only a forest reigns—a presumptuous term for what it does, how it protected me. A home that is no longer my own, one that even if I return to it will not be the same, for I, much like Thana, am forever changed.

After she killed her father, with the blade born from my blood, after she brought me here and kissed away my tears, she declared her love and proposed. It all happened so fast. Before I knew it, I said yes. Before I could process the way my life would change, she told the gods that I would become her queen, she told me that this was my home. On the tenth night of her coronation festivities, our investiture will occur. We will be crowned queen and queen. Thana will be handed the keys to this kingdom and take her father's throne.

Three nights from now.

I am filled with dread.

Mother would finally be proud. This is the life she wanted. To have power, to be worshipped, to be adored. But what about me? I want to focus, for once, on what I want.

Thana. Her face is clear in my mind, as if she's before me. The way she makes me feel when it's just us snakes its way into my heart.

She makes me laugh at the simplest of things, she latches onto my every word, and remembers them, too. How even here she filled my bedchamber with plants, trying to re-create the forest itself. The chamber was so filled with vines, and trees, and red roses, and violets that she carried me across the threshold, battling plants all the way. Even last night, when she sensed I was still homesick, she bade a young sea goddess to build me a lake on the castle's grounds, one that only I can access, where I can be alone.

She will do anything to protect me. After all, she killed her own father just to be with me. So, maybe, it happened a little too fast for me to be certain that what I'm feeling is love. But if what I'm feeling isn't love, whatever could it be? No one's ever done such things for me, she must love me very much.

Of course she had to bring me here—how else were we to be together? How could she rule from the forest's depths when most of her citizens live near here? And of course she chose to keep her throne. After all, hadn't I shown her that path—a way for her to have everything she wanted, a way for us to be together unobstructed?

The nobles' laughter crescendos and reaches me even here. To them, I will always be the girl who doesn't belong. Supposedly, they whispered about Thana's mother the same way. For Morowa was but a commoner, the daughter of the royal gardener who caught Kovnu's eye. The whispers only died down after he grew tired of her and took his first mistress. I imagine Thana inside the great hall, surrounded by nobles desperate to impress. Will one of them seduce her? Is that also to be my fate?

No. I push those unhappy thoughts away as I gather my skirts and begin my return. No one has ever done such things for me, she must love me very much.

"It'll be worth it," I whisper to myself. It'll be worth it in the end. To have the love I always dreamt of, love Mother never gave to me.

Flecks of light dance in the corners of my eyes and I glance down, far past the homes of the nobles and the forest. Down to the lands of the living, where my mother came from—where the humans are. A world, she'd said, without hierarchies, without nobles, without kings and queens.

I pocket my diary and drop my glass, letting it shatter, as I'm filled with a yearning no drink can quench.

As night gives way to day, I sit in Thana's bedchamber twisting my hair as two servants bring forth another human. Her third. My chair rests in front of a window where I can soak up the beginning of the sun's warmth, the only time I'll feel it today. I take longer than I need to ready myself for bed as Thana feeds.

The human whimpers as she draws near. Gone is Thana's dress of volcanic ash from the party. In its place is a burgundy silken robe with feathers on the sleeves and a hem that falls upon the ground, like froth flowing out from a too-full bath. Strands of hair slip out of its pearled caul as she places her finger over the human's mouth, shushing him.

I refocus my mirror so I can't see them and set again to doing my hair.

At first, the servants brought them dead, having killed them before leaving the lands of the living. But they stopped when she said it soured the taste. Too much like the fresh blood of animals, which, at my request, she had tried after killing the servant who'd brought her a dinner of veal roasted with a red-wine mushroom sauce, a meal she tried to eat but could no longer stomach. When he asked if she'd like something else instead, she'd drained him dry. A queen picking off her own just wouldn't do, so, by the third day, when the hunger didn't leave, she was feeding upon live humans. The very beings her father loved so much.

The human moans. It's always like this—fear then pleasure. As she pierces their veins, something calms them, like the venom that courses through a rattlesnake paralyzing its prey.

My stomach twists and knots at the sound and smell: her tongue lapping up the blood, the coppery stench permeating the air.

When she's done, the human slumps to the floor, chest barely rising and falling. Eyes fluttering closed. Thana rings the bell beside our bed, and two servants rush in from a secret passageway behind an armoire to carry him out—the same corridor Kovnu used to sneak in his mistresses, the one Thana used to kill him.

Her eyes meet mine through the mirror, brown irises rimmed with a red circle that's grown wider and brighter over the past several days. At this rate, they'll be ruby red by her coronation. "You've been quiet." She takes a handkerchief from a servant and blots the blood in the corners of her lips. "Favre, what's wrong?" Her brows knit together in concern and before I can say anything, she's in front of me.

She kneels down, and her hands caress my hips through the smooth silk of my gown. Heat rises from within me at once, distracting me from my thoughts.

"Favre," she whispers softly. Her eyes twinkle with another hunger.

She draws near, slowly at first, and her lips brush against mine. Lightly, just barely touching, seeking my permission. I reach my hands up and completely pull off her caul, letting her hair spring loose, twisting my fingers into her locks, pulling her closer. She kisses me, deeper now, sucking at my bottom lip before trailing kisses along my jawline. I tilt my head back and moan.

She chuckles against me, her mouth below my ear. "Shall I continue to make you forget? Or"—she draws the word out—"you can tell me *who* it was, and I'll bring you their head."

Playfully, I push her away. "If I asked for their head every time someone spoke ill of me, you'd have no subjects in this realm."

She pauses as if considering it—annihilating her subjects just to please me.

I think she knows I'm not serious, but remembering the way she drained those humans, one after the next, I add, "I'm joking, Thana," to be certain.

She rolls her eyes. "I know that. Can't be a queen if you don't have anyone to rule over." She scoops me up and places me on the bed. It's heaped with satin pillows. "I shall just have to make it so they can hear us all the way in the guest chambers and remember that you are mine and to mock you is to mock their queen."

Heat rises to my cheeks, and I start to protest. She leans in for another kiss, silencing me. The sun's rays reach in through the window and beam down upon her cheek, the way it did so many months ago on the day we first met. I close my eyes, remembering the moment, but Thana screams.

I open my eyes. "Thana?"

She jumps back, falling onto the ground. Smoke rises from her face, her cheek sizzling as if a branding iron burned her skin.

I reach over and ring the bell even as I pull a blanket from the bed and throw it over her.

Three servants rush into the room.

"Your highness," the first one says. He glances at Thana's shape under the blanket, confusion and fear in his eyes.

"Close the curtains," I say. They hesitate, waiting for Thana to confirm my command, still not used to me. "Now," I yell. "Before she dies and then you do." At that, they lurch into action, drawing the thick curtains closed.

"Leave us," she growls, rising from the ground, freezing me in my place. Her eyes are fully red, and her fangs have dropped. Her face is twisted in rage and pain, looking more monstrous than I've ever seen her. They're gone before she finishes her command, their fear palpable. The wound on her cheek is already knitting together—we gods are near impossible to kill.

She brushes past me and sits at the edge of the bed, her eyes full of rage, yes, but also sorrow. A sorrow that pulls me from my fear, one I understand too well—it's a sorrow born from a longing for a life that she cannot have. The princess who used to wear gowns of the sun's rays, relegated to the shadows. She lowers her head into her hands. "He just had to have the final laugh, didn't he?"

There's no need for her to say who. Kovnu. Her father. He who controlled the sun. "Maybe there's a way to reverse it?" I sit beside her.

She shakes her head slowly. "No. He said it with his dying breath. He commanded the sun to turn away from me. His final act as its king. Only he could undo one of his commands." She sighs. "It is my pound of flesh. Nothing is gained without sacrifice; it was he who first taught me that."

"*Love requires sacrifice*. It's what my mother used to say." She gives me a small smile. "No wonder our parents, for a time, got along."

I rest my head on her shoulder as I push away those thoughts, trying to drown out Mother's voice and remind myself that we are not the same. "Was it worth it?"

"Yes." She kisses my brow and takes my hand. "Yes, it was. I will not forget your sacrifice, too."

My shoulder blades ache at her reference to my wings. *Love requires sacrifice.* Mother used to say it all the time after draining some part of herself for whatever godly lover she had at the time. Gods who stayed for what she could give, who showered her with empty promises but never gave her anything lasting in return.

Thana and I sit like that for a while, my head resting against her, her grasping my hand. At peace. And yet, I can't help but think back to the lights that twinkled below me as I wrote in my journal, the fires down below from a different world, unbound by the ways things have always been and will always be.

Thana stirs beside me. "What's really on your mind, Favre?"

I don't want to ruin the moment, but the weight of the coronation urges me on. In three days, it'll be too late. The time to act is now.

I take a deep breath, mustering up my courage. "What if there was somewhere else we could go? Where we could just be us, a place where we wouldn't have to worry about any of them?"

She goes still next to me, and I remember that Thana has secrets of her own, ones her servants have been sworn, and threatened, to keep.

"They don't even know the truth about you, the food you pretend to eat. The real reason everything is at night." She told the court she wanted nightly festivities to set her coronation apart from her father's because, after all, she's the goddess of night. "What happens when they find out?"

"When I'm queen, it won't matter. This is my blood right. I—*we* have sacrificed too much for this."

"Why stay here, though? Why be bound to the way things are and have been done? Become queen of a new realm, build a legacy that no king of the gods before you can ever touch—a legacy of your own, undefined by these gods."

She shifts and turns to face me, her eyes flickering with curiosity. "Where would this new realm be?"

I let her question linger in the air, closing my eyes as I remember what it was like to feel the sun on my skin, to rise with the day. To walk without whispers at my back and a smile upon my face. A world largely undiscovered, where my own mother came from, back when she was just a girl, uncorrupted by the gods. "*The lands of the living.* Where the humans are."

CHAPTER FOUR

Najja

Present Day: The Kutmenian Sea

"The tapestry started shredding three days ago." Simi runs her hand lightly over it, as if afraid to damage it further. "The threads literally started to unravel, as if fate itself were changing—as if our present and our future are being rewritten even as we stand here."

I furrow my brows. "But that doesn't make any sense." The tapestry is indestructible. According to our stories, it was originally at our easternmost temple—just outside Tssaia, where the vampire queen lives. Learning of the queen's orders to outlaw our kind, the yamaja there locked themselves inside as soldiers surrounded them. They burned everything, including the tapestry, preferring to die, to destroy our legacy, rather than let the vampires get their hands on anything. But on the day that Mama took over her mother's role as high priestess, at only sixteen, the tapestry appeared here, in this room, intact, and it has been ever since.

I later learned that it wasn't that simple but was nonetheless a miracle. That Mama's first duty as high priestess was to ask for volunteers brave enough to go to the temple and retrieve any remnants of the tapestry that could be found. Four went. They swam the great Kutmenian Sea and forged a dangerous path to the temple. Only one survived to bring the tapestry—somehow undamaged by the fire—home.

We do not control fate, even we are subject to it. The tapestry shows us the fate of the world, how one path will lead to the next. For every major event, there is only ever one outcome. Our job is—or used to be—to ensure that it comes true. Once, we used to visit nobles and royals and commoners alike, giving them peeks at their future, guiding anyone who had a role to play in the tapestry's chosen direction.

"According to our records, this has happened once before." She goes to her desk and slides the massive book off. It dominates her tiny frame. The spine creaks as if letting out a deep sigh when she opens it. The book is a ledger full of dates that Simi traces her fingers across, flipping the pages until she reaches what she's looking for. "It was when Thana killed her father, left the Heavenly Realms, and came to our world where she crowned herself queen." She places the book down, leaving it open on the desk and looking up at me. "The one thing I was able to decipher from these threads is that there's a princess at the center of it all, one who has an important role to play in shaping the future of our world."

"A princess?" I laugh. "What is this, some bedtime story?"

Simi crosses her arms. "All stories are rooted in truth, Naj. We are living proof of that. Besides, this isn't just any princess. She's the crown heir of Mnara."

I recoil at that. If it weren't for the vampires and their queens, we wouldn't be where we are to begin with. As Mama used to say, vampires only care for themselves and the human blood that keeps them alive.

I motion to the book. "You say the last time this happened was when Thana came here?"

Simi nods.

I pace back and forth. "It makes sense, then, that a vampire is at the center of this. Thana became the first vampire after killing her father. She *created* them. Her direct descendants still sit upon the throne and look at the havoc she wreaked. What if this princess is worse? Maybe that's what the tapestry is trying to say?" I shudder with fear at my own suggestion. Thana wasn't just ruthless; she didn't just rule unchecked. Thanks to her, the beings she created thought it was their right to rule over humans—to rule over all of this land. Humans, of course, disagreed. So, a thousand years of war between vampires and humans followed until they decided to end the war and carve up our world as if they held the deed.

"How do we know this princess won't become evil as Thana?"

"I don't know who the princess might become," Simi says. "Just as none of us know what we might become. What I *do* know is that she's in danger, and if she dies as a result, something terrible will happen. What that might be, I don't know. Which is why I brought you here. I intend to seek her out. I resent vampires just as much as you, but it is my duty to save her life."

My body grows cold when Simi's words register, my legs freezing in my pacing. "No," I say, my voice shrill. "You can't, I—"

Simi holds up her hand. "I know you question our ways; I know you've had your doubts since Mama died; bu—"

"It's not just our stupid ways, Simi. You could be killed!" Though over a hundred years have passed since our grandmother told the vampire princess something she did not like, we remain condemned and bound to this place. That princess became the queen and she wiped all mentions of us from her lands. With each day, we are further forgotten by those who once welcomed us. With each year, we become more of a myth, until one day, as Mama often feared, we won't even believe in ourselves.

"I need to do this," Simi says. Her eyes plead with mine to understand; the zeal for the yamaja way of life and the yearning for who we once were shine through. "It's about more than just a princess. More than fate itself. If we save that princess, if the queen hears of this, she may undo what she did before—this is our chance to reclaim our place in our world, to fulfill our purpose."

It's a purpose Simi has always believed in, never questioning the traditions Mama passed down. Never doubting everything like I have. Maybe that, more than anything, is Simi's power—to be loyal to a cause she can't fully see, to believe in a duty that got our grandmother killed and could kill her, too. "It's not worth the risk," I say, biting my lip to stop its quivering. But when Simi's mind is made, I'm never able to convince her otherwise.

I can't lose you, too, I want to say, but I stop myself. If I say it, she might not go, she might stay because of me. And if she does, she might eventually lose hope in all the things that make her *her*, until she is but a shadow of herself. And then I'll lose her anyway.

Simi gives me a small smile, likely meant to be reassuring. But it isn't, it can't be. I don't want to lose the only family I have left.

"I know the risks"—she wraps her hand around mine—"but I fear we're at the precipice of war—a war that—"

I gasp sharply, grabbing my head as pain shoots through my skull. I double over, falling to the ground.

Simi rushes to crouch by my side. "What is it? A vision?" Her eyes flit across my face.

I grimace as the vision hits me in wave after wave of pain and terrifying images. The creatures, towering and gnarly. The sea stained blood red. "Simi—" The massive bell on the lower level interrupts me, chiming ominously and echoing through the tower. The last time the bell tolled, the hurricane hit. It's our sign that danger—that death—is near.

The spirit I forgot about lingers besides Simi's desk. She opens her mouth in a scream.

Simi barrels out of the room as soon as we hear the bell. "Wait!" I yell, hurrying after her down the stairs, my ears ringing. The heat from the metal railing burns my hands as I grip it, trying not to trip as I quickly descend the tower. I run after my sister to save her life.

"Simi!" I call, reaching out for her. My voice is ragged from calling her name over and over.

I look up to the sky. It has darkened to a bluish gray. *No.* My breath catches in my throat. From where I stand, at the tower's entrance, I see it all.

Monsters are falling from the sky.

They appear out of the air and land on the sandy shore—one minute, it's calm; the next, it's chaos. Yamaja run and scream, trying to find shelter. Our livestock bleat and cluck, fleeing their pens.

Simi is on her way there. Toward them—the monsters, the creatures I saw in my vision. She skips across the sharp rocks surrounding the tower and onto the wooden bridges that connect the tower and floating homes to the shore.

She runs away from me, hurling herself toward death.

The wind howls, stirring up the sand. The air chills, pushing goose bumps onto my skin. The connecting bridges creak and flap. The sky darkens to shades of gray—only pockets of light shine through.

"Simi!" I scream until my throat tightens and burns. These creatures are nearly twice as tall as us. Their heads are shaped like jackals but fleshless, revealing only bone. With ligaments that are thin and gnarly. Nails like broken glass.

One sweeps its arm to the ground and swoops up a yamaja. I cry out, calling her name, but it's too late. It brings her to its mouth and pierces her throat with its fangs, like those of a vampire but thicker, longer, and fiercer. Blood gushes down her neck as it drinks from her, blossoms as its nails dig into her chest, ripping her in two. The creature laps up the blood with its slender red tongue until she fades, body evaporating into sea foam awash with crimson.

I stand frozen on the rocks, knees locked, unable to move. The destruction is playing out just as it did in my vision moments earlier in the tower room. Waves crash against the rocks, slapping against my ankles. My heart beats in heavy, rapid thuds. A cold sweat slicks my brow. Simi has reached the edge of one of the bridges that connects to the shore. She grabs a passing yamaja's hand. "Get the children," she commands. Then she runs back to me.

"You need to leave." She swiftly closes the distance between us, placing her hands on my shoulders, shaking me until I jolt out of my trance—out of the shock of witnessing the creatures' senseless wrath upon my homeland. "Go, now." She shakes me again.

Screams puncture my ears. Everything is red.

I have to do something. "Whatever you have planned, I won't leave your side." My hands tremble. This can't be happening.

Simi grimaces, shaking her head. "You stand no chance against the Reapers." She places her hand on my cheek. I flinch at the coolness of it, the absence of warmth. "Not now," she says. "Not like this."

"Reapers?" I falter, nearly tripping on the rocks. The merciless creatures of folktales. But they are just that: a tale. No one's actually seen them. I swallow slowly. *Just like some have never seen us.* "How could you know that? You say that like you expected them to—" Then it hits me. Simi calling me to the tower. Her telling me about the princess and our duty. "You saw this." The tapestry shows us a desired outcome, the way something is supposed to happen—the way the world is supposed to end up. But Simi's power allows her to see the steps leading there, the many paths that lead to that goal.

I shake my head. "I—I don't understand. You saw it and you didn't warn anyone? You could've prevented this. You could've saved them—We—"

She looks away, unable to meet my gaze. "By protecting you, I am giving everyone a chance. I saw it just before I summoned you—I saw you and this princess. None of it made sense but then it started to. It is not me who must go to find her." Her knuckles are pale as she grips her dress. She takes a deep breath as if mustering her strength. "It's you."

"No," I snap. "You can't stay." The words tumble from my throat, the future I was afraid to voice. "If you do, you'll die." I grip her arm. "I can't lose you. If you come with me, if we stay together, we can—"

"No," she says. "My duty is to protect you, to protect us all. Trust me. This was the best-case scenario, the best outcome not only for us but for our world. I will give you as much time as I can. You have to get away from here. This has to be worth it. Find the princess. Save her. Stop this evil. Come back and rebuild. You are both at the center of whatever is coming." She shakes me off and unties the sword at her side, one she found in the sea many months ago. She hands it to me.

"Simi, no." I try to hand it back, but she pushes it toward me more firmly.

"Sometimes the only way to find out the truth is to go along for the journey. Have faith. Believe. Trust in yourself." She hugs me, kisses me on the cheek even as hers stain with tears. I reach for her, but she turns away, and I slip on the rocks, hands barely catching myself as I fall. A creature catches on the movement and steps onto the bridge before us, crushing it down into the sea and wading through to the shallow end.

"Simi, watch out!" It lurches for her. She jumps swiftly onto its arm and pulls a knife from her boot, stabbing it in the back of the neck.

"Run," she calls as she straddles the creature to yank the knife out. "Run today. Fight tomorrow. Don't fear your powers, Naj. One day you will have no choice but to trust them. They will be there for you. They will help you in the end."

Then the creature picks her up by the collar of her dress and slams her onto the shore. "Run!" She releases another choked cry. She raises her knife, facing the creature head-on as other yamaja do the same.

"*Najja,*" the sea calls as it hits against the rocks. *"Don't be afraid."*

Simi struggles against the creature, fending it off. "Najja, please," she says, voice breaking.

Biting back tears, I heed the sea's calls, knowing that is what Simi wants. I dive in and begin to swim.

When I look back, her death plays out once more, like it did in my vision—only this time it's real. The Reaper grabs her, hands tightening around her waist as her bones are crushed, as her lungs collapse, and she coughs up blood. Simi gasps, taking her last breath, and vanishes into sea foam, just like Mama.

I urge myself to flee as a sob catches in my throat and a sickening sensation settles in.

Mama and now Simi . . . My family is dead.

I am alone.

On the twelfth day, in the nine hundredth year of the Thousand Years' War, by the grace of the goddess Morowa, the vampire bloodlines united to form a nation: Mnara.

Only the sixth bloodline, the Mora, declined, preferring instead the desert, calling the war not of their creation.

On that day, Nandi, leader of the Adaeze bloodline, was crowned Mnara's queen. Granddaughter of Clea the Queenslayer—who gave her life to kill her mother, Thana—Nandi had distinguished herself by becoming one of the greatest vampire generals.

In welcoming her new nation, Nandi said: "In exchange for your independence, we shall gain strength. Peace shall grow among us. Together, we shall defeat the Kingdom of Lienne—our enemies: the humans."

—LONG HAVE WE WARRED: AN ACCOUNT OF THE THOUSAND YEARS' WAR
FIRST EDITION, 1200 AD
MERKESH ROYAL ARCHIVES

CHAPTER FIVE

Najja

The Nation of Mnara: Tssaia

I arrive in the Nation of Mnara within two days and quickly make my way to the capital. It reeks of death.

Tssaia is on a hill, surrounded by a stone wall on one side and the Sabahir River on the other. Guards are posted alongside the wall, and it's too high to climb, so I swim up the unguarded river and crawl through the bank's high grass. There, I crouch, waiting for the sun to set, not wanting to stand out by walking around when the city is at rest.

As soon as the sun dips below the horizon, the city crackles awake. Hooves beat against the pavement and retailers unlock their shops.

I slip into the city.

The way the vampires tell it, Tssaia was built by the gods—the fallen ones. Thana and her godly companions after they came to the lands of the living and she crowned herself its queen. Of course, as Mama used to say, they didn't actually build it. The humans they subjugated did.

Vampires pour onto the paved streets from their homes. Town houses made of timber, three or four in a row, side by side without space, are cluttered together near freestanding homes made of stone. Paths connect the homes with the local shops, all leading up to a castle, at the hill's highest point, where the royal family lives.

Two women exit a stone house that looms three stories high. They wear gowns of colorful silks and satin shoes so delicate they'll be soiled by the day's end. Back home, stone is too expensive to use for our homes and we wear our leather shoes until they're worn through the sole.

I pull my cloak tighter around me, shaking off a chill. Not from the air—it's warm here—but from the thought of home. A home that may not exist when I return.

Though the war ended only a year ago, Tssaia bears no sign of it. The nobles and royals and merchants who make their residences here were sheltered from the brunt—all while living in a city built by humans, the very people they sought to kill.

Vampires brush past me as I walk through the city, taking it all in. Back home, I could cover our entire village in minutes. Here, it would take days.

The deeper in I get, the more I see. Temples erected to our gods. Shops selling fabrics and ceramics. Hairdressers and dressmakers. Booksellers, apothecaries, financiers . . .

Unlike yamaja, vampires must not bathe in the river for there are bathhouses on every corner. Just as frequent are shops selling blood. The vampires receive it per their peace treaty with the humans—gold from vampire mines for blood from human veins.

An unfair trade. The price is too steep and the risk too high, and I highly doubt the very people who signed the treaty are the ones making the sacrifice. A human king who isn't giving blood of his own and a vampire queen who has never toiled a day in a cold, dangerous mine. These royals make decisions without thinking about how they'll affect others. Much like how the vampire queen killed my grandmother simply because she didn't like a prediction.

I put as much space as I can in these crowded streets between myself and the vampires. But I can't avoid *them*—the spirits, some older than a millennia. Unlike the few spirits in the tower, which I could easily sidestep and avoid, there are too many here, flitting in and out of the crowds. They brush past me and I catch a glimpse of their former lives, their feelings . . . pain . . . heartbreak . . . sorrow . . . *fear*. Humans who died here, building this great city. Vampires grieving losses of their own from a war they thought would never end.

I close my eyes and try to separate myself from it. I focus on the present, as Simi taught me to do. The ground underneath my feet, the roughness of my hands, the pacing of my breath as it moves through my body. All the things Simi would do when her visions overwhelmed her. When they came out too jumbled, too fast to understand. But our visions are not the same, and she learned how to control hers from Mama, who shared the same powers. There *was* a record of the first yamaja like me—one of my ancestresses—but I have never seen it. It's held in the royal archives that the Merkesh maintain.

Once, our histories flowed freely between us, because the Merkesh and the yamaja are descended from the same goddess, who believed in knowledge above all else. They shared their texts and stories and we shared ours. But when we were outlawed, that stopped. They ignored our requests to return our records.

I know nothing about my powers. I can't control them.

I take another breath, but it doesn't help. My chest tightens more the quicker I breathe, my hands growing clammy, and something sharp shoots through my core. I gasp, stumbling back.

"Watch where you're going." Firm hands grip my shoulders and shove me away. A vampire with large black wings, so large they could consume me, glares at me. The vampires all have symbols on their necks denoting the bloodlines they belong to. Some also have features that mark them, like the Oorvain and their wings. Natural-born warriors. He wears black armor with an insignia printed on his chest. Not just a soldier, but a member of the palace guard.

Quickly, I avert my eyes. I bow ever so slightly and mutter an apology.

He turns away before I'm even finished. I dart through the crowd, creating as much distance between us as I can. Lest he remember my sea-colored eyes, recall the stories the Merkesh might still tell, and realize what I am.

Makeshift booths are being set up in the city square. A harvest festival, I surmise from the chatter around me. An annual market where merchants from all over come to Tssaia to trade. Merchants stand in front of their wares. They hold up fleeces and garments lined with fur. Gold rings and bracelets and brooches. Burlap bags heaped with colorful spices of every hue sit on the floor. Cured meats hang that make my stomach growl.

People mill about, their laughter carried in the air. But I'm filled with a heaviness I can't shake. My people's blood is caked under my nails. My ears still ring with their screams. The same memories play on a loop, reminding me why I'm here. To carry out Simi's last wish—to find the princess whose life is in danger, whose death will affect us all. But from what I overhear, the queen won't be making an appearance at this year's festival. The crown heir also won't be here. Which means I must find a way in—a death sentence at best—or I have to lure the princess out.

I know what Simi would say: pray. When my sister prayed, the gods listened. A sign here. A whisper there. They showed her what she needed to know. When I pray, only death follows. Visions sent by the gods who gave me this cursed gift.

I stopped praying to the gods the day they let Mama die. And now they've taken Simi. What have gods ever done for me?

Something dark eats at me, hollowing my soul, tainting it with something other—something I can't name. Confusion? Anger? Hunger to punish those who hurt me, who took everything away from me?

What is my purpose in this world? What is the point if the outcome will always be death for those I love? I look to the stars, searching the sky for a sign, but the stars are silent.

Mama believed fate was its own force. That even gods do not control it. She cautioned us against blaming them—not that I ever listened. She encouraged us to pray, because though the gods are not all-powerful, they are not powerless. *They are always listening*, she would say as she did my hair, my back flush against her chest, her legs snug around mine like a cradle keeping me safe.

Inhale. Exhale. I begin to pray.

I pray to the very gods I've cursed.

Time passes without me realizing it.

I walk through the festival, deeper into the marketplace, wandering without thought as to what path I'll take. A breeze rushes past me. A star shoots across the sky.

I find myself on the outskirts of the market, where dozens of empty tents are staked for vendors not yet here. One billows open, like the wind is rustling through its golden-yellow fabric, beckoning me near.

I walk toward it, holding my breath. *This is ridiculous*, I think. And yet, still, there it is: the smallest glimmer of hope.

"Please," I whisper to the gods. Then I enter the tent.

CHAPTER SIX

Leyla

The Nation of Mnara: Tssaia

The castle looms overhead, its flying buttresses casting shadows onto the starlit streets as we walk down the hillside to Tssaia's square. The scent of blood clings to the air as the annual Mnaran harvest festival sprawls before us. The one time of year when even my guards are free to leave their posts and I can slip out undetected. When merchants come from the farthest parts of my nation's borders to trade. When I can find the yamaja.

My best friend, Danai, walks beside me, dressed in a cotton gown as plain as the one I'm wearing and a fleece-lined hooded robe. We slip into the throng of vampires. The festivities have been in full swing since the market opened earlier this evening. Revelers jostle together, their bodies a blur of black and brown, letting the djembes' sounds lead them to the heart of the festival, where my people dance, giving themselves over to the night.

"So, the kitchen servants—they didn't happen to say where you could find this yamaja?"

"No." I shake my head. "I overheard them gossiping about how they saw a girl in the market hours ago. She had skin as black as the Kutmenian Sea's depths and her locs were red with clay only found in that sea. Her nails caked with it, too. Who else could it have been but a yamaja?" *They're the only ones able to swim so deep.*

"And so, we pick the most crowded time of night." She sighs dramatically. "How are we going to find anyone here? I knew this was a fool's mission."

"And yet you agreed to come." *Not that I gave her much choice*, I think, letting my recent actions sour the moment.

She opens her mouth, likely to say exactly what I'm thinking, to remind me of the only fight we've ever had, but I stop her before she can begin. "Thank you." *Where would I be without her?*

She gives me a small nod. "Who else is going to help you out of the trouble you always cause?" The moonlight catches her eyes: brown and human but rimmed with red. A hallmark trait of the Zamiri bloodline—due to centuries of intermarriage with the Lienne. "Fine," she grumbles. "We'll start here on the outside and work our way farther in."

The deeper in we get, the more the sharp smells of spices, meats, and perfumes collide with the coppery scent of stalls selling blood snacks. I run my tongue across my fangs as my stomach rumbles. The valley is packed with colorful tents, and fellow vampires from our nation's five bloodlines pulse throughout the crowded stalls, touching trinkets and jingling jewels.

Children chase one another through the market. Their sticky hands latch onto our legs and those of other passersby as they hide from one another. In a nearby stall, a Sintu metalworker sells bronze weights—each one sculpted into a figurine that represents Mnaran stories, adages, and proverbs. The Sintu bring only the finest metals from their legendary mines, ones they unearthed with their retractable iron fingernails like hooks.

To my right, a Zamiri woman haggles for silks in front of a tent draped with them. The silks billow in the wind, a rainbow of colors. To my left, an Adaeze nobleman pays for his purchase with gold. Gold dust for seasonings, for cloth, for land—gold is the currency of our world.

A group of girls our age giggle over a pamphlet. I catch sight of the front page: a gossip sheet detailing the most eligible Mnarans. A wicked look crosses Danai's face. "I bet you're in it, Ley."

She brandishes her hands before her. "'The crown princess of Mnara. Age: eighteen. Positives: set to inherit the royal treasury. Negatives: mommy issues, a bit of a pain in the ass.'" She grins.

"*Really*, that's my only positive? Not my loyalty. Not the many times I've saved *your* ass."

"You're not bad with a sword."

I roll my eyes, knowing full well that I am almost as good as she is. After all, I graduated second from our military's academy—second only to her. We trained side by side for years, dreaming of the day we'd go into battle to avenge the deaths of family members that the humans killed.

Until the day everything changed. One evening, I was preparing for our upcoming deployment. The next, I was lying in bed, physicians swarming around me. Instead of where I should've been, preparing to fight alongside my best friend and proving to Mama that I could be the strong queen she wishes me to be.

As if my body's listening, tingling shoots through my leg—pain that's ever-present these days. I stop and rub my leg that feels like it's fallen asleep. My nerves are acting up again.

Danai places a hand on my arm. "We can take a break."

"I'm fine." I cut her off.

She opens her mouth as if to protest, but instead stops and carries on.

On the outskirts of the market, Merkesh storytellers weave tales for children gathered at their feet. One storyteller plays a kora. Her hands delicately pluck its twenty-one strings, its somber notes setting the tone for "The Tale of Amma," a fisherwoman's widow who drowned her village in tears sprung from her grief, forming the Sea of Sorrows, which all souls pass through on their way to Nekros.

Papa used to say that vampires are made of our stories. That stories are the foundation of our nation. Seeing these children, mouths open, eyes wide, and so focused on the storytellers, reminds me of being a little girl—of a time when it was easy to believe in such tales.

"Come, come," another storyteller calls, clinking his gold rings together. Like the woman, he's draped in the signature black-feathered robes of the Merkesh. "Do you know the story of the yamaja?" he asks.

Blood-red eyes wide, the children before him shake their heads. "Begin, begin," they beg.

He stands and begins to act it out. How an old woman saved an alligator in a swamp, but that alligator was actually the goddess Anae in disguise. The goddess granted the woman one wish. The woman could've asked for jewels and gold, to be a queen and to rule an empire. But she only desired a child.

"The gods never give you exactly what you want," Mama often interjected when Papa would tell such tales.

Instead of granting her one child, the goddess of knowledge granted the woman two daughters. Daughters who the villagers swore had legs that transformed into fish tails in water and who knew events no one should've known, well before they happened.

"The first yamaja," I whisper to myself.

Created long before the vampires. Women who foretell fate—a fate we're all bound to.

"Leyla." Danai's voice grows serious. "You really think a yamaja will be here?" Her voice is so soft it could be buried in the winds. She purses her lips, and the faded gash that runs along her left cheek becomes more pronounced. Not from the battles she fought during the war, but from times she never speaks of—before she became like a sister to me.

I twist the gold ring on my middle finger. "Every woman in my family was visited by one when she was eighteen." If Papa were here, he'd say that once the yamaja were more than stories. *Once they were as common as you and I.*

"But why would one come back here when they're outlawed? What if the servants were lying to you?"

I shake my head. "What would they gain from that?"

Danai shrugs. She knows they would gain nothing and lose everything if they were found to have lied to their future queen. I don't say what I'm thinking, what I'm hoping deep in my bones: that maybe, just maybe, one is here for me.

"A yamaja told my great-great-grandmother that she would end Thana's bloodthirsty reign and she did—she tracked her mother to the end of our world and killed her. One told my grandma that she would unite our nation and she did—she brought the bloodlines together under one queen, herself. And one—"

"Told your mother that she would end the war and bring peace to our lands but die young," Danai interrupts.

"Well," I say, smoothing out my dress as my hands grow sweaty at the reminder of Mama's present fate, one she keeps from our people. "They were right, weren't they?" I blink back tears, not wanting to think of the inevitable. Soon, she will be forced to make me queen. It is not the yamaja that I fear, but who I am destined to become. I am not strong like her. I'm the first of my bloodline to not fight in the war. I am not the crown heir Mama wished me to be.

"That's not my point, Ley. Yes, we are bound to fate, but what if by searching it out you uncover something you don't like? What will you do if the yamaja tells you something you don't want to hear?"

"Such as that I'm going to be a failure queen?" I laugh. "'Leyla the Floundering,' they'll call me." The fact that I am nothing like my mother is a point Mama often makes.

"The *floundering*?" Danai lifts her brow. "We'd come up with something better than that."

I shoot her a glare, and she doubles over laughing and then she sobers. "You're not going to be a failure. Just like you don't need a yamaja to tell you what the future holds. Fate is for the gods to know, Ley. For you to know it will only trap you."

I groan. "You sound like her." Danai, like everyone else, practically deifies Mama, praying to her in the same breath as she does Morowa, the queen of the gods.

In our nation, Mama is a legend. She ended the Thousand Years' War and brokered the peace treaty with our once enemies, the humans.

But me? A queen who's never led armies . . . what kind of queen is that?

"Knowing your fate prepares you for the unknown. As soldiers, you and Mama should respect that. I want to proudly meet my fate. I need to know what the future holds." I go through great lengths to avoid discussing Mama, to avoid reminding myself of how I fall short of her every expectation. If the throne wasn't passed down from mother to daughter, she'd probably make my brother, Malike, king.

Danai touches my shoulder, turning me to face her. "Yamaja cannot change the pas—"

"I'm not trying to change the past," I snap. "I just want to be a good queen, Danai." I throw my hands up in frustration. "How many times do we have to go over this? I need to be ready for when . . ." I stop myself as Mama's chiding slips into my head. *A queen must always be in control of her emotions.* I take a deep breath, steadying myself. "I need reassurance that when she passes on and passes the crown to me, I won't let her down." I glance at the ground, at the dirt coating my white slippers. Heat rushes to my cheeks as the real truth slips out, hanging tensely between us. "I just want to make my mother proud."

Danai's disapproval grows thick between us as the night darkens. She thinks I am too tough on myself; I know I am not tough enough.

"Pies? Treats?" An elderly woman's calls pierce the silence. I take Danai's hand and drag her towards the stall dripping with salt-cured animal meats that only a Zamiri like her can digest—most of our bodies cannot break down meat the way a human's can. Blood sausages also hang in thick ropes from overhead. The table in front of us is lined with Danai's favorite treat: pies on sticks, made of rice soaked in human blood, stuck together, and then fried. In the back, behind the woman, are several iron pots sitting above firepits in which blood boils to thicken it for soup.

"Two pies." I push a gold coin with Mama's face on it into her hand. They're made mostly of blood, so I can have them, too.

The woman bows in thanks and hands me two on a stick. "Thank you." I bring one of the pies to my mouth.

Danai snatches it from my hands before my fangs can sink in. Without hesitation, she takes a bite. "Not bad."

I snatch it back and eye the chunk taken out of it. "Was that really necessary? I bought two."

"Quality testing." She grins and takes the unbitten treat from my other hand and stuffs it down her throat. She licks her lips—"That was delicious"—seemingly at once back to her pain-in-the-butt self.

We walk past several stone buildings. They reek of blood nights old; death's stench coats their walls. During the war those taverns were where vampires went to feed, where desperate humans who needed extra coins were paid for their life force by the ounce. Now they're required to have a license that shows that their blood is legally sourced from the monthly shipments the humans send.

I bite into the sticky treat, trying to push Mama and our past from my mind. Blood gushes, running down my arm and dripping onto the ground. I lick my fingers, stuffing the flaky pastry into my mouth and tuning out Mama's nagging voice until all I can hear is the thudding of Danai's heartbeat syncing in time with mine. I close my eyes and take it all in, the silence that comes with the absence of Mama dictating how a princess should act and who I must be.

The distant drumming grows to a deafening roar—a prelude to the celebrations that will last all night. My eyes follow their sound to a large patch of earth where even more vampires are packed side by side. Each wears their hair shorn or pinned up to proudly display the marks denoting their bloodlines, on their necks, on their shoulders, on their backs.

There, more vendors seek out buyers, pushing carts of food and bubbly, bloody drink. The drummers walk through the crowd, djembes strapped to their bodies and decorated with bells that jingle with each step. The dancers are even more laden with bells. They are tied around their ankles and wrists, shaking as they pulse to the beat. Here, rank does not matter; Mama does not preside. Here, and only here, I can be just me.

We walk deeper into the market, through more vampires. But everywhere we look are more vendors promising "never-before-seen" trinkets instead of what I really want: fortunes told, and futures known.

We reach a line of stalls draped with shawls made of the most delicate silks, embroidered with intricate designs. I touch a shawl, taking in its hues, which range from violet to the lightest lavender.

Firm hands grip my shoulders.

"Danai?" But when I turn it's not her. My brother meets my eyes, wearing Mama's favorite scowl.

CHAPTER SEVEN

Leyla

"What are you doing here, Ley?" Malike's voice is sharp with fury. He furrows his brows as he peers at me. His scrutiny comes down like a thick fog.

Danai slides up beside me, and Malike hovers over us both.

"Malike," says Danai. Her voice trails off as if there's more she wishes to say.

"Danai." His lips turn up in a smile before he realizes it and soon he's back to his usual frown.

He glances at me. "Mama specifically forbade you from attending this year's festival."

"Mama is always forbidding me from doing things. That didn't used to stop us. Why should it now?" Though a few years apart, once, *we* were inseparable. *What changed?* I want to ask, but I already know. After all, I was there on that day, the moment I became the crown heir and Mama became queen.

"Hilarious." His lips form a thin line, barely moving as he speaks.

Gold-dyed ostrich feathers shoot up like rays on top of his helmet, a general's regalia.

He reaches for me, but I sidestep away. "I'm not going back to the castle. If I'm to be queen, I should be able to spend time with my people." Ever since he achieved the general's rank, he's treated me less like his sister and more like another soldier to order around.

"*When* you are queen, you can do as you like." He wags his finger at me just like Mama might. "Until then, you're my responsibility." He scowls at Danai. "And yours."

He reaches for me again and I dodge him. "Be serious, Leyla. In case you've forgotten, the war just ended. What if there's another attack? What if something happens to you? What of Mnara then?" Every word echoes Mama's; he becomes more like her every day.

"Then you can take the throne," I snap.

His face falters. I think to take it back, but the words have already found their mark. He grabs my elbow, jerking me toward him. "We're leaving." He drags me past a vendor selling history scrolls and another selling heaps of rice. I grab a handful and throw it at him.

"What the—"

"Run!" I yank at Danai's arm, pulling her along.

"Come back here!" he yells. "Leyla!" He points at two guards. "Catch her!"

I dart through stalls, like the children earlier. Danai sprints beside me. "I knew this was a bad—"

"Don't." I lead us toward the drummers and dancers and through the crowd, pushing past bodies pressed against one another. The earth shifts beneath our feet, and all around us vampires dance.

The coppery smell of blood grows thicker.

Beside us, a Zamiri woman, bloodied knife in hand, drinks from the neck of another Zamiri, whose brownish-red eyes glow in the night as he cries out in pleasure mixed with pain. Three Oorvain kiss, passing blood from goblets, running their hands into one another's hair—their skin glows bluish-black in the moonlight like their wings. Just ahead of us, a Sintu girl sways. She reaches her arms up and runs them across the sky. Her brown curls stick to her face, dampened with sweat as the moon illuminates her skin in a soft, umber glow, highlighting each one of the freckles that trail down the plunging neckline of her dress. My breath catches in my throat. I jerk my eyes away.

We crouch in the middle of the crowd as the guards search the perimeter and work their way in.

"They're going to find us." My heart thumps against my chest.

"No." Danai shrugs off her cloak, a deep purple to my red. "They're going to find me."

"Danai."

"Listen." She grabs my shoulders, steadying me, making me meet her amber eyes. "You want to find this yamaja." She takes off my cloak and wraps hers around me before shrugging mine on. "I'll lead the guards away from you." Our skin is the same shade of warm brown with pink undertones, our bodies are sculpted with the same curves, and our tiny, coiled curls are cut close to our heads—from afar we could be twins. We've fooled many in this same way.

"Thank you." I hug her. My hands linger, thinking of our argument just days ago. Of all the things I said and of how she forgave me, how she's here for me as she always is. Whereas I, all too often, think first about myself. "I'm sor—"

She shakes her head. "Later," she says, squeezing my shoulders.

"Remember, ultimately, this life is yours to live—and yours to control. Don't let anyone, even a yamaja, take that away."

I laugh, adjusting her cloak. "Says the girl who believes fate is only for the gods to know."

She smirks. "What can I say? I'm full of contradictions."

"Over here, over here," one of the guards calls.

"That's my cue." Danai ties on my hood and runs to the right. I wait a beat as the guards follow her, then, crouching low, I push my way through the throngs of dancers, through the vendors selling even more goods and the drummers all around, not stopping until I reach the other side.

When I'm through the worst of the crowd, I catch sight of a pendant on a table. I walk toward it as if led by an invisible thread. On the table are many such trinkets, but this one stands apart: though cast in gold like the others, it is the only hummingbird. Even from here I can see the thumbprint pressed into its left side—an unmistakable blemish from someone who touched the gold too soon after the wax cast was poured.

I bring my hand to my chest and touch *my* hummingbird pendant. It bears the same thumbprint. *Papa's thumbprint*. The pendant was once his; he made it himself. But he is long gone. How can there be another just like it? I look to the skies, to the gods, for an answer. "If you're trying to tell me something, a clearer sign would be nice."

I wait a moment and there's nothing; they're as silent as ever.

She who moves with each day is better than another who waits for luck. Papa's favorite saying. I shake my head. Just a coincidence. Like how there's no yamaja here, just a trick of the eyes that the servants fell for.

I turn away from the stall, preparing to head back to the square, and that's when I see her. I clutch my hands over my mouth to stop my scream. A young girl stands before me.

"You scared me." My heart is racing. I look around for her parents, for her friends, but we're the only ones here. "Why are you out here alone?" But that's not the only thing strange about her. Her fingers are wrinkled like a prune while her dress sticks to her skin. Her feet are bare and dirt clings to them like she just stepped out of the water. Like I looked all those years ago, on the night Papa died.

Thunder rumbles, though the skies are clear.

Maybe this is the sign I'd asked the gods for.

The girl opens her mouth, revealing two sharp fangs. She waves her hand, beckoning me to follow, and she runs away. "Wait up," I yell, rushing after her, unsure of why I'm following this girl. It's like something is urging me forward. She weaves through the stalls, turning into another aisle, this one lined with gourds that thud together as she rushes by. I can just barely smell the wisps of cinnamon and sage and other spices wafting over from the market's square. Every breath I take echoes as my slippers grit against the earth.

She disappears into a tent just behind a stall at the aisle's end.

"Hello?" I call, approaching the tent. I take a step forward, then pause. What if it's a trap? I shake the thought away. I didn't come this far to give up now.

I follow the girl into the tent.

CHAPTER EIGHT

Najja

"Thanks for nothing, gods," I mutter as I walk out of the Sabahir River, catfish in hand. The tent was empty. No vampire princess in sight. My stomach growled, reminding me I hadn't eaten in days, so I went to remedy that.

I throw the makeshift net over my shoulder and make my way back to the "borrowed" tent.

As per usual, placing my faith in the gods was a mistake, and it's time to do things *my* way: making it up as I go. Somehow I have to get into the castle—sneak across its moat *and* inside the princess's chambers undetected—without her screaming for the guards as soon as I arrive. A perfect plan, if you ask me.

I huff, letting out a deep sigh. What even would I say?

Hi, I'm a yamaja (yes, we're real) and I think you're at the center of something really bad that hasn't happened and might not ever happen but if it does could result in the end of our world. But first, I'm here to save you.

I shake my head, locs beating against my back. Saving a vampire.

The tapestry shredding. The attack on my homeland. How did the Reapers even get there? Reapers live in Nekros, the island of the dead. They belong to the goddess there. Why would she send them here? Creatures hopping worlds, from the land of the dead to that of the living, is about as ridiculous as gods falling from the sky. Which, to be fair, *has* happened before. But not in my nineteen years, or for over a millennia before it.

One thing at a time, I tell myself, trying to focus. Trying to forget the weariness that consumes me, the ache that hasn't left me since Simi's death. I *will* figure it out. I must. If she believed that this princess is at the center of whatever is coming, then I owe it to her to see this through.

By the time I reach the tent, the sky is gray. Overcast and cloudy, tucking away the sun. A shudder creeps through me, but I shake it off. If Reapers were here, I'd know. This is just a coming storm.

"Hello?" a voice calls from within the tent.

I stiffen, then reach for my sword and come up empty. *Dammit.* It's inside. Bracing myself, I raise what I do have high above me. Net in one hand, catfish in the other, I kick open a side flap to reveal—

A young woman my age.

Her hair is cropped close to her head in tight coils in a way that only accentuates her beauty: her bright pink lips, her strong cheekbones, and her thick, sculpted eyebrows that perfectly frame her face. She looks around the room, her eyes landing on me. Bright red irises—a vampire. Her gaze pulls me in much like the Kutmenian Sea, beautiful and deadly.

"I'm sorry," she says, taken aback. "I-I didn't mean to intrude. I came here looking for a young girl, but . . ." She continues talking, but I lose track of what she's saying.

Focus, Najja. I blink, clearing my head and pull my gaze away from her mouth. The girl stops talking. Her eyes flit over me like a puzzle she's attempting to solve.

I look around the sparse tent. The only things here are my sword, resting against the far side and blocked by the girl; the firepit I dug earlier; and the two of us. Keeping the space between us, I place down the fish and the net. That's when I see it: the edges of an Adaeze heart unfurling behind her neck. I think back to my lessons, to the family trees Mama made us learn. The Adaeze bloodline comprises the royal family, and there's only one girl near my age. "You're the princess," I say, stunned.

Her eyes search over me once more before she breaks into a wide grin, as if the puzzle is solved. "You're the yamaja," she gasps. "You came here for me."

I furrow my brows, thoroughly confused. "How did you know?"

CHAPTER NINE

Leyla

She isn't what I expected from a yamaja. Not weathered and wizened by age, by the weight of shouldering fate's commands. Long lashes frame her eyes, a vivid blue green—a stark contrast to her midnight-black skin. Thick, reddish locs are interwoven into a long braid that hangs down the middle of her back. She wears a simple tunic, tucked into trousers that are soaked up to her knees. They're a deep blue that accentuates her eyes, making them sparkle like the stars in the sky. The long sleeves of her shirt fit over her arms like a second skin, hinting at forearms so smoothly muscular that they are better suited to a soldier, not a seer. The stories never said that yamaja have to be gray haired, but I always assumed it'd be so.

"How did you know?" she asks, staring at me in shock.

Chin up, she unflinchingly meets my gaze, exuding a confidence that is beautiful . . . powerful. Though the goddess of knowledge created her kind, I wouldn't want to face her on a battlefield.

She clears her throat, and I realize she's been talking to me. Heat rushes to my cheeks and I look away, suddenly finding the dirt floor to be the most interesting thing.

"How did you know that I'm here for you?" she asks again.

"Well," I say as I watch an ant trail through the dirt. "You're a yamaja." Perfectly matching how the servants described her, and yet I was still caught off guard.

She raises an eyebrow, as if she thinks I'm the one who isn't making sense. I clear my throat, launching into an explanation. "Yamaja foretold the end of Thana's reign and the end of our Thousand Years' War." My words spill forth, each more rapidly than the last as I recount the many ways yamaja have guided my ancestresses and how it's surely my turn next. "You are blessed to know our fates, yet often cursed to have no one believe you. But I—"

"Would believe me?" she scoffs. She turns away from me but not before I catch her rolling her eyes.

"Did you just roll your eyes at me?"

"Why, yes, I did, your highness." The sharpness of her tone stings. What did I do to her? "So typical of a vampire to think that everything revolves around them," she mutters, loud enough for me to hear. "*Everyone* wants to know their fate. *No one* wants to believe it. Luckily for you, I'm not here for that." She says it so matter-of-factly, with such finality, it's soul crushing.

"If you aren't here to tell me my fate, then what are you here for?"

The yamaja lifts her head, looking tired beyond her years. "I'm here to save your life."

After a few moments of silence, I throw my head back and laugh. "Did Danai put you up to this?" It certainly wouldn't be the first time she's pranked me, creating an elaborate ruse, paying off the servants to go along with it. But she knows how badly I want answers; this seems too cruel for her.

"I don't know this Danai, but I can assure you I speak the truth," the yamaja says.

I look down at myself. "Well, clearly someone is playing with you. As you can see, I'm fine."

"Or . . ." she says, "maybe the danger hasn't presented itself yet." Her blue irises shift to gray. Something is scaring her, and the thought frightens me. Maybe Mama was right; maybe I should've stayed inside.

"What danger are you talking about?"

She shakes her head, as if she doesn't want to voice it, as if saying it will make it come true. "Let's just hope for your sake that my sister is wrong." Her brow furrows, and she moves in front of the tent's entrance. "We'll stay here. We'll wait it out."

"Wait it out? And how long do you propose we do that?" I think of the guards chasing down Danai. Once they find her, they'll come looking for me. They'll tear the square apart until they do, and then I'll never get the answers I seek.

"Until I'm satisfied that you're not in danger." Her tone makes it clear there's no room for argument.

"How long will it take until you're satisfied?"

My voice comes out breathier than I intend, and a suggestive smile spreads across her face.

Heat rises to my cheeks. "That's not—that's not what I mean." I ball my hands into fists and kick at the dirt. I walk right up to her and face her down with my coldest stare. Which would be more threatening if I actually were facing her down, instead of staring directly at her neck. "I command you," I say, putting weight behind my words.

She laughs but doesn't move. "I'm not your subject, your highness. I'm not bound to obey your commands."

Inwardly, I groan. The gods *would* send the most insufferable yamaja to "save my life." I reach up my sleeve and grab the knife I keep there. I step forward and aim it at her chest. "I don't want to hurt you, but I will if you don't get out of my way."

She steps forward, closing the distance between us. In one motion, she maneuvers around me, disarms me, and brings me flush against her chest. "Let me go. I wasn't going to kill you."

"Pointing a knife at me tells a different story." I struggle against her, but she only tightens her grip. I drink in her saltwater smell and her warmth. "Princess," she whispers low in my ear, sending shivers down my spine. Her hand wraps around mine and she wrestles the knife free from my grip. "Don't make me forget why I'm really here."

"You wouldn't."

She pockets my knife with one hand, still pinning me to her with the other. I gulp. It isn't her killing me that I'm imagining. I shake my head free of the thought, of the yamaja whispering other things into my ear, of her kissing me.

"If you mean I wouldn't lose any sleep, that's correct. It's not like I enjoy being a royal caretaker."

"It's not like I asked you to—"

Her screams interrupt me. One second, she's standing, the next, she's on the floor, doubling over in pain. "No, it can't be," she sputters as she rocks and clutches her head.

I drop to the ground at once, understanding she must have seen something. "What is it?"

Her eyes are an even darker gray. She glances at me, clearly confused. "You have a sister? A twin?"

I shake my head. "Only a brother." And then it hits me, and my blood grows cold. "Danai," I whisper. I shake her. "Tell me! What did you see?"

"Death." Her voice is hoarse with terror, just as the ground quakes with a monstrosity and a fierceness I have never known.

I scramble up and dart out from the tent. "Wait!" the yamaja calls.

Thunder cracks open the sky and the drumming that has been constant background noise stops. In its place, screams rip through the air where moments before my people laughed and danced.

"Danai!" My heartbeat quickens and tingles shoot up my legs. I push aside the pain and run as fast as I can.

CHAPTER TEN

Leyla

A howl reverberates through the square. Bodies slam into me as screams erupt and vampires rush past, tripping over themselves and others.

My heart squeezes tight in my chest. *Danai.* I push through the crowd, looking for her. *Run*, every part of my body screams. What if we *are* under attack? Mama told me *not* to leave the castle. Like a fool, I disobeyed and now Danai will pay the price.

Someone slams into me, and I fall sideways, wincing as my knees scrape the ground. I land in a sticky puddle, and when I push myself up, blood drips from my hands. Frantically, I wipe them on my dress—*am I bleeding?* A woman lies beside me. The black lines of her bloodline mark unfurl across the back of her neck. *Sintu.* It's splattered with blood gushing from two large puncture wounds on her neck.

The marks are too large to be vampire.

I glance at my hands and back at her gaping wound—it's her blood that coats them.

Blood oozes out of her neck. I take off Danai's cape, bundle it up, and press down, trying to stop her bleeding. A painful moan escapes from her lips.

"Help!" I shout into the crowd of panicked vampires, but no one stops. I apply more pressure, but her blood keeps seeping through the fabric to my fingers.

Two hands grab my shoulders.

I kick. "Let go!"

"Stop, it's me." My attacker lowers her hood to reveal a face peppered with freckles, a long scar on one side, and two brownish-red irises hardened with terror.

"Danai!" Relief washes over me. "Help me. We need to get her—" But when I turn back, the Sintu woman's eyes are wide and empty, and her mouth is open in a sound that no longer comes.

Danai hooks her arm around mine. "Get up," she snaps. I tear my eyes away from the woman. "We have to get back to the castle." She jerks me up and urges me forward. We dart through the large crowd scattering in every direction. Growing up during the war, I became used to hearing of death. But I was always here, far away from the battlefields. This—this is something new. My body is breaking out in a cold sweat. Adrenaline spikes through my veins as we rush back to the castle—to safety.

Danai's nails dig into my skin, a silent command to move faster. Another howl erupts from the square, causing me to look back. Large creatures, masses of darkness, fight hordes of Oorvain guards on the patch of earth where vampires just danced. The creatures' ligaments are gnarly, like knobby tree branches. Their nails are sharp, like claws, and two long fangs protrude from their fleshless skulls—already red with blood.

More Oorvain fly toward them, slashing down the beasts with their armored wings.

One guard rushes forward, his plume bouncing as his mouth opens in an endless scream. *Malike.* He lunges, his sword aimed at one of the creatures. But the creature is faster. It grabs his arms and flings him into the air. He lands facedown. Malike tries to push himself up, but his arms give, and he smacks onto the ground. The creature takes a step toward him to finish the job.

"Malike!" I yell. I start to run for him.

Danai grabs my arm, yanking me back to her. "That's the last thing he'd want." But all I can hear are his screams that sound so much like Papa's did years ago. The night everything changed. I should've been faster, stronger—I could've saved him had I tried. I am not that little girl anymore.

My eyes dart around, landing on a nearby stall, abandoned, lined with the finest metals and an array of knives. I break from Danai and pluck two curved swords from the table. Their golden hilts glint in the night.

"Leyla, no!" says Danai.

But I'm already gone. I race to where the creature has Malike in its arms again. It brings him toward its mouth, its fangs hovering over his neck. I slash at its knee; my head just barely reaches its torso. I dig in, ripping through its flesh. The creature stumbles back and drops Malike. I crouch over him where he's sprawled out on the ground.

I place an arm underneath him. Danai rushes toward us, yelling, hands frantically waving like she's trying to get my attention, but her words are lost in the sounds of the battle stretching around us. "We're going to get you out of here," I say, trying to scoop him up.

"Leyla, watch out," he says, short of breath.

A thunderous roar bristles the hairs on the back of my neck. Too late I realize my mistake. The first thing Malike taught me during training: never turn your back on the enemy.

The creature latches onto me. Its nails scratch at my legs, ripping off strips of skin. "Please, no," I yell. A sharp pain washes through me. I scream louder as it drags me backward. I reach for the ground, trying to grab onto anything, even tufts of grass. Spots appear in my vision; it yanks me into the air.

The ground disappears beneath me, and I scream until my voice fails me.

I spot a blur of red locs, hear the swishing of a sword. At once, the creature's grip on me weakens and its legs buckle. It falls, shaking the ground like an earthquake. The yamaja slices through its neck, and its head rolls off with a thud. Her silver sword is dripping black with the creature's blood.

I crumple on the ground, heaving as blood oozes from the wounds on my body, soiling the ground red. I gasp as bit by bit the severed creature disintegrates and disappears into the air.

The yamaja extends a hand, and I hobble up. A grimace lines her face as several Oorvain take down another one of the creatures. I open my mouth in thanks, but then I hear it: a familiar scream.

No no no no. The last remaining creature is dragging Danai away.

I sprint after them, pain coursing through my body. "Danai!" My lungs expand as I yell, expending the last bits of energy I have left.

It swoops her up in its arm, cradling her like something precious.

Run. I urge my body forward, pushing myself to my limits. I close the distance between us. "Leyla," she cries, voice hoarse. She reaches her hands out to me. Please gods, no.

Faster, I urge myself to run.

"Leyla," she calls, in one anguished scream.

I extend my hand. I'm so close that I can touch her fingertips, her pulse beating alongside mine. I look up and meet her eyes, quaking with fear.

"It's going to be okay," I start to tell her. *I've got you*, I want to say. But just as I think I do, Malike barrels into me and we fall to the ground. "Get off of me!" I push him away, but when I stand up, she's gone.

"No!" I shake my head as hot tears stream down my face. I fall to my knees, arms outstretched and open to the heavens. "How?" I ask gods who never listen. *Why?* I scream inside.

The hillside stretches before us; the only forest is far behind the castle. One moment the creature was before me, and now it's gone, taking with it my best friend.

Vanished.

As if the sky opened up and swallowed her whole.

Once, long ago, ~~there was a fair maiden~~ the gods were bored.

Truth be told, the gods were often bored. But on this day, they were particularly so. So, instead of the usual fires or floods used to make humans suffer for their godly entertainment, they thought to visit a town in the lands of the living and issue a challenge. A contest of sorts. And whoever should win would be granted one wish. All they had to do was make something *out of* nothing.

One by one, the townspeople tried by parading prized possessions before the gods. But the gods only laughed, for they were not nothing *turned to* something. *Soon the humans stopped trying and the gods grew bored again and returned to the Heavenly Realms.*

But not before a fair maiden happened upon the king of the gods in her family's pecan grove. She picked a handful of pecans, then she purposefully tripped, spilling forth the pecans. Kovnu, in his boredom, helped her.

"Thank you," she said as he handed her some.

He merely shrugged and said, "It's nothing."

For several years, the maiden tended these pecans, prepping them, planting them, growing them. Until they turned into a great grove. Until their branches sprouted high into the sky and people from all over came and said, "Isn't that something?" And so, the maiden climbed up the highest tree and made her way to the Heavenly Realms, where she presented Kovnu with her tale of turning nothing into something.

Kovnu reared his head back in laughter. "Very well," he said, pleasantly surprised. "What is it that you wish?"

"To be more powerful than anything and anyone," she said without hesitation, choosing her words carefully.

Kovnu granted her that gift.

But it was not as she hoped. With the gods, nothing is as promised. Her power came not of the world but of herself. To access it, she had to use herself.

A cup of her blood for a salve that could heal minor wounds.
A few of her toes for a magic mirror.
Her left eye for a powerful love potion.
A great deal more of her blood for a sword that could kill any god.
True power requires sacrifice. No one is ever above the gods.

Over time, she came to live in the Heavenly Realms. "The sorceress of the gods," she was called. She had an affair with a god, whom some say she seduced with a potion. A single child came of this union. A girl who inherited her father's wings and the power that ran through her mother's blood.

The girl called herself an angel. Her mother called her Favre.

—MNARAN TALES: VOLUME I
TRANSCRIBED: 1009 AD
MERKESH ROYAL ARCHIVES

CHAPTER ELEVEN

Favre

Nekros

A small price to pay for love, I told myself over a thousand years ago as I cried out, hacking off my wings.

Now, in this decrepit manor house in the middle of Nekros, as I tend wounds that are nearly as old as me, I can't help but wonder if it was worth it.

The bleeding never stops where my beautiful wings once were. Wings from a lifetime ago.

The dead goddess's bedchamber sprawls around me as I sit on her blood-spattered, pink-cushioned chair. My back faces the shattered mirror. I turn my head, taking in the exposed wounds on each shoulder blade: two deep, jagged lines, scabbed over and oozing blood.

Dab, don't rub, Mother would've said. And so, I dab the healing salve she taught me to make onto each of the wounds. According to her, dabbing makes it hurt less. And yet, I wince at the sting.

Nothing takes this pain away.

If Thana were here, maybe . . . I shake my head.

I followed Mother's instructions precisely, pulling three fingernails to make the salve. Even something as small as a healing salve costs a price I must pay. It's the curse of the power passed down from my mother's blood to mine: I can do anything, I can be anyone, but I must give parts of myself in return. I must sacrifice. Now, at least, the other wounds heal. Thanks to being a vampire. But no matter what I do, the wounds on my back never fully heal. With time, the scars never fade. It's as if, by my act, I betrayed my body, and this is my mother's way of lashing out and reminding me that some prices are too high, too precious, to pay.

You must learn from the past, Mother often said. But Mother should've heeded her own advice. Then she might still be alive.

I wipe my bleeding fingers off, further bloodying my frock, and glance out the window to the bright blue sky. I unlatch the windowpanes and let the crisp, warm air come rushing in. No wonder my shoulder blades are bleeding. When I was trapped, locked away in the bottle tree, they always did on days like this. When the sky is clear and the air is light. As if they knew how badly I yearned to fly, how much I wanted to break free. But even when I had them, all those years ago, my wings never freed me.

No matter how high I flew, no matter how far I went, I always felt the pull to return to the Heavenly Realms. *Home*, as my mother called it. A home where we didn't belong.

My fingers trail along the window sill. I rest my left arm there as I watch the branches billow and sway. In the corner of my eye, I see a spirit drift into this room that used to be hers, and before that, belonged to other goddesses, but was mine first, before any of them. Instead of choosing a more agreeable likeness, as all spirits are able to do, she bears the image of her death. Head bashed in. Legs slightly askew. I place a hand gingerly on my churning stomach. Thankfully, I haven't eaten today.

Only instead of taunting and haunting me, as she's done for the past five days since I killed her, she sits quietly in a chair in the corner of the room. She reaches down into a woven basket and tries to pick up her unfinished embroidery. But her hand glides right through the fabric, so she stares longingly at it instead.

A little white church. A ridge of snowy mountains. Flocks of sheep and goats. Air that is so pure. A view that takes your breath away. Not all of that is reflected in the piece, but it's a place I'll never forget. She captured it so well that she must not be able to either.

"You're from Provignon," I say, the words tumbling out before I can stop them.

The spirit looks up as if waiting for someone else to answer me, but then sees it's just us. "Yes," she eventually says.

"A lovely town."

She doesn't respond.

"How did a girl from there end up here?" I say, feeling the sudden need to make conversation. I hate to admit how lonely I felt in my bottle prison, how lonely I still feel.

"You've been?"

I nod. I bite my tongue just as what I was about to say of a day and a place I'll never forget, the first village we saw after descending from the Heavenly Realms, almost trips from it. "When I knew it, it was a village full of sheep and goat farmers," I say instead.

"After Thana, it became that again." She has a faraway look in her eyes, as if she's there, hundreds of miles and years away. "I was to marry a farmer nearly twice my age—he had one of the largest flocks. Never would I go hungry again. I could provide for my family, too. After I left, he married my younger sister. She died giving birth to her only child." The goddess's eyes are hollow. She's replayed her sister's death over and over again. Likely watched it through the lens of this cracked mirror, racked with guilt and unable to do a thing. Just as I do with Thana and the day they took her away.

"Let me guess, you met a golden-haired boy who turned out to be a god. He promised you the world. You ended up here. A false goddess whose name no one knows," I offer. A story as old as time. Many variations, the same ending.

"My name is Asha. I know it even if no one else does. And now you do, too. And it was a raven-haired girl," she says with a weary smile, closing her eyes as if remembering that very day. "She promised me everything I wanted: freedom from my fate. She would make me a goddess—I could do what I wanted, go where I wanted, love who I wanted to love. All I had to do was accomplish one thing." She glances at the opposite wall that's covered in marks tallying up to four hundred years. A bloody handprint smears across the marks from when I dragged her to the floor five nights ago.

"Five hundred years of playing this role, she promised me four hundred years ago. We'll make you a real goddess. *Like a fairy tale.*" Her eyes twinkle at the recollection, at the hope she once held dear. "Not that she gave me any details of how she'd make me that as I took the blood oath that bound me to this lonely, haunted place. But it didn't matter. I wanted to be free." She looks up at me, meeting my gaze through the mirror with cold, hungry, empty eyes. "I had only a hundred years left."

I pull my gaze away from the mirror, bile rising up inside of me. *It wasn't personal*, I start to say. I stop myself. *You were a means to an end.* I don't dare say that either. I have hurt so many, and saying those words would be more for me than her. Nothing I say will reassure her, no words will make me forgivable. So I settle instead on something true. "It never would've ended up as she promised. The gods never give you exactly what you want."

"Like it was with Thana?"

I furrow my brow. "What are you talking about?"

Before she can speak, a loud crash echoes from below, followed by a scream. I gather my skirts and rush from the room. I hurry down the hall and peer over the banister to the foyer, where a single Reaper waits, holding a young woman in its hands.

Asha appears by my side, her eyes sparkling with laughter. "You brought back the wrong person." She points. "Look at her eyes—she's Zamiri. The royal bloodline, the Adaeze, their eyes are blood red." There's a smug smile on her face, as if she's telling me what I don't know.

"What do you know of the curse?" I ask. "The one on Thana's tomb."

"That it can only be opened by one from her bloodline, which this girl clearly is not."

"Yes, but that's only part of the truth. If they didn't tell the poor girls they made goddesses of the dead, then I'm guessing no one still alive knows the full truth. You can't *bring* someone here to open the chamber—they have to *want* to come here. They must make the journey on their own. They must open that door and prick their finger on the spindle within—only then will Thana's tomb be accessible to us all." I tell her what the mirror showed me, the person the Adaeze princess would do anything to save. "What would you give to save your sister?"

Anything.

The answer's written on her face.

"Exactly." My lips curl up into a smile. "She will come here to save her friend and she *will* unlock that door to do it."

"But why?" Asha says, horror warping her face. "Why bring back someone who has only caused the world pain? Y-you have a second chance. You could leave here, you could start a new life, you could be *free*." She gestures at the place where my wings once were. "Why give up more for her? Why use the vampire and I as your means to an end? She clearly used you."

I flinch at that—her accusation about a love she will never understand. I start to speak, but she cuts me off. "You miss your wings," she says, as if she's divined my darkest secret rather than my most obvious truth.

How high I once soared, all those years ago. How happy flying made me. How the sun welcomed me into its warm embrace.

I look down to my arm that was resting on the window sill, at the tendrils of smoke still rising from it, from where the sun burned my flesh. The skin knits together, healing in a way my wings never will. What good is a second chance when I cannot have that life back? Thana loves me, she *needs* me. There is no point in dwelling on the past.

I turn away from the false goddess and walk back down the hall. "I miss many things, don't you?"

CHAPTER TWELVE

Leyla

The Nation of Mnara: Tssaia

When Danai and I were little, we dreamed of leaving Mnara. Her, to explore the world, to uncover its mysteries, and I, to be free of Mama and her expectations. But we have always been bound to the castle—Danai, out of duty to Mama and me. Me, because of the queen I'm meant to become.

Whether in our dreams or reality, one thing was always the same: we were together. Inseparable since Mama brought Danai into my life seven years ago. The only person who ever treated me like I was just Leyla.

Not Leyla Adaeze, crown princess of Mnara.

Not Malike's little sister, who he was raised to watch over.

With her, I could be myself.

Now she's gone.

Because of me.

I awake to a knock at my door.

I wince as I sit up in my bed. Pain pulses through my left temple. My entire lower half aches. Memories flood back to me.

Malike pulling me off the ground.

Me, kicking and screaming and attempting to go after her.

Guards taking the yamaja away.

I push away my sheets. My legs are already healed. But the pain remains.

A hand raps against the door again. "I'm coming," I say. When I move to get out of the bed, my right leg is numb. I wiggle my toes, trying to wake it up.

Someone bangs on the door again. "Her majesty requests your presence at once," a stern voice commands from the other side.

I let out a deep sigh and force myself to get up. The pain I feel now will be nothing like what I'm sure I'm about to endure.

Moments later, I'm led by several guards to the banquet hall where Mama suppers every morning before bed. Five guards flank me, two on either side with one directly in front—protecting me, entrapping me. I am usually surrounded by guards who wait in the castle's shadows for any sign of danger, ever ready to defend me and attack. But this . . . this is a lot even for Mama; the attack must have her scared. And Mama scared is never a good thing. After her sister's murder, which made her queen, Mama started to turn her fear into anger—anger she takes out on me.

As we walk, the castle's silence coils around me, amplifying the clanking of the guards' metal-heeled boots against the marble floors and the beating of my own heart.

The first rays of sunlight slip through cracks in the stone walls. As we walk past, servants lower curtains over the walls to block out all light—light the eldest among us cannot survive.

We stop behind two large gold doors, waiting for more guards to open them. What critiques will Mama saddle me with this time? What words will she use like daggers to plunge into my soul? I take a deep breath, trying to calm my racing heart. No matter what she says, I must endure it. Danai is gone and Mama is the only one with the power to get her back.

The doors creak open; darkness pours out. Black velvet curtains drape floor-to-ceiling windows throughout the room and hold back the light.

Three chandeliers dripping with crystal and gold hang above a long table. Gold adorns the walls, framing the windows.

Mama sits at the head of the dark wood table that's covered in black lace and laden with food: plums and cherries soaked in so much blood that the fruits they were barely remain. Sausage links, drenched in blood. A line of blood slides down the golden fork Mama holds and splashes onto her hand. Two golden goblets with emerald-encrusted bowls overflow with blood sweetened by clementines. One for Malike, the other for Mama, who sits to his right and cuts into a delicacy—a human heart.

"So good of you to join us." Mama pats the cushion of the chair to her right but doesn't look up. My stomach growls, but Danai's screams ring louder. How I ran toward her, how I was so close, how she is gone because I disobeyed.

"Leyla," Mama snaps, and I realize she's been calling me. The human servant girl who is refilling her glass startles and pours the blood into Mama's lap. The girl starts to apologize, but faster than any of us can breathe Mama has the girl pinned to the table with her hand. The girl quivers and begs for mercy, but it will do her no good.

"A clumsy servant is a useless one," Mama mutters in the same irritated tone she's used to put me down as well. Except I am her only daughter, the future queen, so she cannot kill me.

Mama lowers her mouth onto the girl's neck. Her lips touch the delicate skin there and the girl whimpers as Mama's fangs descend. Shortly after Mama starts to feed, the girl will be still. Only she does not quiet, and Mama does not bite into her. Mama looks up in my direction and curls a finger toward me.

"You lost a lot of blood in the attack." Mama's next to me in a flash, the girl discarded at my feet.

"Drink," Mama commands. She returns to her chair. Then, with another curling of her finger, she beckons a different servant girl closer. The girl replaces Mama's spilled drink, hands trembling all the while.

"Drink," Mama repeats, with a nod to the whimpering girl at my feet. We all drink human blood, we must to survive, but that's exactly what the peace treaty provides—regular shipments of human blood collected from each citizen throughout the year. There's no need for her to feed directly from a human, nor are we supposed to without their consent.

Mama breaks the treaty she signed with her own blood. She does so every day.

If I were queen, I'd never take such a risk—we lost so many vampires during the war, the price if the humans found out we were breaking the peace treaty is too high. Even if the blood tastes better, fresher, direct from the source.

Let it go, Leyla. Just do as she says.

Mama looks up, expecting me to follow her orders, testing me as she regularly does. Making certain my heart is as cold as hers, for *a queen must always be in control of her emotions.* By "control," she means not feeling at all.

"Do it or I will," Mama says, sealing the girl's fate.

The humans might've been our enemies, but it is one thing to meet someone on a battlefield and another to kill them like this.

"No," I say. I am tired of playing Mama's games.

"Please," the girl begs. But Mama is upon her before she can continue. Her hands encircle her fragile neck. Her fangs break the skin. A few seconds later, her whimpering subsides. A satisfied moan escapes her throat as Mama's saliva's predatory toxins hit the blood in her veins. It's the only reason so many humans agree to be fed on by us—it's the best endorphin high there is. If you do it just right, they won't feel a thing. It lulls her into a dreamlike state where she meets a blissful death. Or so I tell myself, so I don't think of the life so carelessly taken before me.

Mama steps back, and the girl crumples to the floor. She sits back down as if she didn't just kill an innocent girl. Guards emerge from the room's shadows to take the dead girl away.

The door has barely closed behind them when Mama begins. "What were you thinking?" she asks, clearly not talking about me refusing to kill the girl. I open my mouth to answer, but she cuts me off. "I ordered you not to go to the festival. I told you to stay within the castle walls."

Malike's silence tells me everything—he agrees with her; this is all my fault.

"Maybe if you didn't keep me locked up here, I wouldn't feel the need to leave." The words escape before I think. Mama stands. In a blur, she backhands me, the slap stinging my cheek. I bite my lip lest I cry out. Though the Oorvain are born faster and stronger, the rest of us gain such abilities as we age. The eldest among us can move faster than a heartbeat. Mama is already back at her chair.

"You put your people at risk. The creatures never would've gotten to Danai had you not snuck out." She wipes her lips with the napkin on her lap as she continues to eat. The heart before her still beats like it was just carved out.

"Aren't you worried?" I ball my hands into fists. "Danai was wearing my robes. They clearly came here for me. What if they come back?"

She slams her fist onto the table, spilling her food and splattering blood all over her face. The chandeliers rattle from her force. The room grows eerily silent. "I am worried about my daughter who doesn't know how to listen. What sort of future queen does such reckless things? If you're right, what if the creatures had taken you?" She takes a sharp breath, then falls out of her chair, coughing into a handkerchief.

"Mama!" Malike rushes to help her up. He glares at me as if I shoved her myself.

I stand frozen at the other end of the table. What if she dies because she was yelling at me?

Mama allows him to help her to her seat. She places aside the handkerchief, now covered in blood.

"You are soon to be queen, Leyla." She takes a deep breath but doubles over again, racked with coughs. "A queen must put her people before herself. Always," she says, her voice hoarse as she repeats her favorite mantra. "You must do better."

Be better, I hear.

"You will come to realize that there are sacrifices even a queen must make. You care too much for that girl. I brought her here to be your personal guard, not for you to befriend her. Caring too much for anyone is a weakness a queen cannot afford. Love makes you weak."

I close my eyes as her words hit me. They're the same ones she always says while teaching me to hide myself from others, telling me it's safer to stop caring, like she clearly has. Voice steady, calculated, I respond, "I don't care for her more than any citizen, Mama. But she *is* a soldier. We should show loyalty to the ones who protected us during the war. I am merely putting our people first, as you have taught me."

"I see," says Mama. She looks to the curtains and the sun hiding behind them. "Regardless, it is daylight. Our guards need to rest. I will meet with my advisors tomorrow night. We will discuss how to best approach the matter at hand."

"Tomorrow?" I scoff. "By then she could be long gone. If she isn't already."

Mama smirks. "I thought you didn't care about her more than anyone else?"

"Well, I—"

"You must accept what may pass. There are protocols even a queen cannot ignore." She only mentions protocols when they're convenient. Her advisors are so old and set in their ways, even the smallest discussion brings forth centuries of past disputes—the simplest decision takes days.

"But Mama—"

"But Mama nothing," she snaps. "My late sister and our ancestresses worked hard to show the other bloodlines that we may be Thana's direct descendants, but we are not the tyrants she was. I will not have my own daughter ruin the peace between the bloodlines because she wants to use military resources just to look for her friend. Stop this foolishness." She grips the fork in her hand, squeezing it until the metal bends. "I raised you better than this. We have more important issues to deal with. The bloodlines united under one queen during wartime to combine resources, to defeat the humans. Now that the war is over there are some who think they don't need us, that a monarchy isn't best suited for all. If we want this nation to thrive, if we want our family to remain in power, we must ensure they still think they need us. We must never lose their trust. Danai was a soldier; she would understand. We must all sacrifice for peace."

"At what cost?" I mutter. "How many sacrifices?" Danai doesn't deserve this.

Mama shakes her head. "Youth makes you reckless. Nothing good comes from chasing after demons. You must stay here. Your people need you. One day soon, you will be queen."

"What of the yamaja?" I say, ignoring another of her ever-present reminders about the queen I'm soon to become. "Does she also interfere with our peace?" I remember the guards dragging her away in shackles from the valley. "We should talk to her. She may have information that could prove useful."

"She's in the dungeons, where she'll stay until she is properly questioned."

"We both know what those *questions* look like. She knew about the attack—she tried to warn me. I doubt she was here to harm us."

"You spoke with her?" Mama lifts an eyebrow. "What else did she tell you?"

"Nothing," I say quickly, not wanting to incur any more of her wrath.

"Good." Mama shakes her head. "It is like I said, never trust a yamaja. Fate is only for the gods to know." She places her fork and knife down. "Besides, what if she tricked you—what if *she's* behind the attack? What sort of queen would I be if I didn't carry out due diligence?" Paranoia pierces her voice. "If she knows nothing further, we'll let her go."

Mama snaps her fingers, and another servant emerges from the room's shadows. The girl walks over to her and bows until her knees sweep the ground. Mama smiles at her. The girl tilts her head to the side and brushes away her hair to offer her neck to Mama. As Mama positions herself, the area between her sleeves and her gloves becomes more visible—the delicate black lines of her cancerous disease unfurl across her veins, marring her once flawless skin. When it spreads to her neck, the physicians say she'll have only days, and then I will be queen.

CHAPTER THIRTEEN

Leyla

I rush past the guards who line the long halls, ever silent, taking everything in. When we were little, my brother and I would entertain ourselves for hours attempting to make them laugh. We would pop out of the curtains and roar, tickle them with feathers, and tell them jokes. But they never once even cracked a smile. They stood there, watching, waiting. Ready to defend us all.

Footsteps chase me as I walk, echoing throughout the hall. "Leyla, wait," Malike calls after me.

I ignore him, continuing past our library and prayer chamber and deeper into the palace. I veer left and then right, until jewels encrust the very path I walk on. Until gold dust covers the walls, until I'm in my chamber—my eternal prison—once more.

"Leyla!" He barrels in after me.

"What?" I snap, spinning around to face him.

Anguish warps his features as his shoulders heave. "I'm sorry," he said. "I didn't mea—"

"To do and say nothing as you always do?" I finish. "Is that all you care about, being her favorite?" I storm over to my bedside bureau, where a dozen rings sit on a bronze tray—all items from the royal treasury, an inheritance for me, the crown heir. "Is this what you want? Take them." I pick up a ring with a golden fish on it and throw it at his head.

"Watch it," he says as it sails toward him. I pick up another, this one inspired by a proverb that reminds me to always watch my back. "What has gotten into you?" he snaps.

I clutch the ring in my hand and curl my fingers around it. "I just want my friend back."

"We're going to get her back."

"When?" I close the distance between us. "Those creatures appeared and then vanished with her like specters. Too much time has already passed. How do we even know—" I stop myself, not wanting to imagine any other outcome than her alive and by my side.

Of course, that's the very problem. Had I not demanded that she stay here when she asked to go, she never would've been taken in my place, mistaken for me. She'd be safe.

The pain of regret must show on my face, because Malike reaches a hand out for me, his voice gentle. "Don't blame yourself," he says.

I yank myself free. "I don't," I lie. "I blame you." I jab my finger at him. "I saved you. You let her go."

He pauses as if struggling to find the right words to say. His voice cracks when he does. "I couldn't risk it. What if that creature carried you off, too?" He averts his gaze to the floor, the pain of the choice he had to make clear. A few seconds later, he turns his back to me and heads toward the door. But when he gets there, he hesitates. He opens his mouth as if to press further, but eventually hangs his head—resigned. "We all have roles to play, Leyla. It's time you accept yours."

I stay like that until his footsteps quiet, then disappear altogether. I think of the guards, the games Malike and I used to play, and the tension now thick between us. I would give anything to be back there again. To be running up and down the halls, trying to make the guards smile.

I curl into my bed, decked high with pillows. I yawn, though the weariness I carry is not from lack of sleep but from the loss that seems rooted in my people's very foundation. The loss that permeates my life. It is from the desire to grieve as Amma, the fisherwoman's widow, did for her lost wife, to cry for Danai without care for others' presumed opinions, to cast off the weight of the crown I don't yet wear.

Loneliness wraps itself around my soul as I'm left among remnants of a childhood that seems worlds away from where I am now.

Paintings are on the walls. Thin and worn and frayed at the edges and commissioned by Papa on his many journeys. They're too painful to have up but would be even more painful to take down. Removing them would be another reminder that he's gone and he's never bringing such treasures back—that there are no more tales he has to tell.

Mama hung each one herself as Papa spun stories of nobles and commoners, of gods and knights. Of Valdis, who journeyed far from her home and followed the setting sun to Nekros to save the woman she loved. Of the yamaja, who dive for the special silk they use to weave the fabrics of fate.

Fate. Was it fate that he died? Fate that Mama is sick? Fate that I'll soon wear the crown? How much of life do we really control?

My eyelids grow heavy, pulled down as if by weights, and for a moment, I think I'm drifting into a peaceful sleep. But I'm not.

I never am.

Screams always haunt my dreams.

It's snowing early this year.

The captain directs the ship, steering us along the river—water bright and crisp, winds thick with salt. I can't help but think that a night on the water is the worst night for first snow—the worst night for the ninth-birthday voyage I begged Papa for.

"To know your world, is to know yourself," he said, readily agreeing.

My cousins' cat darts across the bow, zipping back and forth on the deck. "Kitty!" I say, running toward her.

"Leyla, be careful," Mama yells. Papa comes beside her and lets out a deep, booming laugh. "Let her play," he says softly, taking her hand in his. "She barely interacts with children her age. It's good for her to have something to play with."

"Fine," she says. "But if you injure yourself like the last time, don't come whining to me."

Aunty stands on the edge, dressed in a yellow silk robe that shines against her dark skin. With her head held high, she waves at the vampires who line the riverbank. My cousin, the crown heir, and her brother and sister stand beside my aunt doing the same. Drummers play and dancers call in greeting. Aunty and Papa—her ambassador to the human kingdom of

Lienne—have been in talks with the human king for months. A ceasefire is in place. Hope is in the air. Everyone says peace is near.

I run, knocking into Malike, who's waiting beside the captain. She lets him take over the stern. "Look at me! Mama. Papa." He waves at them, letting go of the wheel.

"Whoa, there," says Papa. "You've got to hold on. A captain must always guard the ship."

The cat zooms past me. I run to catch her, diving between Papa's legs. He scoops me up in his arms, swinging me as the moonlight catches his smile, teeth twinkling. He opens his mouth in a chuckle that never comes. Spears rip through the sky, piercing into him. They pierce Aunty and my cousins, too.

Papa tries to grab hold of the ship, but he loses his grip and slips. I fall with him as arrows whiz past, straight toward Malike. I scream. The captain dives atop him; two arrows bury into her back, and she doesn't get back up. The spears are dipped in poison.

Papa tries to push me away before he hits the water, but I fall into the river, too.

The water shocks my skin. I kick, but I can't stay afloat. Spears strike around us. I let go of my breath; water shoots up my nose.

"Papa," I call. My head bobs above the water as the current tries to pull me down below.

I don't know how to swim.

"Leyla!" Mama reaches into the water for me from the ship.

Papa's hands reach mine, cold and clammy, and he pushes me toward Mama.

"Papa." I try to kick away from Mama and lean back towards him but I'm left gripping only the hummingbird pendant that he wears around his neck. When I look for him, he is nowhere to be found.

Tears run down my face. I cry out. Yet this voice isn't mine anymore.

It's too old, too tired, too broken with pain. And when I turn, I realize that it's Danai whose hands I now hold in the river. Whose chest blooms blood as red as a rose.

"No," I scream. *I ignore the water weighing me down. I press my hands upon her, thinking that if I press hard enough, I can shove the blood right back where it belongs. That if I can just press long enough, the bleeding will stop.* She will be fine, *I tell myself.* She will be fine.

Her blood drains into the water; the river runs red.

I raise my hands to the gods, but they do not hear me—they never have.

"Save me," *Danai says. Blood gurgles out from her, masking her voice. Before I can respond, to tell her everything's going to be all right, her eyes go blank like Papa's.*

Still sobbing, I clutch her hand to my chest as the current pulls me under. My people's screams from the riverbank are so loud I can see them manifest as I drown—faces contorted, the air in my lungs raspy, making it harder to breathe—

"*Leyla.* Leyla!" A sharp voice rips me from my nightmare. I'm shaken awake, and when I open my eyes, Mama is beside me.

"*Mama?*" I scramble back. My mother is here? Did she hear me crying out in my sleep like a child? I meet her eyes, expecting her usual disapproving glare. But instead, her brows are knitted in concern.

Maybe I'm dreaming? I pinch myself. But she's still before me, draped in a translucent, billowing white nightgown and swathed in furs wrapped around her shoulders.

Now I can see what she tries to hide, why she rarely makes public appearances. The black veins are not only across her hands but stretch up her thighs, around her stomach, and stop just under her chest.

I swallow thickly. My mother is dying. I know this as well as I know that I must drink blood weekly to stop the cravings that could consume me and turn me more monster than human. I've known for nearly a year—when the disease's black marks first appeared, when they only lined the veins in her fingertips. Looking at her now makes it even more true. No gold adorns her head and hands, no golden robes surround her body. Just Mama—the woman who gave birth to me, who used to sit on the ground playing hand games with me. She is barely two hundred years old; she should have at least a few hundred more to live.

We stare into each other's eyes; so many unsaid words pass between us. How much time do we really have left?

"What are you doing here?" I rack my brain for the last time she came this way. Two, maybe three years ago? Her chambers are on the other side of the castle. I always meet her in the dining room. The throne room. Or her room. *A queen's room*. Whereas mine is still in the royal quarters where my family once lived. Before the Red River Massacre that haunts my dreams took the lives of Papa, Aunty, my cousins, and countless others.

Before Mama became queen and everything changed.

"I came——" She pauses, as if not knowing what to say. "I came to check on you." She reaches for my hand, then stops midway. "When I got here you were shouting for your father. Do . . . do you still dream of him?"

I nod. I haven't seen the softer side of my mother in so long that I'm unsure what to say, unsure what words might turn her back into the heartless queen I've grown to know.

"I had no idea."

"You never asked," I say softly. She never asks me anything. Not how I'm doing. Not what I want. Not if I'm scared to lose her like I lost Papa. Scared to become queen.

"I was harsh earlier." But she doesn't apologize. I would be more shocked if she did after so many years of not doing so.

I eye her, still not knowing what else to say.

She looks around the room, taking it all in. She flinches when her eyes land upon the paintings beside my bed. She stands and walks over to them. "I didn't realize you still had these up." Her fingers graze their borders, tracing them like she used to every morning before bed as Papa spun his tales.

"Valdis." She stops in front of the one of the knight Valdis. "That was one of your favorites," Mama says softly. "Valdis, who went to Nekros to beg the goddess of the dead for the life of her beloved back." She laughs, but it's raspy, like it's afraid of its own sound. Once, her laugh echoed throughout the castle, booming toward me as she chased me down the hallway and tucked me into bed. "Remember—" She pauses. "Remember how you tried to find the goddess of the dead to ask her—"

"To bring our family back," I finish. Mama's laugh is gone; there is only silence as the memory is soured by what happened next. "I barely got to the forest before you found me. You brought me back here. Had me pick out a switch from his garden. Then you whipped Danai in front of me to remind me the cost of my life. To remind me that there are always others who will suffer. That a queen—"

"Must always put others before herself," Mama finishes, softly. "I know." She blinks back the tears pooling in her eyes. We both know those tears will never fall. They fell the night Papa was murdered, the night soldiers fished her sister's bloodied crown and her nieces and nephew's bodies out of the even bloodier river, and handed the crown to Mama. Oh, how she cried. How desperately she clung to me and Malike. How fiercely she rocked us to sleep.

And then she stopped.

The mother I know now does not cry. Is it her strength that people love? That Malike seeks to imitate? Is that why she reminds me so often of my weaknesses?

"My sister was always the perfect one, always winning my mother's praise," she says, surprising me as she sits back on the edge of the bed, as if it's story time again. Her eyes have a faraway look in them. *The perfect one*, I think. *Just like Malike.* "When my sister died," Mama continues, "it was all on me. I wasn't supposed to become queen, so my mother never taught me anything. I wasn't prepared like I've tried to prepare you." Her hands are shaking. She balls them in her gown and twists until they stop.

"Like you, I wanted to find a goddess who could grant me their lives, who could take it all back to how it used to be. But we were in a war. Morale was low. The Red River Massacre dealt us a grave blow. What our people needed was a leader, someone who seemed unaffected, someone who was strong." She reaches out and grips my hands. It takes everything in me not to recoil—hers are frigid to the touch. "When I die, they will still need that leader. You mustn't cry for me. Not in public. Not in private. The other bloodlines will see you as weak, and if they do, they could overthrow you. Your brother can only protect you so much."

Her eyes are watery and wide with fear. She waits as if expecting me to agree, to promise her that I will not cry, that I will be strong. And if Danai were still here, I probably would. I would say anything to please Mama, to reassure her that I will not let her down. But now, I can only think of Danai's absence. How saying things to please

Mama will not bring her back. How Danai always cradled me after Mama tore me down. *Strength*, she would say, *comes in many forms*.

"How do you know that is what our people need?" My voice is small like a mouse.

"Excuse me?" Her voice deepens like a lioness's roar, making me want to cower beneath my sheets.

But I do not.

"I mean," I say, a little louder this time, "our people didn't ask for you to lie about how you felt. Maybe we needed to grieve as a nation. To mourn those the humans took from us." I think of that red river and the hundreds of bloated bodies floating on it. We are a nation of stories, yet we never speak of that night. "We lost family, but many others lost loved ones, too. Maybe they needed to see you grieve so that they could grieve. You raised us to keep our feelings to ourselves, but keeping it inside has changed us, changed yo—"

"I thought you were ready to hear the truth," she interrupts, shaking her head. Her blood-red eyes are heavy with disapproval. "You're still playing pretend, Leyla." *Still weak*. The way she says my name sends shivers up my spine. She yanks her hands away from me as if my weakness is contagious.

I shift my gaze to the wall beside my bed, refusing to let her see the tears forming. My eyes land on a painting of a lion in a net with a mouse on the forest floor just below it. A mouse, who, as the story goes, saved the lion from the hunter's trap. A mouse who diligently chewed through the net when the lion had lost hope—all while ignoring the lion's taunts that such a small, weak creature could not save him. But, of course, it's easier to ignore a stranger than your own family. Over the last year, I've had to grow used to living with pain. Her words should no longer be able to affect me like this, and yet, they do.

"Do you hate me?" I ask the question I've wanted to for years, ever since Mama became queen and always seemed so disappointed in me.

She shakes her head. "This is love. You have no idea what I've done for love. Just as you have no idea what you may one day do." She stands from the bed.

"Mama, wait." I reach for her, instantly consumed with regret. I should've bitten my lip, kept my words to myself. But it's too late; she's already walking toward the door.

"You are not a child anymore. It's time to act like it." She slams the door behind her.

My hands shake as I reach over to my nightstand and grab the glass of blood from where my handmaids left it. I slip back into my sweat-covered sheets as the blood coats my throat. *I am not enough.* Not enough for her, not enough to wear the crown, not enough for this world. Why can't I say what she wants me to? What can't I be who she's trained me to be?

I wrap my arms around my body, rocking myself back and forth. *Breathe, Leyla*, I tell myself as tears slide down my face. *Breathe*.

I take another gulp and finish the glass. As I do, I hear Mama's words echo through my head once more. *You have no idea what I've done for love. Just as you have no idea what you may one day do.*

I get out of bed. I refuse to lose Danai as well.

On the fifth day of the ninth month, a mere hour after dozens of vampires—including her husband, sister, nieces, and nephew—were pronounced dead, Karina Adaeze was crowned queen. The ceremony was quick, hurried even, with only the nobles already present in attendance.

The next seven years became the bloodiest the war had ever seen. Karina led her troops into battle, hunting down everyone who had a hand in the death of her family members. Karina the Ruthless, she came to be known. No prisoners of war were ever returned. No survivors left in her wake.

Until the eighth day of the Siege of Tamor when, against the advisement of her generals, Karina ordered her troops to lay their weapons down and rode toward enemy lines. She carried a single white flag. Her advisors thought she had gone mad, that she would be killed without even an heir of age. But the Lienne's king lay his weapons down, too. And so, peace talks began anew and this time a treaty was signed.

Forever after, she would be known as Karina the Broker of Peace—the Lioness of Mnara.

—LONG HAVE WE WARRED: AN ACCOUNT OF THE THOUSAND YEARS' WAR
FIRST EDITION, 1200 AD
MERKESH ROYAL ARCHIVES

CHAPTER FOURTEEN

Leyla

I walk to the courtyard just beyond the royal chambers to Papa's gardens, although they shouldn't be called gardens anymore. Lush green vines no longer sway—instead they're brown and hang knotted like fishing nets. They stick to me as if I'm walking through a spider's web. The grass is all but nonexistent; dirt covers the ground. Not the rich brown of moist soil, but ashen. It's dry and crumbly from years left untended. After the Red River Massacre, Mama ordered that the gardens be left alone.

The Merkesh say that in the month after our death, our souls travel west to Nekros to await the goddess of the dead's judgment. There, she peers into them to see how we lived. Those who were fair and honorable travel through Nekros to the Heavenly Realms, to our gods above. Observing from a distance, watching over us, I suppose. But I've always felt that Papa lingers here—whether in the tiniest worm squirming beneath my toes or in the rush of a passing breeze. These gardens were his sanctuary, so it makes

sense that they are also mine—the one place where I can escape from her scrutiny, the one place where I can still find traces of him. Where I come to clear my mind and think and plot as I need to now.

At the garden's edge are two oak trees. Papa planted the first when Malike was born and the second when I was. But you'd never know it from how the second towers over the first, its branches fanning out high above it. Malike used to joke that my tree hogged the sun—stealing nutrients from his.

We all have roles to play.

His words from earlier push to the front of my mind. Maybe he and Mama are right. Maybe I am causing more problems by searching for my fate. Maybe I should accept it's something I cannot control, something I shouldn't seek to learn.

The soothing sounds of a kora rise into the air, and my ears perk up at the music. The notes wrap around me, warming my soul. Papa used to play. He tried to teach me, but unlike Malike, I never had the patience. I would pull too hard and the strings would snap, or too softly and the sound could barely be heard. I never sat still long enough to learn how to pluck each string just right to get anything resembling a melody.

I follow the tune deeper into the gardens to where a crumbling fountain stands—white marble crusted with mold—a pool drained of water that used to flow here all the way from the Sabahir. The gardens face the north, allowing the plants just enough sunlight to grow, but not so much that Papa couldn't tend them. The more we age, the less resistant to sun we become. By the time we reach two hundred years, the sun is not only a nuisance but a threat: it can burn us in an instant. And so, we live at night and sleep during the day to prepare ourselves for the inevitable. How curious that Papa loved something so temporary—had he lived for half a century more, he'd never have gotten to see his gardens in their full daytime glory again.

Malike sits on the fountain's edge, plucking the strings as well as any storyteller at the market—just like Papa used to before bed, spinning tales with his music.

Of Valdis, a brave knight. Of Amma, a mournful wife. Garoux, four-legged creatures with lethal bites. Beasts who make your worst nightmares real. A mouse brave enough to save a lion. And a scorpion who defeated a renowned hunter. The stories of our people, our world.

Gone is Malike's usual armor. He wears a simple white linen tunic, embroidered with gold silk along the hems of his sleeves, and matching loose linen pants. No sword lies at his waist, no helmet snug on his head. The sun strikes his shaved head, surrounding it in a golden glow. Even without the words, I recognize the tune and the story that usually accompanies it: one of a girl who gave half her soul to her sick sibling, blessing them both to live, one only in the night, the other only in the day. The story has many iterations—sometimes it's lovers instead—but the ending is always the same: they can only meet for a few moments, as day gives way to night and night to day.

The music fades. "I can see you," he says, pulling me out of my thoughts.

"I didn't know you still played." I step out from behind the bushes where I stand.

He sets the kora aside. "There's a lot about me you don't know." He pats the space beside him. Slowly, I walk over and take a seat. I place my hands in my lap, waiting for him to speak, but neither of us utters a word.

"I'm sorry," we say simultaneously after several moments.

I smile at him, heart heavy with regret. "Papa wouldn't want us to fight like this."

"You're not the only one who misses him, you know?"

"I know." I lean my head on his shoulder as he lets out a sigh that fills the space around us. After some time, I raise my head. "You used to play in public all the time, though. Why did you stop?"

He shrugs. "There wasn't any time. Becoming a soldier made me useful to Mama when suddenly I was not, so I put all my energy into becoming the best one I could be." Instead of meeting my gaze he looks off into the distance, as he sometimes does whenever he talks about the war and his time in the army.

I snort. "Yeah, right. You've always been her favorite. You've always been the one who's done everything right." He's always been better than me and, ever since Papa was killed, has never let an opportunity to remind me of that go to waste.

"Because I had to, Leyla." He interrupts my thoughts, voice strained. "I wasn't given the leeway you have. While you were handed tutors, I was shipped off to war. She doesn't value my life in the way she does yours." He rapidly blinks his eyes. They cloud while looking down at his hands—rough and scarred with gashes. I remember a time when they were soft and smooth, when the sounds of the kora could be heard from his chambers late into the day. "I became the unnecessary child, the boy who can't be king and carry on our people's legacy."

I flinch at the sharpness of his tone. If it were a knife, it would strike true. "I-I didn't know you felt that way." I've never once thought of how it must've been to grow up on the battlefield instead of at home.

"You never listened. It was Leyla's way or none at all . . . But you're still my sister"—a smirk plays at the corners of his lips—"even if you are a pain." He takes my hand in his. "I didn't mean to let Danai get taken. I didn't consciously make that choice. I just saw you and acted. I've lost so many . . ." His voice trails off and grows distant as if he's back on the battlefield and not here. "I can't lose you, too."

Memories rush forth of him checking in on me every evening after bed. Cradling me when Mama was too busy, when the nightmares of Papa's death didn't allow me to sleep. Giving me my first sword, patiently teaching me to fight.

He is tough on me, but he always shows me love. How have I never realized what he was going through? What do I say? What can you really say to the person who's always been there for you, when you've never been there for them in the same way?

He holds his head as tears roll down his face. I place a hand on his cheek, and his lips quiver. "I'm sorry, brother," I say to him. I bring his face down to my shoulder and cradle him in my arms. All the words I should've said before, all the things I should've done rush into my head. I wasn't there for him. He was alone. I blink back tears, yet still they come, running down my face and under my chin. I squeeze him tighter, wrapping my hands around him, pulling him in as close as I can. "I'm sorry," I say again. "I never knew you were hurting, too." We stay like that for what seems like hours but is likely only minutes. After a while, he pulls away and throws his head back in a laugh.

"What's so funny?" I sniffle, wiping away my tears.

"All he ever wanted was for us to be there for each other." He reaches his arms up, stretching them into the sky, before bringing them down and placing them in his lap. "What are you still looking for, Ley?"

"Forgiveness," I say without thinking, without even realizing that the word slipped through my lips. "For not doing more . . . for not knowing what to do."

"You're doing all you can," he says.

"But wouldn't it be grand if we had power over our fates—if we could change the future and turn back time?"

"Yes," he says softly, brushing his fingers along the kora's strings. "But life is not a story. You cannot control fate." He snaps back his hand, placing it once again in his lap. He turns to me, red eyes watery and wide. "You can only control what you do with what you have."

I sigh, looking out into the garden that Papa perfectly cultivated from the journeys he took before having us, when he first met Mama. He shared his knowledge with us, teaching us which plants could be boiled into a soup to ease a broken heart and which flowers could stave off even the deadliest of poisons. *To know your world is to know yourself*, he'd often singsong, reciting a common Merkesh saying from his days as one. Before he fell in love with Mama and renounced the Merkesh way of life.

Theirs was a story I used to love to hear, before Papa was killed. Mama was supposed to marry an Oorvain noble, a marriage that from her birth had been arranged. But her mother—the queen—was still alive and her eldest sister, who would inherit the throne, had already given birth to an heir. So, when Papa proclaimed his love for Mama and when my grandmother saw how much Mama loved him, too, she granted Papa the right to choose: his life as a Merkesh or a life with Mama, as her husband.

Danai has a similar spirit, an eternal quest for knowledge. She always knew what to say and do, even if such advice was wrapped in a snarky edge. "I wish Danai were here." I bunch my hands together as if praying. "I just want to feel a little less alone."

"We're going to find her," he says after a long pause. This time, he wraps his arm around me, and his beard scratches my cheek. It smells of lavender oil—Papa's favorite. Papa would've known what to do.

But he's not here.

Something awakens deep inside me, my despair turning into determination, into hope.

I raise my head to meet Malike's gaze and remember my earlier promise to myself. "I'm going to find her." My voice is steady and firm. "I am going to bring her back."

He lifts his eyebrow, likely struck with disbelief. "You can't be serious. You don't even know where she was taken."

"No, but the yamaja knew more." I remember how she raced after them, how she knew exactly how to strike to kill. She was fearless, breathtaking. I think back to her words. "She expected an attack; she saw it."

He snorts. "That's ridiculous."

"And mysterious creatures turning into ash when killed and vanishing into thin air isn't?" I place my hands on my hips. "We live in a world whose very backbone is stories." *All stories have some truth*, Papa used to say. "What if there is more to this yamaja? What if she can help me find Danai? I need to try."

Malike shakes his head, a firm no. "You are always getting into trouble. You never listen to me or Mama."

"Why do you always have to take her side?" I throw my hands

up in frustration. It's as if our earlier reconciliation never even happened. I should've known better; he's just like her.

"Whoa." He holds out his hands. "No one is taking anyone's side. I'm just stating facts. Why do you always think so badly of me?"

"Because you do take her side. You always remind me of the ways I don't listen. Don't you think I get it? Don't you think I've beaten myself up enough? First Papa, on my birthday. Then Danai, when I sneak out. I know it's my fault." Tears run down my face again and my anxiety sends me into a panic. "I know it's my fault," I repeat in between sharp breaths. "I'm the reason that Danai is gone. I don't need to be constantly reminded of how I've failed. I want to fix this—I need to."

Malike grabs my shaking hands. I try to pull away, but he pulls me closer. "Leyla," he says, ever so softly. He rocks me in his arms, saying my name over and over.

"I'm not ready, Malike. I'm not ready to be queen. I'm not ready to—" I stop myself from saying what comes next: *lose her*. I'm not ready to lose Mama. Regardless of everything, she's the only parent I have left. "I just want my friend back, and I can't do this alone."

"You don't have to." He wipes my tears. "Mama said she's meeting with her advisors tomorrow. They're going to figure this out."

I push away from him. "When have they ever reached a solution in a day? I have to go after her *now*. I have to try."

"I don't know what's worse." He stands and starts to pace. "I could let you, but if something happens to you, I'll never forgive myself." He pauses mid-speech as if the solution suddenly dawns on him. "I'll let you go. But on one condition."

I gesture at him to speak.

"I come with you."

"Absolutely not, I don't need a babysitter."

"No, but you do need someone to go along with you. Ley, you've never left the capital unguarded, you've never fought outside of a training exercise—"

"I saved your ass from one of those creatures."

He lets out an exasperated sigh. "That is not the point. If you want to try to find her then I'm coming with you." He crosses his arms and glares at me. "Do you want my help or not?"

I shrug. "It depends—can you get the key to the dungeons?"

He nods. "I know the guard who's on shift, I can swap with him, but why?"

"Perfect." I smile as my plan clicks into place. "I need to break out the yamaja."

CHAPTER FIFTEEN

Najja

After the attack, I was dragged to the dungeons that are located within the castle's depths. Not because I did something wrong, but simply because I'm a yamaja and the queen hates my kind.

The dungeons smell of misery and pain. Of vomit and lost hope.

I'm shackled, hands held high above my head; I can barely touch my toes to the floor. I weep, new tears falling over old ones and drying on my cheeks, as I have every night since Mama drowned, since Simi died at the Reaper's hand.

Why did I come here? Why did I risk my life for people who would imprison me just because of who I am? I put my duty first, as Mama and Simi did, and that was my mistake. They believed in something greater than themselves, in a way of life passed down, and how did the gods reward their loyalty? They let them die, just as I surely will, too.

I adjust myself, trying to find some comfort, but the shackles rub against wounds from the Reapers' attack, exacerbating my pain.

My cries reverberate against the walls, creating an echo chamber of my agony. I will die here, alone, because of powers given by gods who can't be bothered to hear.

I fall into a daze. Everything looks the same. There's only one tiny window from which slivers of light pour, but whether it's from the sun or the stars I can't tell. How much time has passed? A few hours? Days? The dungeon is otherwise dark and absent of warmth. And of other prisoners, too. At least, I don't think others are here. If they are, they stay silent, hope long abandoned.

The more time passes, the more uneasy I grow. I close my eyes to sleep. But sleep only brings forth dreams that are even darker than the dungeons I'm in. Something about this place has taken hold, pushing forth memories that are not my own.

Memories of people who should've passed on through Nekros, but out of their pain, their sorrow, their misery, did not. It's as if by being trapped here, I'm connected with this place's spirits.

A human general who was captured in battle.

A servant who stole from the queen.

A vampire girl whose mother attempted a coup.

Dozens of spirits visit me in my dreams. Their memories, and others like them, flash through my head. They all died here.

I am doomed.

I *will* die here.

I never should've come.

Keys rattle, and I let my eyes flutter open. The door creaks. My body stiffens. I clean up my tears, wiping my face on my arms, not wanting to show my vulnerabilities to whomever it is. I suck in a deep breath, dreading what's to come. When the footsteps reach me and I set eyes on my visitor, it's the vampire queen. The very one who killed my grandmother for giving her a prediction she did not like.

"Hello . . . yamaja." She pauses after hello as if determining what to say next, and when she says *yamaja*, it comes out like bile's stuck in her throat, a bitter taste she wishes to be rid of. Her body is gaunt, her cheekbones cutting sharp angles, and she's tall, taller than me even. She's draped in black lace robes that are too loose and laden with pounds of gold that weigh her down, making her look . . . frail. A sharp contrast to the power in her voice. Karina the Ruthless, she used to be called. Even now, with her body ailed by sickness, I can see why the moniker was bestowed.

A shudder ripples through me.

"What is your name?"

My strength swells as I look upon the queen my mother despised so much. Anyone who really wanted to know my name, who saw me as someone of any value, wouldn't have put me here to begin with. "*You* can call me whatever you like."

Slap.

The back of the queen's hand hits my face, the stacked rings on her fingers dig into my skin. I cry out as she rakes over the impression they made, widening the wound. She pulls back. Blood oozes out and trickles down my left cheek. I bite my lip, stopping my scream, as rage consumes me.

With a flick of her tongue, she licks her rings. "Yamaja blood." She smiles. *Smug.* "I haven't had this in *years*."

I stare right at her, unflinching, as my cheek burns. I won't beg, if that is what she wants. I won't give this woman who calls herself a queen that satisfaction. A queen who was so scared of what was to come that she took another's future is not worthy of being queen.

I hack, then spit. "My bad," I say, barely missing the queen's gilded slippers.

Slap.

I bite my tongue so hard the coppery taste of blood fills my mouth. "I came here to save your daughter's life," I manage. "You should be thanking me."

The queen grabs my neck with her hands, lifting me above the ground, putting to rest any doubts about her strength. Her nails press into my jugular, just enough to make her message clear. "What did you tell my daughter? Why are you really here?"

"I told you," I say through gritted teeth. "To save her life."

"Why would you risk your life to save hers?"

"Trust me, if I could go back in time, I wouldn't make the same choice twice."

She laughs at that but doesn't release her grip. "You yamaja don't know how to leave things alone. You don't know how to keep fate in the hands of the gods. I, too, was excited when a yamaja came to me. But I learned there is harm in knowing one's fate—it only drives you to obsession. A day hasn't passed where I've not thought of it. And so, you see, yamaja, I don't want my daughter to fall into the same trap. It's better she does not know what is to come."

Her body shakes then, as if in an involuntary shudder. She immediately releases me, and I slump against my chains. She closes her eyes as if steadying herself, and that's when I see them, black lines tracing across her skin, following her veins. The thing about seeing death so often is I've grown accustomed to its signs. These are the marks of an illness that is consuming her, and will soon claim her life.

The queen sees me looking and quickly turns away. "I know that

I will die soon and the gods will judge me. But my daughter will not follow down my path, she will not grapple with her fate, she will not waste her life trying to undo what is already in motion." She turns back to me, holding my gaze, her blood-red eyes blazing. "We'll continue this conversation later. Perhaps some time in here will make you more . . . forthcoming. When I return, that will be your last chance to share what you know. If you do, I'll let you go." A small shiver ripples through her body, and she leaves without another word.

I let out a deep breath and slump against my chains. I thank the gods for sparing me before I've even realized what I've said. I look around the dungeon to reassure myself that she is in fact gone, but when I do, I'm met with guests of another kind. Shackles clank from where I cannot see, and then, one by one, the spirits I thought I'd only dreamed of step forward.

"She lies," they hiss. "She will kill you," they say—before they disappear altogether, leaving me alone, bleeding in the dark.

CHAPTER SIXTEEN

Leyla

When I was ten, a month before I met Danai, Mama made me watch a man die.

He was a Lienne general, captured after the Battle of Verdan. They had him strung to a rack, strapped in without the chance of escape.

The dungeon was dark and dank. The stone tiles comprising the ground were uneven and sunken in at places. Stale liquid pooled in the spaces between the tiles—water that trickled down from cracks in the walls, blood that spilled forth from the humans imprisoned there.

The chains rattled along the walls as if the spirits of the dead never rested.

I was sick to my stomach. I liked to imagine that Mama was sick to hers as well. That every time she gritted her teeth—urging the commander to turn the lever attached to the rack that stretched the human, pulling his joints farther apart—she mentally clutched her stomach, trying not to throw up breakfast.

After, I asked her why she made me go, made me see things I could never unsee. *A queen must never turn away from the decisions that she makes*, she said. And then, in boots splattered with the man's blood, she walked away from me.

I liked to imagine a lot of things back then. But the truth is that the year after the Red River Massacre changed her. Hardened her into someone I didn't recognize—one she probably didn't either. Maybe she has been trying to prepare me like she claimed. But I didn't need my mother forcing me to watch a human tortured. And I don't need her barking orders at me like she did her soldiers during the war.

Every step I take farther into the dungeon pushes me back closer to that moment. How the general's blood leaked from his body and trickled down the floor. I tried to move and squirm away from it, but my back was already pressed against the opposite wall. The blood soaked into the sandals Papa had given me, leather ones with little bells that jingled when I walked.

I couldn't get the blood out; I had to throw them away.

The dungeon is eerily silent now.

I'm hit with a putrid smell—the stench of piss and blood washes over me. I bite my lip to stop from gagging. Though we rarely use these dungeons anymore, apparently no one decided they needed to be cleaned.

"By the grace of Morowa," I utter. But it is clear that the gods left these parts long ago. Rusty, cobweb-covered chains line the walls next to buckets collecting water dripping from ceiling cracks.

I shudder beside Malike, who too easily navigates the space. He takes me to a separate chamber, where the yamaja stands, hands tied up high above her, left cheek scarred and dried with blood that looks too fresh to be from the attack. "You could've at least brought food." She cracks a laugh that comes out like a wheeze. Her lip is swollen twice its previous size.

I yank the keys from Malike and fumble with them until I find the one that fits. I unlock her chains and she slumps forward. I catch her before she falls. She rubs her wrist, bruised from the chains' too-tight grip, and pushes away from me, leaning against the wall. "What is it this time?" She looks at me, eyes burning with hatred and heavy with exhaustion.

I reach my hand out toward her and she flinches, a movement so slight I barely catch it. Her eyes widen as if afraid and then the rage is back again. I step away, giving her space. "Who did this to you?"

She glares at me and says nothing, but from the way she looks at me, like she's seeing the person's reflection, I already know. Mama. Clearly the conversation she wanted to have with the yamaja has already begun. She must've gone to the dungeons after visiting me. "I'm so sorry," I say, wishing that I had gotten here earlier, that I could've stopped Mama from inflicting such pain. Mama hates yamaja so fiercely that you'd think one tried to kill her or someone she loved, instead of telling her that she would die young. But still, I didn't think . . . I naively hoped that—

"I don't need your pity," the yamaja says, cutting off my train of thought. "Let me guess, you want something from me as well? I already told you, my gift is not in seeing any future you want to know about."

"I'm not here for that," I say, still not quite understanding how her powers work, but certain this isn't the time to ask.

I gesture at my brother. "We need your help. You clearly know more about the creatures that attacked. What are they? Why were they here?" My voice turns sharp like Mama's. How easily I command her. How easily I order her, a stranger, to do something for me. "Please," I add, trying to soften my directive. "I'm trying to save my friend."

"And what if I don't? Will you leave me strung up here? Shall I become your plaything, too? What if I say no, your highness?" She draws out "your highness" in the way Danai jokingly used to, but this time it's a vile thing—a curse.

"We'll get you out of here no matter what."

Her eyes widen in surprise. She gestures to Malike. "Swear on his life."

He makes a sound in protest. "Swear on your own." He looks at me. "I'd like to keep mine. Besides, maybe we should make sure she wants to help us before we go swearing away lives, your highness."

"Why does everyone keep saying it like an insult? That's my title," I snap back at him.

The yamaja lets out a mock yawn. "I'd rather stay locked up than listen to you two bicker."

Malike growls at her. "That can be arranged, yamaja."

I step in between them. "You have my word," I say, more to him than to her.

"So much for leverage," he mutters.

She purses her lips, as if considering what I said. "What's in it for me?" she says after a while.

"Not spending another night in the dungeons," snaps Malike.

She rolls her eyes hard enough to get them stuck in the back of her head, as Mama would say. "First, my name is Najja, not yamaja, *malichora*." She emphasizes the name the humans use for us, a reference to the demon they believe us to be. She looks directly at Malike while she does, her eyes a searing bright blue.

Malike starts to draw his sword, but I stop him. "Najja, it is," I say.

She continues to glare at him, as if challenging him further, but then shifts her focus to me and meets my eyes with such intensity it sends shivers up my spine.

"Second, I came to the capital because my sister—" She pauses as if the word pains her, like something so common has become loaded. "My sister," she says quickly, as if not wanting the syllables to linger on her tongue. "Like me, she has visions, but hers are of possible steps leading to an event. Before my homeland was attacked, she said that you were in danger, that you and I are at the center of something important. But then the Reapers came before she could say anything else."

The mention of my fate being foreseen by a yamaja is quickly replaced with one thought, one fear. "Reapers?" I must've misheard her. Every vampire knows of Reapers. Reapers are the creatures in dark tales told to children to make them go to bed—to make them stop asking questions. *You'd better be good, or Reapers will get you*, Mama would say when I was little, referencing the creatures bound to Nekros, bound to serving the goddess there.

Malike scoffs, but a shudder creeps up my spine. I drop my hands to my side. "Oh, Danai. I'm so sorry." I swallow down my emotions. "But I don't buy it. Why risk your life?" I say. "Why help people you knew wouldn't believe you?"

She laughs. "Your mother asked the same question, as if helping a stranger is such a foreign idea to you." Malike starts to protest, but Najja cuts him off. "It's my duty. One I've rejected for years. But my sister believed in that duty—she died in service of that belief. I owe it to her to do something." The chains in the dungeon rattle, as if the spirits of the dead still linger and are sending condolences to the living. "Surely, even if you don't understand the concept of helping other people, you do understand duty, prince."

Malike scowls at her, at the derision in her voice, but I pick up something else. *Pain.* Not from the scars she visibly bears, though I'm sure there's that, too, but from ones not so easily seen. A pain that speaks to my own, to a helplessness that festers and eats at your soul.

"I understand," I say. "It's why I'm here. I have a duty to my mother, yes, to the throne I'll inherit. But I also have a duty to my friend. When my mother wasn't there for me, Danai was. I have to save her even if it means going up against the creatures of nightmares. Even if it means risking my life."

Najja locks eyes with me, and I have to force myself to not turn away from the intensity of her gaze. An understanding passes between us. "But all the stories say that Reapers come from Nekros. This is going to sound ridiculous, impossible even, but what we thought was impossible has already happened, so maybe not. What if they took your friend to Nekros, to the island of the dead? How will you find her? It's like the Heavenly Realms, it's a world away—you can't just follow a map," she says, voicing my very fears.

"She has a point," says Malike, reluctantly agreeing. "You go to Nekros when you're dead. No one alive has ever been."

I gasp. "That's it!"

"What's it?" says Malike, a panicked look in his eye. "You want us to kill you?"

I roll my eyes at him. "Of course not. *All stories have some truth*," I repeat the words Papa would often say. "And look, it's come true. A yamaja, someone who's only existed in our stories."

"Technically," starts Najja, "we've always been here."

"Exactly!" I say. "Reapers likely always have as well. Which means that maybe all stories *do* have some truth to them. Valdis's story is made of truth as well."

"Valdis?" Najja and Malike say at the same time.

"The human knight who helped defeat Thana? Who went to Nekros to save her beloved?" Najja asks.

I nod in confirmation. Valdis, the knight I grew up hearing tales of, who became more than just a tale—she became a guiding light, a reminder to never give up. "There are, of course, many variations of the tale, but they all have one thing in common: Valdis always follows the setting sun to reach Nekros. What if her story is like a map? If we could go there, I could save Danai. You could bring back your sister."

It would be too late for us to save anyone else. It takes twenty days after death for a soul to truly depart this world. Twenty days in which a soul travels to Nekros and waits to receive an audience with the goddess there, to receive judgment and be sent to their final resting place. It's why Danai and I tried to go to Nekros when we did, right after Papa and Aunty were killed, right after she was brought to the castle, after surviving an attack that took her parents' lives—we only had so much time.

Najja shakes her head, sadness again coloring her eyes. "It wouldn't save my sister. Yamaja don't go to Nekros. We return to the sea when we die. But I will help you. It's what my sister wanted, and if it's what she wanted, it's what I'm meant to do."

"You go to Nekros when you're *dead*," repeats Malike. "Some places aren't meant to be found before their time."

"Thank you for stating the obvious," I say, my words edged in sarcasm, "but if there's a chance to save Danai, I'm going, and I happen to know exactly where Valdis's journal is. Maybe it can lead us to Nekros and back."

CHAPTER SEVENTEEN

Leyla

Several long, tense moments later, we find ourselves safely in the library via the secret tunnels that run throughout the castle, ones Malike first introduced me to that Danai and I used to spend hours exploring. A bookshelf in Malike's bedroom that leads to the kitchens. A trapdoor in the throne room that leads to the courtyard. And a tunnel just outside the dungeons that leads to the library. All secrets that we uncovered, only for Malike to tell Mama, who, bit by bit, has been having them sealed. I never expected to use them to sneak in a yamaja.

Weak sun seeps through the library's domed ceiling, casting an eerie glow over the circular room. Shelves of scrolls and books line its walls, some reached only by the wooden ladders that climb up to the highest heights.

The library's walls are gilded like near everything else in the castle. Its deep, oaken wood is layered with gold and adorned with paintings of Anae. And the black marble floor is inlayed with golden lines spiraling out like the roots of a tree.

Bright blue stained glass comprises the dome. A single symbol lies in the middle, a stone tablet that Anae used before she joined Thana's rebellion, back when she was just the youngest daughter of a sea god and the goddess of wisdom, back when she created the yamaja.

In the center of the library, a map is etched onto a table. The Kutmenian Sea in the northeast. The Kyiri Desert in the northwest. The human kingdom of Lienne in the east, and the Nation of Mnara beside it. The Wastelands, where no one goes, in the west. And beyond them, mountains and a sea, rumored to be the Sea of Sorrows. Every territory, every nation is intricately drawn.

Danai used to sneak away, saying she had training, but would return with ink stains, not cuts, on her hands. Eventually, I found out the truth: she'd been studying for the Merkesh test—the exam required in order to join the Merkesh bloodline, the only bloodline you cannot be born into but to join means renouncing one's past.

Afraid to lose her, I begged her to delay the exam and stay another year. Begging turned into yelling, and yelling turned into crying and into the worst fight we've ever had. How desperately she wanted to go. How badly I didn't want to be alone. But it seems I was to lose her anyway. How much better it would've been on her own terms.

I trace my hands along the papers strewn about the map table. All items she left behind. With a sigh, I brush them aside.

Najja walks over and taps her finger on the Kutmenian Sea. "This is where I first saw them." She pauses. "In my homeland." Her eyes have grown heavy, their irises darkening into a cloudy gray, like a storm brewing on the horizon. Little did we know it was Danai that would need protection, simply for looking like me.

Regret is my constant companion.

"Years ago," I say to Najja, as Malike looks on from the other side of the table, "Danai and I tried to go to Nekros. Danai had Valdis's journal. The head archivist gave it to her. This library was like a second home to her, and I always assumed it was something the archivist had fictionalized to indulge a child." I head down one of the overflowing aisles, running my hand over books and scrolls until I find Valdis's section and the many written accounts about her. Next to a transcribed account of how she came to be part of the group that killed Thana is the journal, right where Danai always shelves it.

I bring the book to my nose, catching her scent on its pages. Then I pull back and open the journal, letting Valdis's words create a map of the journey we must undertake. Monsters and haunted woods. Vicious spirits and never-ending deserts. The legends that filled my bedtime stories and stoked my imagination. All part of Valdis's journey to the end of our world. And now they're more than legends, more than just stories—they might be real. The fear of that settles within me, intermingling with dread. To go on this journey will be to risk certain death; after all, wasn't that the point of Valdis's own journey, to prove to the gods her devotion to her beloved, that it was a love she was willing to risk it all for?

Danai was taken because she was mistaken for me. How can I allow others to suffer the same?

As if sensing my thoughts, Malike appears beside me. "We need to get going." He places a hand on my shoulder. "The sun is rising. Most of the guards are asleep. We don't have much time to leave undetected."

I think back to the gardens, to our conversation there. My brother has always had my back, has always tried to protect me. But this is my journey. I won't lose him, too. "You can't come," I say, barely louder than a whisper.

His brow furrows as my words reach his ears. "What?" He shakes his head in objection. Could he, for once, be less stubborn? "If you're going, I'm coming. I would never forgive myself if anything happened to you."

"I know," I say, louder this time. "But I need you to stay nonetheless." We each have our duties to the throne—mine to inherit it, his to protect me. "Someone has to stay behind; someone has to be here."

He opens his mouth to protest, but I grab his hand, squeezing. "What if something happens? What if Mama needs you? Malike, I know you care for me, I know you need to watch over me, but I won't be able to do this if I don't know that our nation will be okay if something happens to me." I say *our nation* even though I really mean him. But saying that truth would only make him protest further. I will not have my brother sacrificing himself for me. Not again. I raise my head to meet his eyes, dark red with deep dark circles underneath. He studies me, taking me in.

"You're serious," he says, like he did in Papa's gardens. Just like he did when I asked for his help, when I asked him to initiate what could lead to my death.

I nod. "A queen must put her people before herself."

"Mama's words, not yours," he says, lips barely moving.

"Still," I say, taking his hand in mine. "It's the truth nonetheless."

"I'm going, too," Najja says, walking toward us. "If my sister felt that I was meant to undertake this journey, then I would dishonor her death not to do so."

At that, I say nothing. There's nothing else to say. Determination blazes in her eyes, one that speaks to my own. Like mine, her mind is made up, and it would be futile to try and change it. It is alluring, her energy that matches my own.

I turn back to Malike. "Please," I say. "Please give me the comfort of knowing that you're okay."

He shakes his head. "You're my little sister. It's my job to protect you."

"Not this time." I give his hand a squeeze. "We have a duty to each other, yes, but we have a duty to our people even more," I say, uttering the words that I know will convince him. Malike, more than me, has always heeded duty's call. "Someone needs to be here if—" My voice catches in my throat; I don't want to think of what will happen if we don't succeed. I raise my eyes to meet his, trying to communicate with my soul more than I can with words.

Silence passes between us as our souls speak. "I'll stay," he says finally, and relief overwhelms me. My brother sweeps me up into a giant hug as his face grows wet with tears. He hugs me like he did all those years ago on the night our father was killed—fiercely, knowing that when he lets go, the weight of the present will come crashing down upon us and our lives will never be the same.

Najja and I slip from the castle as the sun stretches above the horizon, slowly illuminating the sleeping city in its amber glow. Its rays sparkle in the corners of my eyes, beaming down on my back as sunspots appear in my vision. It warms me, yet still I shiver—not from the cold, but from the thought of it all, of Danai alone, of what we must accomplish and where we must go.

The Wastelands are several days from the capital on horseback. I carry a single pack, given to me by Malike. Both Najja and I have one; they're filled with food, drink, and other provisions. Filled with everything Malike says we'll need until we can restock at Vurness, a three-day journey from here.

Everything we *think* we'll need for a journey like this—one rarely undertaken.

Nothing is certain.

I glance down at my left hand, at the gold rings on my middle finger. The Adaeze heart, the mark of my bloodline—a heart fused with a sword identical to the one Thana used to kill her father that her daughter later used to kill her—is engraved on one. A scorpion is on the other. Within the center of the scorpion ring is a gem holding a lethal poison, easily injected into my veins. It has been passed down from mother to daughter—from queen to future queen—in case of capture during the war. Now, like most everything else, it's a decorative piece. Mama passed both rings to me on the night she became queen. They have always served as reminders not only of our past and who I am, but of who I'm meant to become. Reminders of my duty not just to myself, but to my nation—to my family, to Mama.

One day soon, she'll pass her crown to me. That I do know. But I also know that I cannot—could not—rule Mnara having left my only friend to die.

Tsassia's gates are open wide, unguarded like Malike promised. We walk through them, quickly, not daring to hesitate. As soon as we pass through, however, I can't help but turn back, feeling the pull as Valdis must have when she left her home for Nekros to save the one she loved. I look up to the tower where Malike stands guard, watching for any sign of trouble, keeping an eye out for me. Our eyes meet, and before he changes his mind, before he insists upon coming along and one more person's life is in danger because of me, I turn around and leave the only home I've ever known.

CHAPTER EIGHTEEN

Favre

1,201 Years Ago: The Heavenly Realms

I run my sweaty palms down the sides of my dress, across details painstakingly embroidered over the course of ten days—ever since Thana brought me here and proclaimed me her future queen. The royal dressmaker is a god, of course, a weaver who can predict the future and also creates some of the most beautiful outfits ever worn. Normally, she could've created such a dress in the blink of an eye, in seconds, but to make this dress—and Thana's—both one of a kind, she crafted them with her own hands, one thread at a time.

Thana's gown, the richest red with beaded gold appliqués, is the inverse of my own, which is gold detailed with red. Each thread tells a story—of our love and the kingdom we'll one day rule, but not that of our futures. According to the goddess, some things should be lived—*never* foretold.

Never foretold, I repeat to myself. Trying not to itch under the weight of the heavy fabric, under the weight of my new life—a life in which my old life ceases to exist. I take a deep breath to calm myself. I would give anything to know. To know how this will all play out. To be reassured that this is what's meant for me, that like in the stories Mother used to tell about girls saved from dragons and demons by knights in shining armor who were secretly princes, we'll marry and live happily ever after.

"Ready?" Thana slips beside me and places her hand in mine. She's icy to the touch, and the cold pushes shivers up my arms and down my spine. Once, I used to sit for hours soaking up the sun. Now, night is my companion, and its goddess and I are to be wed.

We wait behind the ornate double doors that'll open at any moment. The doors separate us from the throne room and the hundreds of nobles already in their seats. Nobles who whisper about me, saying I'm not worthy to be here. Nobles who hope that I'll trip, or likely something worse, with every step I take. I shiver, this time from the panic coursing through me. "You'll be great," Thana says, as if my fears are written all over my skin.

She squeezes my hand lightly and draws me closer. She leans toward me, her lips grazing mine. She sucks on my bottom lip, biting down softly and then hard. A coppery taste fills my mouth. She pulls back slowly; a single droplet of my blood sits on her tongue. She licks her lips, taking in my blood. She closes her eyes, as if savoring it, and lets out a sigh. When she opens them, they're an even brighter red. "You taste so good," she whispers into my hair, pushing bumps onto my skin, awakening both fear and desire.

A trumpet sounds. The doors open. We pull apart. We walk, not touching but side by side, just as we practiced the night before and the nights before that. I look up to the square windows, equally spaced around the throne room, letting through the moon's light for the coronation.

It's only been ten days, but it feels like an eternity. An eternity since I felt the sun on my back, warming me to my core. An eternity since I flew so high in the sky. Since I was free.

The nobles who are packed into rows of seats alongside and leading up to the thrones fall silent. The absence of their whispers, ones I've grown so used to hearing—a stark contrast from the peace of the forest I grew up in—stirs me from my thoughts. From the lies my mind weaves about how my wings freed me, about how they made me feel alive. I glance beside me to Thana, who is basking in their attention, glowing in the moonlight. She takes my hand and smiles down at me.

My wings never freed me; Thana did. And now, I am to be her queen.

I hold my head high for the rest of the procession, stopping as rehearsed before the god who was ordained centuries ago, by Thana's father, to transcribe the history of his rule, his customs, and his traditions, including this ceremony. As such, Thana chose this same god to crown us, to preserve a legacy, to legitimize her rule.

The god addresses me and Thana and then the nobles watching on. He leads us through the ceremony that Thana's father created after he slew his own father and had himself crowned king. *Rituals,* Thana said her father told her long ago, *are important to keep up. They legitimize us and as such are the glue that holds us together. Our people see this opulence and they think that the one who has this must be important and deserving of their reverence and respect. Furthermore, they'll strive to uphold our rule because maybe, just maybe, one day they can have a slice.*

Without looking, I know this is true. The silence of the nobles is their respect, of not just this ceremony but the entire institution. An institution they think I am not worthy to be at the head of, because I didn't play their games, I didn't bide my time. To them, I skipped the line they've been waiting in for centuries. No amount of ceremonies will make them respect me. Thana's hand brushes against mine and I realize I was lost in my thoughts. In her hand is the chalice that will finalize our union. We will drink, and then each noble, representing a quorum of all the Heavenly Realms' gods, will drink as well, thus completing the ceremony and crowning us queens.

I take a deep breath and reach for the chalice and the golden drink within it that will seal my fate.

Thana steps forward, her face going ashen.

"Stop this at once!"

I turn around, following the booming voice. Vines erupt from the doors at the throne room's entrance. They hurl toward us, knocking the chalice to the ground, spilling the golden liquid on the floor.

I expect Thana to do something, but she's frozen in place. In the middle of the room is the only one of the nobles I haven't yet met. *Morowa*.

"Mother," Thana hisses. "What are you doing here?"

Thana's mother saunters over, stopping in the middle of the room. Her gown, made of roses and thorns, fans across the floor. Her skin is sun-kissed, a warm brown, even though there's no sun. "Hello, daughter. It was so lovely to receive an invitation to your wedding." Her tightly pursed lips make it clear that it wasn't lovely at all. She turns her eyes on mine. "And to meet your"—she scans me up and down—"bride. However, I'm afraid there's been a change of plans." She snaps her fingers, and a quivering servant walks through the doors and stops before her. I glance at the servant, certain I've seen him before.

"Tell them what you told me." The servant's eyes dart from Morowa to Thana to me. That's when it dawns on me, and dread starts to seep in. He was there the night Thana started to burn in the sun.

"Tell them," Morowa prods him. "Tell everyone the truth."

The servant raises his head, likely realizing that it's too late; there is no turning back. He is entrenched in this mess and the only way out is forward. "The princess is changed," he whispers. "I saw her, burning at the sun's touch. I saw her drink human blood and . . . and her eyes turned blood red like that of a . . ." He clutches a pendant around his neck, a small effigy of Kovnu. "Like . . ." He swallows loudly. "Something not of our world."

"Thank you," says Morowa. She bends down, caressing his head as a vine slithers up from the ground and encircles his throat. Before the servant can protest, before he can beg for his life, the vine strangles him. Morowa removes her hand, allowing his body to fall to the floor.

"A servant who so easily betrays his mistress is of no use." She shrugs as she beckons over the guards.

Murmurs rise among the nobles. Not about the servant whose life their former queen so easily took—the last thing anyone cares about is a dead servant, a lowly minor god who was a nobody to these nobles, a god whose name they—*we*—never bothered to learn, but about the words he said, the accusation made against their future queen.

"Am I wrong?" Mororwa looks at Thana. "Shall we wait until morning to see?"

Thana balls her hand into a fist, but she says nothing.

Her mother nods solemnly, but I catch the twinkle in her eyes, the smile she's trying to suppress. "I take no pleasure in doing this. Thana is my dear child. But one cursed by the very sun her father used to rule . . . We might have ignored how she took his life, but this is a sign we simply cannot ignore. As his queen, I swore to uphold these realms, to protect the sanctity of them. A princess who is no longer a god cannot become our queen."

"Banish her," a noble cries, and that cry gives way to another. "She must not be queen."

"We cannot subject our people to this."

"Only a god can sit upon this throne"—Morowa points at it—"and a god you are no longer."

Thana lets out a shaky breath. "You want it so badly? Take it." With that, she throws the crown to the floor. "I'd rather not be queen if I'll be stuck under your rule, forced to abide by these silly rules of what a god is or isn't and what a god can and cannot do." She bends down to pick up the chalice, just as Morowa's roses and vines latch onto it.

Thana rips it away from them, her hand bloody from their thorns, and turns to face the nobles. "We are gods and yet we allow ourselves to be reined in like this? Better to not wear this crown than be a servant to it."

She holds out her other hand and I take it. What life do I have here without her?

We exit the throne room just as Morowa picks up the crown and places it on her head.

We flee the palace and go to the only place in the Heavenly Realms we can trust: the forest that was once my home. We sit inside the cabin where I was raised, where on the good days, Mother spun me stories while gently doing my hair, and on the bad, well . . . there's no point in dwelling on that.

The cabin is small. As if in the ten days that I've been gone, it shrank itself. As if saying that I do not belong here. In reality, the cabin is the same size. Two bedchambers, barely big enough to hold the modest beds inside them, and one other room, holding the kitchen and the space where we dined, which we sit in now. The floorboards creak under our weight. Thana stands, looking out the room's lone window, her gown tattered from us fleeing through the forest. She gazes to the trees, to the stars in the sky. As if searching for someone.

"Where will we go?" I ask, but Thana says nothing and merely continues to look out the window as if she's searching for someone. She pulls back and begins to pace up and down the small space.

There's a knock at the door.

"Are we expecting someone?"

Thana brushes past me and opens the door. Spilling forth are five gods, ones I barely know.

"It took us a while to find the place," says the first, wearing Thana's favorite smirk. "This forest has a mind of its own."

Her own, I think to correct but don't.

"Hello to you, too, Lexa." Thana pulls the woman in for a hug. I recognize her instantly. She's Thana's sister, but by a different mother, and the goddess of discord and strife. "It's good to see you."

Thana goes to greet the others. First, Neferain, a war goddess, specifically of the hunt, and one of Thana's oldest friends. Tall and slim, dressed in all black, hair in braids close to her head, and huge black wings unfurling from her back. A goddess whose family was once high in command but fell from favor after siding with Kovnu's father instead of Kovnu in the war between them that Kovnu won.

Next came Anae, the young sea goddess who created my lake; the daughter of the royal dressmaker and a goddess of knowledge. She wears her hair shorn and a gown of the sea, reflecting the waters she controls.

Then Vzira, who would always be the most beautiful in the room and, if it weren't for her powerful family, would've been executed by Kovnu years ago for daring to claim that he was unfit to be king.

Finally, a man I don't quite recognize, whom Thana is surprised to see. "Uncle?" she says. It must be Suty, the god of deserts, a minor health diety, and Kovnu's half brother.

"Morowa never liked me, and my brother didn't either. You did me a favor." He kneels before her. "I am at your service, my queen."

"When do we leave?" says Vzira, a fierce look in her eyes.

"Leave." I turn to Thana. "Where will we go?"

"To the lands of the living," Neferain says plainly, as if I should know.

I stare at Thana, putting it all together, realizing she made plans without telling me. "Was this always your intention? Were we never to become queens?" I think of all I've sacrificed for her. The life I can never have back.

"Shh," she says, closing the distance between us. She runs her hands up and down my arms, soothing me. "Don't be mad. I was going to tell you after the coronation. A place without hierarchies, just like you said the other night. It was to be my gift to you.

Ideally, we would've been ruling both worlds, but now we shall at least have one."

I hold her gaze, searching her eyes for deceit. But she only smiles at me, still rubbing my arms, trying to calm my raging storm. Of course she didn't tell me, it was to be a surprise. But why did the others need to know? Was there really a need to tell them before me? She pulls me to her chest. "I love you," Thana says. "I just wanted to make you happy."

At that, I smile up at her. Her declaration of her love. Three words not even my own mother had said to me. I push away my worries. "I love you, too," I say. She kisses my forehead and then she walks over to the window sill and picks up the chalice.

She turns toward us, hunger's gleam in her eyes, and brings her left hand up to her mouth and bites down. Blood trickles from the wound into the chalice, until it runs down the side and drips onto the floor. The wound heals, her skin knitting together to close it.

"Drink from this cup and I shall give you the power you seek." A wicked grin spreads across her face. "Then we shall go to the lands of the living, where we shall be gods again."

One by one, the gods step forward. One by one, they drink from the chalice and then Thana drinks from them. There they lie on the ground, as if in an endless sleep.

Finally, she turns to me and holds the chalice out my way. And, for once, I'm not thinking of what I've lost or could lose. I'm thinking of all I could gain. Acceptance, a family. The power to never be forgotten ever again.

I take the chalice and drink. I lick my lips, taking in the last drops of her blood. Sweet and sticky and rich.

She pulls me close to her and the chalice falls to the ground. Her hands caress my head, stroking my hair. She trails soft kisses down the side of my mouth, her hand sliding up my throat, encircling it. She tilts my head back and pushes my hair gently to the side. And then she bites me. Her fangs sink into my neck. A sharp sensation, like tree branches clawing at me, overtakes my body. I want to scream, I try to. But I'm unable to make a sound. She pulls back, and I'm still burning. She trails her fangs across my skin, from my neck to my collarbone, to the soft skin just beneath where she sinks her fangs in again. This time, I feel no pain. Only warmth as the heat builds, spreading all around me, rising up from my core.

"Favre," she whispers, as if worshipping me, as she comes up for air. I inhale sharply as she does, then she sinks right back in. I moan as the heat builds, as I move demanding more, as darkness overcomes me, and I relax into her hold.

FAVRE'S DIARY

Later That Night

As Thana drank my blood, she promised me two things: one, that I would never again be alone, and two, that I would know power beyond my wildest dreams. And with that power would come security, would come peace.

She drank and drank and drank and drank, until I feared I had nothing left, until I was stiff, lying on the floor, looking up at the sliver of the moon through the cracks in the roof.

She smiled down at me as I faded out of consciousness. As my eyelids grew heavy and started to close.

The last thing I remembered, though, was not power or peace. It was the smallest flicker of doubt as something old and hungry awakened within me.

What have I become?

PART TWO

CHAPTER NINETEEN

Favre

Present Day: Nekros

At midnight, I wake and stare into the darkness. I slept fitfully after hours of tossing and turning. Hours of the dead goddess's words rattling through my ears. Hours of anxious thoughts slithering into my mind and creating doubts where there should be none. Thoughts about the girl I used to be, a girl so full of rage at the god that her mother had served, a girl trapped in circumstances not of her own making, a girl willing to do anything for the life and love she felt she deserved. Even if it meant giving up my wings to create a sword, born from my own blood and pain. A sword that could kill that very god.

A life I gave to you, comes Thana's voice. Quiet and gravely, she seamlessly slips into my head as if her voice is my own. *A life you shall have again*, she reminds me, *when we are together once more*.

I close my eyes, trying to get her voice out of my head. The voice of the woman I love, who has caused the world, and me, so much pain. But with that pain also came happiness . . . A caress against my cheek, kisses trailing down my neck, strong hands gripping mine, reassuring me that she will never *ever* leave me in the way that Mother did. Then, just like that, the memories fade and my mind is empty of her words. *Gone.* I could resent her for that, but she's the one trapped now, in an actual prison that she needs me to unlock. So we can be together again. So things can be how they once were—*better* than they were.

And so, I'm alone in the darkness. Alone with thoughts that won't quiet and doubts where there should be none.

I pull the bedsheets up to my neck and wrap them around me, trying to reassure myself that everything really will be okay. Like I used to so many years ago. Back when I was small and Mother was still alive.

I glance at the cracked mirror, and my own fractured face stares back at me. It is the face of a woman, not a girl, who has done terrible things and become someone she never thought she'd be. I pull the covers closer, snuggling under them, hiding what I see. I exhale slowly and think back to when Mother was the only monster I knew.

I'm cocooned within the covers. *Safe.* But there is nothing safe about this world. I have known that since I was a little girl, since I learned that those closest to you can hurt you the most. And so, that illusion quickly falls.

Earlier, I was dreaming. Only I can't remember what it was about or if I am still in it, suspended between my desires and reality, never close enough to reach one, never far enough to quit trying. After a while, I sit upright in the bed that once belonged to me, since tainted by the goddess I killed and those who came before her in ushering the dead home.

Remnants and reminders of my time in this manor house are all around me. A bedside table my initials are etched onto; a window seat sunken from many days spent curled upon it, gazing out into the woods, counting down my days; and a slightly bent floorboard where I'd stored my diary, where all my thoughts and my doubts live. Items from a millennium ago when Thana and I were last together—just before the end. Before the hunting party led by our daughter, Clea, and the human knight Valdis came. Before we were tortured and trapped for what was to be eternity.

I shudder at the thought and let out a sigh. I'm clearly not sleeping tonight. I slip out of the bed and into Asha's silk robe, the perfect shade of cream, and then out the door and into the long hall. Guided by my memories and doubts, I descend downward, not knowing if the creaking noise is the staircase or my aching bones, and into the dungeon where the vampire girl is.

I stop just before the dungeon's iron door and press my back to the cool metal, letting my eyes and nose adjust to the dark and musty dungeons. I stay there, hidden, my breath syncing with the girl's, for what feels like an eternity. Through the door's small window, I watch clouds whisper across the moon. Much like my time locked in the bottle tree, one moment blurs into the next. The minutes pass without my knowledge of them.

I don't know why I came here, of all places, when I couldn't sleep. Nor do I know what to say to the girl I've made my means to an end, just like so many made me.

Nothing.

The realization hits me like a stab in the chest. There's nothing.

Nothing to be said, nothing that will make it okay, that will take away the feeling inside me. It's grown too loud over the years, much like my hunger, and become an unsatiable beast.

This sickening feeling that lives within me has made a home within my bones.

It consumes me, making me toss and turn each night, unable to stop reliving the past and to think about anything but every choice I've ever made.

Suddenly, the air in the room grows thin. I'm gasping for breath, but with each breath I still can't take in enough. And I'm back, all those years ago, to when I was a little girl and telling myself that if I could just do this one thing right, be less of a burden, then my mother would come back home. My mother would love me.

Then I'm running, away from the dungeons. As fast as my legs can carry me, away from this house and all its memories. Thinking that if I can get out, if I can just *breathe*—maybe, just maybe, the thoughts in my head will quiet.

I run, my bare feet thumping against the stone. I run, pushing open the house's large double doors. I run, stumbling into the woods and over knobby roots and rocks and hollow logs. I race through the woods, deeper and deeper. The air is thick with fog, so thick that I can't see where I'm going until I'm there: the edge of a lake. I stop myself just as my toes touch the water. Just before I fall in. I stumble back from the shock, ice-cold water jolting me to the present. The damp earth underneath my feet. The cool air rustling through my hair. The woman in the lake staring back at me.

A woman who was everything to me yet made me feel like nothing.

Who cared more for the gods in her life—the men she tried

and failed to satisfy, for they could never be satisfied—who always ended up leaving her in the end.

But I was there. I was always there. Waiting for her to return.

And, sometimes, she did. After a god left, after she tried everything to win him back, she'd come back home to me.

She braided my hair. We played games, hide-and-seek within the forest where we lived, only the two of us. She spun me fairy tales. Of girls like me, who had nothing, who, through many trials, eventually got more than they'd ever dreamed of. All they had to do was never give up, all they had to do was wait.

And just as I got comfortable, right when I started to imagine, to want more—a life of only she and I. A life of not chasing after gods who only wanted her for the power her blood possessed. A life in which we could go anywhere, become anything—she'd meet another god. *Bewitched him,* they'd later say. One day she'd be there, styling my hair, and the next she'd be gone.

Sometimes, she'd come back to see me. Weaving stories that felt like a fairy tale, of the gorgeous mansion the god lived in, of the daughters of his I'd surely befriend. But that only lasted so long. I always ended up alone in the forest. The bastard daughter of another god, who no one wanted.

I sit on the cool ground and stare into the lake. The woman in the lake still stares back at me. Mirroring my every move. The more I look at her, the more I can't look away. Soon, my mother's face and mine blur together until I'm staring at only me. Until I'm left with a single thought that chills me to my core: I can't tell where my mother ends and I begin.

Should not a king lead by example? Setting the standards by which his subjects follow. How can one call themselves a king if they disregard for themselves the very rules they expect of others?

To commit such a sacrilegious act is to lose the respect of their people, thus deeming themselves unfit for the crown.

If a king is unfit for the very object embodying his supreme authority, he should not long possess it. He should no longer be king.

—VZIRA'S THESES, OR DISPUTE ON THE SOVEREIGNTY OF THE KING
WRITTEN 29 BD
MERKESH ROYAL ARCHIVES

CHAPTER TWENTY

Leyla

The Nation of Mnara: Vurness

"Heads up!"

Najja yanks me to the side just as a Sintu woman tosses the contents of a chamber pot out her window. The stench hits me right as it splashes where I stood, and I bring my hand up to cover my nose and mouth as I gag.

"Not what you'd pictured?" Najja says as we push past the throngs of vampires that fill the narrow streets of Vurness. My shoes are caked with mud, and likely something else I don't want to think about. Houses are crammed together on either side of the road, built with barely enough space for an alleyway between them, and there, clotheslines hang above, advertising undergarments for all to see.

I shoot her a glare, but she's right. It is definitely not what I had in mind when I pictured the legendary city Danai has always wanted to visit. Even during the war, they kept their market going, to ensure vampires everywhere weren't cut off from necessary supplies. Danai could recite facts about it at a moment's notice. And she often did. Detailing the structure, its impenetrable iron walls that loom over us, shrouding the city, and its trade routes deep underground—a web carved within the mines, known only to its residents. Mines that became the key to the peace treaty Mama brokered with the human king. The mines the Sintu once controlled are a source of survival for all of us—human blood for our gold. I take it all in and sigh. To see all this, without her . . . I stop walking and close my eyes, trying to stop myself from spiraling before I begin. I touch the hummingbird pendant on my neck. I can't lose anyone else.

Vampires mill about, picking up cloths and stools, trading glassware and linen. At every stall are statues of the goddess Vzira in her many forms. A young girl. A middle-aged woman. An elder. And then there are the metals. Iron and bronze crafts like I've never before seen, metals that never tarnish, by craftswomen who can make anything upon request. The sharpest blades. The sturdiest pots. All items made by the Sintu from the metals they gather from the mines that they work with their iron-sharp nails. The Sintu are the best metalworkers in the nation. Those who do not work in the mines, harvesting the gold that is essential to our world, go to schools to learn trades.

We blend seamlessly into the crowd of merchants and their horse-drawn carts, of families shopping about, and of nobles carried on palanquins by human servants throughout a market spanning as far as I can see. Everyone is consumed by their own worlds, never lingering our way.

Though my feet still ache and my back and shoulders are stiff from all the walking and the uneven grounds on which we've slept, the past three days of traveling with a stranger haven't been as bad as I expected.

Though few words have passed between us, the care she's shown me has spoken volumes. Whether it's walking just ahead of me, paving a way for me as we've woven through tall grass, while pointing out snakes and other creatures lying hidden along the way. Taking breaks as I needed to, even though she clearly did not. And always volunteering to take the first watch, so I can sleep. There's been kindness . . . gentleness . . . exchanged. As if we both realized . . . all we have during this time is each other.

I take a deep breath, unclenching my jaw, as ease settles within me. This is not my home, but I *am* home—my people are my home. The sounds of them bartering and laughing. The many shades of brown blurring together as they mill about. And the smells. Perfumes at one shop, herbs at another, and of course the sweets.

As if I am suddenly transported back in time, Danai is before me taking a sticky sweet from my hand and stuffing it into her mouth. She throws her head back and laughs—it's as if I am there with her again and not here.

"Spare some coin?" a woman calls. The memory slips from me as soon as it appears.

I look down at the Sintu before me. Her linens are soiled, covered in dirt and hanging too loose on her bone-thin frame. Her wide, hungry eyes stare back at me as she holds her hands stretched out. "Coin, please, miss," she asks. I dip into my dress pocket and hand her several gold coins. "Thank you." She gives me a toothy smile then vanishes in an instant.

That's when I notice that there are people like her all around the market town. That unlike at home, many people are wearing rags. There are the nobles and merchants, with the carts and horses and palanquins. They are laughing, bartering for goods, and trading their wares. But there are also others, some covered in dirt like they've just come from the mines, others with hollowed cheeks asking, no, begging for coins. The nobles ignore them. The merchants turn up their noses.

Mama always taught me that a queen takes care of her own. That a queen must lead by example.

A cry pierces through the crowd, one rife with rage. I whip my head toward the sound. It grows louder, as if coming near, and my eyes land on a mass of people just ahead of us in the town's square. They're facing a podium where a girl presides, her stance fierce, and everyone around her is chanting, "Down with the queen."

Goose bumps rush up my arm as I freeze in place. Najja gently places a hand on my arm, jerking me out of my trance. "Something tells me we shouldn't wait to find out what that's about." She motions to the left, and I follow her, trying to go around everyone. But the crowd is too large, and the more we try to push past, the more we're caught up in it. Soon, we're in the middle of it with no way out.

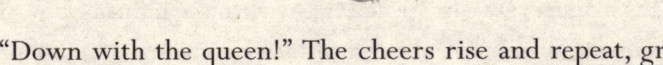

"Down with the queen!" The cheers rise and repeat, growing angrier with each chant, and fear courses through me.

Don't panic, I tell myself. *They don't know you're here.* So, I do the only thing I can do. I try to blend in. I stop pushing against the crowd, I stop trying to get out, and I face the podium and wait, nervously anticipating what's to come. The chants grow louder and louder until suddenly they stop.

A girl around my age steps onto a platform that looks like gallows, the very ones used during the war to execute captured humans. The girl is Sintu—her mark, Vzira's hand balancing two scales, representing the morals she always upheld, unfurls on the back of her neck—with pitch-black hair in a braid that's coiled into a bun atop her head. She's not tall but rather of slightly less than average height. If not for the fountain, which adds a few feet, she'd be lost in the crowd. Her eyes burn red and her lips are set in a satisfied smile. She radiates with power, she is stunning, and I can't look away.

She's followed by two other girls. Held high above their heads are banners that say, "STUDENTS FOR JUSTICE." They must be enrolled in one of our universities. Similar to entrance into the Merkesh bloodline, these require passing a rigorous test, but instead of studying history and religion, university students study law, medicine, and the arts.

The girl in the middle clears her throat and everyone quiets. Some stand, arms crossed; others lean in; all are waiting.

"Next year marks one hundred years since our inter-bloodline agreement," she says. She doesn't yell; in fact, she's quite soft-spoken, which only makes the crowd gather closer.

She's not referring to the peace treaty with the humans, but to an agreement my grandmother forged after convincing the other bloodline leaders to stop fighting one another and combine forces to defeat the humans.

"We became one nation under a queen descended from a legendary war hero, Clea," she continues. "But her bloodline—the Adaeze—conveniently let you forget that they're direct descendants of Thana, that Clea was Thana's daughter. The daughter of a queen who had entire villages burned, who killed others like her, who killed her own children just because she felt like it."

The crowd boos and a few people near me grunt and nod, agreeing.

"We, the Sintu, *we* mine the gold. We mine the iron, the bronze, and all the metals. It's *our* metals that keep this nation going. Our metals are one of our nation's most traded and desired goods . . ." She raises her voice. "Where do they come from?"

"Our mines!" everyone yells.

A shudder creeps across me as their fists go up at once, creating a fearsome image.

A warm touch at my elbow jerks my gaze away from the girl. I sigh with relief to see Najja by my side. "We need to get out of here," she says, her voice low and steady. "If this goes south, you don't want to be here."

"I know," I say, "but I need to stay."

"What? Are you mad?" she says. Her eyes flit across my face as if looking for a sign I'm unwell.

"I need to be here," I whisper. "They are my people. All my life I've been in the castle, thinking everyone loved Mama, thinking that because the war was over, our people were prosperous again. All my life I've believed a lie. But now, I have a chance to hear another side." My feet remain firmly planted even as I shove my hands in the pockets of my dress to hide their trembling. "These are my people"—my voice cracks—"I *need* to hear this. I want to stay."

Najja opens her mouth, as if to protest, but she only sighs. "It's your funeral," she says gruffly. But she steps a bit closer to me and moves her hand to rest on her sword. I shoot her a grateful look.

The girl begins speaking again and the crowd quiets. "Those

mines now belong to everyone, a concession we agreed on for peace. A concession that became a sacrifice, a sacrifice of our way of life. Who lives in luxury now? Her. Our gold, our metals, all around her castle. And what do we get? A lifetime of working in the mines and a barely livable wage. If we're lucky, some of us make it into the university." She motions at herself and the two girls below her. "But even there we are silenced and shunned by our noble peers who bought their way in. Yet they think we're not deserving.

"We are rationed out blood, forced to either pay for it with the hard-earned coins we make working *our* mines or wait for shipments from the Lienne—shipments that only come four times a year. And yet the queen and her nobles keep human servants, which we are not allowed to do."

"Kill her! Let's kill the queen," someone yells.

The crowd rowdies and someone knocks into me, pushing me forward, but Najja catches me before I fall. She leans in so close I can smell the saltwater scent that permanently clings to her clothes. "Ready to leave now?" she whispers.

Before I can respond, the girl at the front tugs at her shirt collar and cocks her head to the side, revealing two bite marks. "I am one of the last to be turned in this way—born human and gifted a new life. But now, thanks to the queen's laws, we are regulated, only able to turn a few humans a year, and so our bloodline, once a bloodline of strong women, weakens. We, the Sintu, used to be feared. Now we, the Sintu, scrape by thanks to the generosity of our queen—and soon a daughter who is only my age. A daughter who, instead of being forced to fight in the war her ancestress started—like the rest of us—was spared from it. Sheltered from the horrors, the traumas the rest of us still bear."

A pit of sadness grows in my throat at the ever-present reminder that I did not live up to my duty. The only one in a line of warrior queens who hasn't bled on the battlefield alongside my people—who wasn't strong enough to.

"What say you of her ability to rule us?" the young Sintu asks the crowd.

The crowd laughs. "Get rid of her, too," someone yells.

"Kill them both," someone else suggests.

I flinch at that, but maybe they're not wrong. What kind of leader sends others to fight on her behalf?

Someone screams, pointing to the sky. "What is that?" they cry.

I look up, and the sky is swarming with blurry black figures like oversized birds. The crowd ducks as they come crashing down.

Oorvain.

In addition to their mark—a knife wedged between two wings—each bears the Adaeze heart embroidered on their cloaks.

They're not just any Oorvain; they're the royal guards. The guards slam into the crowd, and it scatters.

I grab Najja's hand and yank her toward me, running back through the crowd as it disperses into chaos. Someone bumps into me and Najja, separating us and knocking me to the ground. I fall into a puddle, mud splashing onto my face. As people run, a horse pulling a cart startles, rearing its front legs.

"Leyla," Najja cries, pushing through the crowd, trying to make her way toward me.

Get up, I tell myself, but fear has me in its grip and I freeze. All I can think of is the Reapers' attack, of the Sintu woman I fell beside, who lay dying—bleeding out—on the ground, of how Danai saved me, of how I tried to save her, and of how I failed.

Run, I tell myself, but I can't move. I can only look up, wide-eyed, at the horse in front of me. Rearing his front legs, preparing to stomp all over me and send me to my death.

The horse shakes his head, mane thrashing, then brings his legs down.

I'm pushed to the side just as the horse hits the pavement, hooves cracking the ground. Najja lays beside me, chest heaving. The horse breaks free of its harness and gallops away.

"The princess, where is she?" a guard questions a shop owner only a few feet away, holding a rough sketch of me. Mama must've sent them. They are here for me.

Najja pulls me off the ground so swiftly that I collide into her chest. She holds me there for a beat, eyes the color of a raging wave meeting mine. "I've got you," she says softly, then she lets go, leaving me reeling from her touch. She takes a quick look around, scouting out an exit. Her eyes latch onto an alley and she drags me toward it. We zigzag down the alley, Najja leading and pulling me along. The alley twists and leads into another. We run down it and then another and run right into a guard.

I skid to a stop. Another guard jumps from the roof and lands behind us. The guard in front of me opens his wings, as does the one behind us, blocking any way out. The one in front looks at me and his eyes widen with recognition. Then he envelopes my body within his wingspan, cradling me in a way that might comfort me if he weren't a guard sent to drag me home.

The other guard knocks Najja down with his wings. She screams as he grabs her by the throat. She squirms, trying to get away. But he's stronger; the more she struggles, the more tired she grows, and the less she kicks.

"Let us go." I kick. The guard's wing-grip on me tightens. Najja gasps for air.

"I command you," I cry. "Let me go." But my guard doesn't budge, so I'm forced to watch as the other guard suffocates her. Unlike a few days ago, when fighting off the Reapers, she doesn't look fearless or fierce. She's frantic, she's scared. And it is completely my fault.

I kick harder, desperate to free myself. Desperate to free us both, to get us to safety far away from these men. But no matter how hard I struggle, I can't escape.

"Duck!" A melon falls from the roof and slams onto my guard's head. He falls to the ground. I barely duck in time. The Sintu girl from before jumps from the roof, landing on the back of Najja's guard. She sweeps her legs around his neck. He's caught by surprise, giving Najja enough time to slip from his grasp and whack him with the blunt end of her sword. He falls, unconscious. Meanwhile my guard is already knocked out cold, yellow melon guts splattered onto his face.

The Sintu girl jumps down from the roof, landing between Najja and me.

"You're welcome," she says. Her eyes linger on us as she sizes the two of us up. "I would've thought a yamaja and the daughter of the Lioness of Mnara could've held their own against two guards. Apparently not." She steps forward, toward the end of the alleyway, where strings of clothes hang on a line. The girl brushes aside the towels, revealing a hole in the wall. Then, without waiting to see if we follow, she steps into the dark.

CHAPTER TWENTY-ONE

Leyla

With no other options, we follow the girl into the tunnel. It's so dark that it takes my eyes longer than usual to adjust and make out the path we're on. The tunnel looks like it was carved by hand. On the walls and on the ceiling are chisel marks in the shape of the long, iron fingernails the Sintu have. The nails are retractable, a hereditary feature—fearsome yet so easily hidden away.

As my eyes adjust, I see other tunnels shooting off from this one. On the floor are broken iron beams, like those of the rails used for mine carts. I remember Danai gushing about them once, showing me sketches from a book about the design of the mines. The Sintu make intricate transportation systems for the sole purpose of carting miners in and minerals and miners out. She was riveted by the concept and wondered if it would be possible to build these rails on a larger scale, to construct some sort of self-powered cart to transport people between cities and towns and villages faster than horses and carriages could.

The hand-chiseled tunnels, the iron rails—we must be inside one of the mines.

"Do you have any idea where we're going?" Najja whispers from behind me as I follow the girl.

"What were we supposed to do? Stay there and run into more guards? We didn't even see her up there on the roof. If she wanted to, she could've just as easily knocked us out. This seems like the safer option."

Najja gestures around us. "Oh yes, walking through a dark tunnel with a girl we don't know. Definitely safer."

The girl laughs, the sound reverberating throughout the tunnel.

"Something funny?" Najja asks.

"Oh, just the thought of me sitting on roofs with melons and thwacking passersby with them."

"I don't know your life," Najja mutters.

The girl continues to speak. "To answer your question, this is an abandoned mine. One of several, actually. Officially, it's boarded up and could collapse at any time. Unofficially, we use it for transport."

"Could collapse at any time?" says Najja. "I think I'd prefer to take my chances with the guards."

"Transport what, exactly?" I say. The Sintu girl leads us down a path to the right. I hear it before I see it. The sound of many voices bustling around, like a city underground. As we near, the tunnel brightens with candlelight and I see that's exactly what it is. Hundreds of Sintu are underground.

To my left, women load containers full of food—blood and other things, like seeds, rice, and beans—onto carts. To my right, women sort through piles of clothes. And, in front of me, several women melt gold candelabras, jewelry, and cutlery in a special pot, a crucible—I learned what it was called after Danai begged me to convince Mama to allow us to visit the royal treasury in the capital for a day. She wanted to shadow the royal goldsmiths and learn more about their processes. Though these women don't have the fancy tools those goldsmiths had, the process looks the same.

First, they melt the items down until they're liquid. Then the molten gold is poured into coin molds to create blanks, discs of metal. The Sintu sort the blanks into two piles. One of the piles is melted down again—those must be the blanks that are too heavy or light—and the other is hammered into coins. The head of the royal goldsmiths, who gave us a tour, took every opportunity to praise Mama, saying that thanks to her, we no longer had to worry about counterfeit coins and the negative affects they could have on our economy. In the early days of her reign, Mama standardized Mnaran coins: the weights and size of each must be the same. To make batches of coins of the same size took great technical skill. There were only a handful of vampires gifted enough to do it, he'd boasted, and they all were employed by the crown and had been trained by him.

At the time, I couldn't understand why anyone would want to counterfeit coins. In Tssaia, there's always more than enough. I pause, trying to recall if that was actually true or if I hadn't bothered to notice.

Clearly these women learned the skill. Mama's face is on one side of the coins, and on the other is my great-great-grandmother, Clea the Queenslayer. Clea is depicted as Morowa, but instead of holding the goddess's traditional scepter, she holds a sword—the very one she used to kill Thana. After the women are finished hammering the impressions, I can't tell the difference between the coins before me and they ones I carry.

"What is all of this?" I ask.

The Sintu girl who led us here mock bows. "Welcome, your highness, to the underground."

"The underground," I repeat while searching my mind for reference to such a place. I come up blank.

"If you've never heard of it, then we're doing our job," she says, answering my puzzled stare.

I nod in the direction of the girls melting down the gold. "That's illegal, you know."

She shrugs. "Technically, it's more like a gray area. You see, your mother became so confident that no one would learn how to make the coins that she never really came up with a punishment for anyone who did. And before you ask, no, we didn't steal the gold. Everything here was given to us by our allies, all to support our cause."

"And what cause is that?" I cross my arms across my chest. "Overthrowing my mother?"

She laughs, shaking her head. "If we wanted to do that, we could've years ago. Overthrowing one ruler isn't that hard. If someone really wanted your entire family dead, they could figure out how to do it. But the thing is, another ruler would eventually take her place. We seek something more permanent. Sanctuary, for all."

Before I can process what she's said, a bell rings, pulling our attention to a different tunnel, an offshoot of this space we're in. The bell continues to ding until a cart rolls to a stop at the tunnel's entrance. Two Sintu stop sorting clothing to go help a woman and her child disembark. The woman has a bruised eye, the child has bruise-covered arms.

"They're human," I say.

The girl before me nods. "We help those who need helping, no matter who they are, in the way that our founding mother, the fallen goddess Vzira, once did. An escape route, food, clothing, and money to start a new life." As the Sintu help the woman and her child down, they bring them over to the piles of clothes and allow them to take whatever they choose.

"Why keep this a secret?" I say. "It's not like you're doing something bad. I'm sure my mother would—"

"Your mother doesn't care about us. She only cares about those rich enough to make her richer—her merchants, her nobles. Do you know what war leads to? Trauma. Domestic unrest. And so much more. Even with the war over, there are no programs to help those who fought in the war readjust to life, to find jobs, to settle back in with their families and loved ones. We tried to bring these concerns to your mother, and we were turned away at the castle gates. That's why we lead these protests—they're the only way our voices are heard, they're the way we get more supporters and donations. If we could get what we needed from an audience with the queen, we would've done that years ago."

I start to argue, to say the words Mama has said to me many times—that a queen always cares for her people, that she puts them above all else. But then I remember the many meetings she's had me sit in on, to learn how to be a queen. The ones Mama says I will one day run, in which citizens bring Mama their concerns and she hears them out. I've only ever seen nobles and merchants in the throne room. Complaining about land disputes, about workers who want to be paid too much, about how there should be nicer inns erected alongside the roads the merchants use for the blood-gold trade. The meetings I sat in on passed by painfully slow, with Mama spending the time sorting out mostly petty squabbles.

"I see," I say. "But then why would you show this to me? Why bring us here if I am the very product of the thing you despise?"

"Raina," someone says, as they approach us. The Sintu girl turns in their direction. Raina must be her name.

The person takes one glance in our direction, then whispers something into Raina's ear. "Thank you," she says before turning back to face me. "I heard a rumor that the princess's friend was taken and that the queen refused to send a search party. Unsurprisingly, even at her own daughter's request, the lioness does not bend. And yet you went anyway, determined to find your friend, even though those who took her are the very things from our nightmares. I'd assumed the lioness raised another, but maybe she instead gave birth to a mouse."

I flinch. But the girl holds up her hand. "Remember, it was the mouse who saved the lion." I think of the tale Papa used to tell me, the one she is referring to, of a lion who got trapped in a hunter's net and the mouse who freed him by chewing through the ropes. The lion, full of rage, struggled, and the more it did, the tighter the ropes became. But the mouse was thoughtful and resourceful. The mouse was unexpected. "Maybe you are what Mnara needs.

"Your mother believes a queen's duty is to rule and that a people's duty is to follow. Like her, we were raised during the war, but unlike her we will also grow up during peace. There are many who believe that the same alliances needed in war are not needed in peace. We deserve to be heard, not treated as if it's our fault we're poor when the very reason we're poor is because we sacrificed so much for this nation. We sacrificed so much for peace." Her eyes get a faraway look in them that makes me think she's not just talking about the mines, that she's lost more than that, that the war took from her as it did from me.

A young woman appears by Raina's side. Raina motions to her. "Ida will take you to the living quarters. In the morning, we'll transport you out of here. We've thrown the Oorvain off your scent—by the time they realize, you'll be long gone."

She nods at one of the other Sintu and they take us to the waiting cart.

"Thank you. I won't forget this."

"I know you won't." Raina grins. "You owe me, princess. *If* you survive this journey, I intend to make sure that our paths cross again."

CHAPTER TWENTY-TWO

Leyla

Ida leads us through a series of winding tunnels until we reach a long hallway of wooden doors—the living quarters Raina spoke of. She stops at the third door on the right. "Someone will be by later with food." She opens the door and then scurries away before we can say anything else.

"After you," says Najja, as she opens the door. A single candle is lit on a table, and there is one bed.

Najja wastes no time in placing her pack down on the left side of the bed. She unlaces her boots, kicks off her shoes, and lifts her shirt just high enough to reveal an under tunic so sheer it's basically see-through.

"What are you doing?" I ask her, holding a hand up to avert my gaze.

"Getting ready for bed," she says without looking my way as she proceeds to take her shirt off. "They'll likely have us up early in the morning. Might as well get some sleep while we can." She folds her shirt and then looks over at me. She lifts her brow. "Why are you just standing there?"

I look from her to the bed, trying to avoid glancing at the undergarments she wears. Her sheer undertunic and shorts held loosely together with a single cord of rope. The gap in between them giving way to her midnight black skin. I pull my eyes away, ignoring the heat rising to my cheeks. "You're just going to . . . get in the bed . . . dressed in that?"

She raises an eyebrow. "You expect me to get in bed in the clothes we've been traveling in for three days?"

"No," I say, "of course not. I just didn't . . ." I let my voice trail off as I search for the words I'm looking for. How I didn't think through the logistics of this, not just traveling with but sleeping right beside a person I barely know. I wasn't afraid of her; after all, she'd just saved my life. But the past few days, one of us was usually keeping watch, so it felt less . . . intimate. I didn't expect to be close enough to notice the way the candlelight illuminates the softness of her curves. Or to feel her warmth. Our bodies, side by side. My eyes flit over to her and then quickly to the floor.

Slowly, a smirk spreads across her face. "I see," she says. She grabs the pillows on the bed and begins to place them in a neat row, dividing the bed in half. "Is this better, princess?" She draws out every syllable in a way that unnerves me.

I grit my teeth. "Like I keep saying, you can call me Leyla."

She chuckles and the twinkle in her eyes confirms that she knows she can and yet is calling me princess anyway, to see how I react.

I take a deep breath to clear my head. I should be focused on why we're here, not how sheer her shirt is. "Fine." I turn away from her. "Don't look," I say, before undressing to my chemise. I climb into bed next to her. Despite being so close to a near stranger, my body relaxes at once. Most days, it's easier to ignore my nerve pain like I do the constant noises of the old castle that's my home. But the past few days of sleeping on makeshift pallets has been harder than I anticipated. My whole body aches. I stretch out my tingling legs and sigh.

"Getting comfortable?" Najja pats at the pillows. "Make sure you stay on your side," she says, eyes still twinkling with laughter. "Wouldn't want to compromise a princess's virtue." Her lips slowly twist into a smile. "Unless . . ." she says, her gaze sliding from my eyes to my lips, "you would."

A knock on the door saves me from answering. "Come in," says Najja. She gets up at once to open the door. As if she caught me staring, she turns around and winks. I sink into the covers. Now would be an excellent time to disappear.

After a few moments, I feel the bed shift as she climbs into it. The smell of blood pulls my thoughts out of the gutter. "Your highness," she says mockingly. She adjusts the pillows ever so slightly to put a tray between the two of us. Chicken and rice for her, blood for me.

"Freshly donated, I was told," she says.

Our eyes connect across the pile of pillows as she hands it to me. She watches as I take a sip and then another. "How do you drink that?" she finally says, wrinkling her nose in disgust.

I laugh, trying to make light of it, of her discomfort with me drinking human blood. "At least all my blood has always been donated by live sources. What did that poor chicken do to you?" But my joke fails to make its mark and her eyes never leave the glass of blood in my hand. "Go ahead, ask the question you clearly want to ask," I say, as it's all but written across her face.

"Have you ever taken a life, fed from someone who didn't donate? Someone who didn't have a choice?"

I grit my teeth, thinking back to the human girl Mama killed without a thought, as she has countless others. The humans were our enemy, but on the battlefield, for survival, was one thing; in the comfort of our home is another. I frown, recalling how easily that Sintu cheered for me to be killed, too, all because of my mother's sins. "Before I knew better, I drank what was given to me. But then I saw my father killed before me and my mother driven to war by revenge. I will not be part of the death of another simply because they are human and I, vampire." I think of the words my mother commands of me but never truly lives by herself. *A queen should put her people's needs before herself.* "My duty is to my people." I stare directly at her. "I would not so easily jeopardize our peace."

I am not my mother.

Najja looks away from me and into the flickering candle beside her. The silence wraps around us, until I feel the need to speak, to smooth things over, to apologize like I would with Mama though I have done nothing wrong.

"I'm sor—"

She holds her hand up, before resting it on the pillows dividing us. "Please, no," she says quietly, then she clears her throat and speaks louder. "*I'm* sorry. That wasn't fair of me. I made assumptions, taking out my anger at her deeds on you—much like she did on my people, after my grandmother told her of her fate. But an eye for an eye doesn't solve anything."

"No, it does not," I say, staring at her.

After a while, she holds out her hand. "Truce?"

I stare at it for a beat.

"I don't bite." She gives me a small smile.

"That's my line," I laugh. Slowly, I take her hand and shake it, letting her warmth wrap around me. "Truce," I say quietly.

"You're freezing!" She clasps my hands between hers, as if to warm me up. I let her, some part of me not wanting her to pull away.

"We're terrible at producing warmth," I offer as explanation. "That's where the myths come of us dying at night and sleeping in coffins to hide from the sun."

"Coffins?" She snorts at that. "Thankfully those aren't true. It'd be a pretty tight fit." She wiggles her eyebrows at me. "The two of us . . . side by side . . . in a coffin."

At that, I burst out laughing, and she follows. "If that's the best you've got, we need to work on your finesse."

That's when I realize it's the first time I've laughed in days—since Danai and I were at the harvest festival together. I grow quiet at that thought and immediately try and think of something else—anything that will bring me out of my sorrow.

"Danai once found a coffin. We were visiting some noble's house and they had one on display." I start to smile at the memory. "Everyone else was in another room. She dared me to climb into it. We got stuck. It was terrible." I laugh. "Luckily my brother found us, not my mother." I swallow slowly, Mama would always discipline first and ask questions later.

"How did you two become friends?" Najja asks.

"She kicked my ass." I laugh even harder at Najja's shocked face. "It's true." I explain, "She was an orphan, taken in by the castle. That was how we met. We all trained together. Me, my brother, the children of the nobles, and the orphans. We trained from age twelve for a war that was just beyond the capital, a war we feared might come to us at any moment." I take a deep sigh at the irony that the war never once reached the capital, that there was never an attack there—not until the day the Reapers came, after the war, and stole Danai away.

"I was top of the class. Not because I was the best." I shake my head. "I could hold my own. But much to my mother's dismay, I wasn't a natural like her. It was just that everyone else was too afraid to actually beat me. Until Danai. I guess she didn't get the memo that you're not supposed to kick the princess's ass, and so, there I was on the ground, bloody lip and blackened eye." I grin, remembering the day I finally made a friend. "Everyone stared at her, but she's didn't care, the orphan who had the audacity to defeat the royal heir."

I close my eyes, and I am back there, on the mat. "Danai reached her hand out to me. 'About time,' I'd said once I'd finally dusted myself off. The best part?" My grin widens. "She didn't apologize. She critiqued my form." I place my glass down on the side table as sadness overtakes me again. "We were inseparable after that," I say, tears already prickling my eyes.

"We'll find her." Najja squeezes my hand. I nod, reassuring myself more than her. We stay like that for a while, side by side in the bed, sharing stories. Soon Najja falls asleep. But sleep does not come easily to me. I lie there, looking up at the ceiling, wondering: *Will she be alive when we do?*

CHAPTER TWENTY-THREE

Najja

The Wastelands

We're woken from our sleep just before dawn and placed in a mine cart. The cart winds through the tunnel, climbing higher the farther we travel. Finally, we reach the end of the line, a door is opened, and sunlight bursts in. The Sintu hand us back our packs, refilled and heavy with supplies, before disappearing into the mines without another word.

Over the course of the next day and the two days after that, the landscape changes drastically. The trees become leafless with gnarly branches and at times not even that—just trunks hollowed from the inside out by the black beetles that swarm within. The lush green grass turns to brown, and where it exists at all, it's in patches. Some places there is only dry earth. The days are humid, and the nights cold. I find myself missing the cool spray of the sea on my face.

Then there are the ruins, the rocky remnants of places that used to be. A pile of stone that might've once been a tavern or a temple. A house, stables . . . an open space that could have been a market square. All things that might have been. That probably were. Now reduced to dust and stone thanks to a thousand years of war. A thousand years in which humans and vampires fought. Pillaging the land and altering life for us all.

"The Wastelands. We're here," says the princess.

I glance around, taking in the barren place that connects vampire and human territories. This place represents the worst of it, the physical aftermath of a war that spread like wild flames. As my mother used to say, the Wastelands was the site of many legendary battles between humans and vampires. And when all was said and done, both abandoned it—not wanting to control such a desolate place, where the wind sounds like howling spirits, where vines snake out of half-buried human and vampire skulls and cracks form on the ground where streams used to be.

The princess swings her bag off her back and sticks her hand inside, rummaging around. A few seconds later, she pulls out Valdis's journal, quickly flipping through the pages until she finds what she's looking for. She holds it up to me. An illustration of a mountain ridge is etched across the pages. It's just visible from the Wastelands, its peak hovering over the horizon. She turns from me and points to a similar mountain ridge, at least a few days' journey from here. "Those must be the Typhian Mountains, where the entrance to Nekros is." Her joy is palpable. Not just joy, but relief. Relief that soon we'll find her friend. That soon, we can return home.

Or at least, she can.

Though we left Vurness a few days ago, my mind is still there. The poverty that afflicts many within that city reminds me of home. A home that I so badly wanted to leave. But not like this; on my own terms. Now I want nothing more than to return, but my home may not exist anymore.

When Mama was alive, she tried to hide it from us. How wetness still clung to her gown because it didn't have enough time to dry between her washing it and needing to wear it. Any extra fabric she could buy went to clothes for us, ones she made and mended by hand. How our meals were always meager and often consisted of only what we fished or grew, and how our catch and livestock were not ours alone—any excess had to be sold to local villages for profit to pay taxes to a lord we'd never met. When our catch was low or livestock scarce, Mama would say she wasn't hungry and watch us eat instead.

After Mama died, there was no point in hiding anything.

My childhood ended with her death.

Thoughts of home mingle together with everything else. The Reapers' attack. Losing Simi. How fiercely that guard in Vurness had grabbed me, not caring whether I lived or died. I, however, did care, surprising even myself. As I felt my breath fading and my vision dimming, I wished to live then more than I have these past few years. That, more than anything else, scared me. The guilt from that single thought threatens to consume me. That I wanted to live when everyone I love has died. *Selfish*, a voice in my head said. And I couldn't help but agree. As if she can sense my thoughts, Leyla shoots me a concerned glance. I look away, not wanting her to see the tears that prick my eyes.

The farther we walk into the Wastelands, the darker it gets.

Soon, night is upon us, and the sky is painted with stars—each twinkling brighter than the last, crafting patterns in the sky.

When Simi and I were little, Mama took us to the top of the tower overlooking our homeland and pointed at the stars. We watched with awe as her fingers traced across the sky, naming each and every one of them. With each name followed a story of how the stars came to shine, how the sea came to be so vast, how the whole world was formed. She always began with Polaris—Morowa's son and the god of travelers, who created the first stars as beacons of light to guide those journeying home.

Our mother taught us to look to the stars. When we are sad, when we are lonely, when we are afraid. The stars are our constants. The stars will always guide us. The stars will lead us back home.

The morning after Mama died—after she was drowned in the hurricane's wrath, killed saving me—Simi took me to the beach. Dragged me out of our hut and to the sandy shore. The sand soaked into my toes that were being suckled by little currents rippling far underneath as my feet sank, slowly, into the wet sad. The wind blew, combing through our hair. And the tide rose, trickling over our feet, receding, then returning. We stood that way for hours, arms wrapped around each other, feet planted, remembering Mama, mourning her and saying goodbye.

I glance up at the star-smattered sky. The stars I saw then are almost the same ones above me now. *You can follow them home*, I tell myself. But, instead of hope, instead of some sort of relief, a shiver creeps through me as the night darkens. I know the thought is a lie.

After this, Leyla will go home, and she will one day become her people's queen. But after this, what will become of me?

I find the star that always points north, the one Mama called the

Star of the Sea. I close my eyes and whisper my fear to it.

Where will I go?
What home do I have left?

I bat away yet another mosquito buzzing in my ear and coming for my blood. Though the sky is dark and the night is cooler, it's still swarming with bugs. Their bites cover my arms and legs; it takes everything for me to not scratch. It will only make the pain worse.

I unroll the sleeves of my tunic and tuck my trousers into my boots, hoping it will, at the very least, ward some of them away. The farther we walk, the closer together the trees are planted, and the branches weave until they're intertwined and we're in the middle of a thick wood that claws at my hair and scratches my neck.

I duck, just avoiding a low-hanging branch. The princess walks underneath it, undisturbed, the branch barely grazing the top of her head. I look ahead to where she is, navigating us with Valdis's journal, which describes a forest Valdis crossed through—a lush, life-filled forest, a far cry from what this is now.

Out of the corner of my eye, something flickers. I turn my head, but there's nothing there. Nothing but the shadows cast by the trees illuminated in the starlight and a cacophony of sounds from the cicadas and crickets around us.

I rub my eyes. We've been walking for hours. Maybe I'm just tired.

But something flickers again before me. Stark white against the dark woods.

A woman in white.
White soaked in red.
Drenched in her own blood.

She stands to my left, in between two trees.

"Is everything okay?"

I jump. The princess is standing beside me, looking in the same direction I was. She furrows her brow and glances at me. She sees nothing because it is nothing *she* can see.

There's a spirit here, but when my eyes search for her, she's gone.

A mosquito loudly buzzes in my ear. I swat at it and miss, slapping my own shoulder instead. "I'm fine," I say, a little too quickly. "Just these annoying bugs."

"What bugs?"

At first, I think she's joking, but then I look at her arms. There's not a single bite blemishing her skin. "How is it possible that you aren't being bitten at all?"

She laughs and then gives a quick shrug. "I've never been bitten by a mosquito a day in my life. This is the first time I'm seeing one so close. They tend to avoid us—maybe there's something about our blood they don't like."

Another comes buzzing toward me and I step forward, avoiding it, but nearly smack into the princess. "I never thought I'd be envious of a vampire."

It's not until she tilts her head to look up at me, eyes twinkling in the moonlight, that I realize how close we are. I think to take a step back, to put space in between us—so that she can't hear the racing of my heart—but it's as if I'm pinned in place, not wanting to break the moment. Her eyes meet mine and then they trail across my face, as if mapping every feature.

"Is that a request?" She lets out a laugh that softly echoes between us. "I've never turned anyone before." Her eyes linger on my lips and then hers curl up into a smile before trailing down to my neck and the vein throbbing there. "But I know how."

"How?" I ask. Before I can stop myself. Not really wanting to be vampire, but also not wanting to create distance between us.

Her lips curl up into a smile, eyes still sparkling, teasing me. "I'd drink your blood, leaving you at death's door, and then offer my own blood to you." She closes her eyes as if imagining it, tasting my blood. My heart rate quickens. "All you'd need is a taste. After that, the transformation would be instant. You'd be a vampire. Although"—her gaze flickers up, meeting my eyes with a palpable hunger—"a yamaja's never been turned, so who knows? It might be different with you."

The night has grown cooler and yet I'm flushed with heat. "So you don't have to be buried underground?"

She laughs. I love her laugh. "No. Some stories might be true, but those were definitely made up by humans who say we are the undead and use that to justify our deaths." Her smile fades. "If something's already dead, are you really taking a life, they say." Her voice rings with anger. And then, as if realizing herself that we are nearly touching, she steps back. "It's late," she says. "Like you said, we should keep going and find a good spot to camp for the night."

I silently curse at myself for ruining the moment and fall in beside her as we continue to make our way through the forest. While we walk, I check around me, but there don't seem to be any more spirits. Maybe that was the only one. I begin to relax again. "At Vurness, Raina mentioned that turning humans is restricted."

"It is. It was part of the peace treaty terms the human king required. My mother didn't want to agree at first. I think the only reason she did is it doesn't really affect us. In fact, the Sintu are the only vampires who can't birth their own. My bloodline, the

Adaeze, can birth vampires, and though we age much slower than humans, we still do. The Oorvain appear as adults—new ones are born from the ashes of the previous. The Merkesh, though considered a bloodline, aren't technically united by blood. They're chosen from the other lines. And the Zamiri have intermarried with the humans, so for them it is possible.

"It used to be that we could turn whoever we wanted. Now, it's much more complicated. There's a list and a bunch of requirements that must be met even for consideration."

"Like what?"

"Making sure they're in a good mental state before agreeing to the turn. Before, vampires used to turn people who didn't really consent or understand what they'd become. It's one thing when you're born this way, but I can imagine it must be another to be turned, to suddenly crave the blood of the very people you once were."

"Why do people do it, then?"

"For one, we live for a long time. There's very little that kills us. For example, we're immune to all poisons, except that of the Deianira plant. The older we get, the stronger we are. But being turned can't cure an ailment that was present before the turn—it can't regrow a limb that wasn't already there. It's not a magical cure. But tell that to the humans. They hunt us, taking our fangs, thinking they have magical properties to cure ailments. It's illegal to do so, of course, but their king looks the other way." She grows quiet. "As I guess my mother does with many things, too." She lets out a deep sigh. "It's not so simple as us being the bad guys and them being good. Maybe once it was like that, centuries ago, but war means atrocities have been committed on both sides. It's now up to us, the present generation, to acknowledge our past while also healing the scars that remain."

My heart squeezes. The love she has for her people is so clear. "Is that what you'd do as queen?"

She smiles at me. "I'd try. Don't get me wrong, I was raised to hate humans. But I was also raised to hate you. You're not so bad. Except for your fondness for chicken, but I guess I can forgive that."

She laughs, and I do the same. How easy it is to laugh with her, to forget about my worries in these moments. When I first arrived, there was so much anger in me, but this journey has somehow soothed me. Maybe it's feeling like I belong here, like I'm needed here. Maybe it's her.

"It's so easy to be driven by fear," I say. "And for understandable reasons. Our people haven't had the best interactions."

"Exactly. But fear can't drive us forever."

Suddenly my head is jerked back by the hair. I pull myself free and spin around, sword raised and ready to fight. But there is nothing there, nothing but a branch bouncing behind me, around which is wrapped a strand of my hair.

"Are you okay?" Leyla asks. She walks back to me. My hand is covering my heart; it pounds against my chest. My breath comes out unevenly.

I take a gulp of air and nod. "It's nothing."

She eyes me warily. "Maybe we should stop here for the night and rest?"

Something else flickers ahead of me. Another spirit. "No!" I say, a little too loud. "I mean, let's not stop now—it'll be hard to sleep here. Let's find a clearing." I'm afraid of what dreams may come if I am to sleep in this haunted place.

She rolls her eyes but cracks a smile. "If you're afraid of the woods, just say so next time."

I place my hand on the trunk of a tree in front of me, taking a beat to catch my breath, to calm myself. That's when I see him. Another spirit in the woods. And after him, another.

The more I look, the more I see. Sitting on the ground, hovering in between the trees. Walking around, sure to brush up against me.

"Najja, are you sure you're okay?" Leyla asks. Her eyes crinkle with worry.

I try to speak, but I can't. Dread coils within me as I take in what must be hundreds of spirits surrounding me.

This is not a forest but a graveyard for the war's dead.

CHAPTER TWENTY-FOUR

Najja

The princess stands beside me, staring up at the spirits she cannot see. Then she looks at me for answers I cannot give. Words I have never spoken to anyone.

So instead, I start walking. Through the woods. Trying to make myself small, trying to not take up their space. Trying everything to not have their thoughts overtake me. Their memories coursing through me, like the sea during a storm. Their pain, their suffering. All at once, overwhelming me.

The only clear thoughts running through my head are those of the place I call home—a home that might not be there for me when this journey is over and when I return.

Slowly and then all at once, it hits me. Everything I've been trying to hold back. All the pain I've been trying to keep in.

Tears burn my eyes. My breath comes out in ragged gasps. Like it would get when I was little and was just learning how to swim. How to dive deep. It was so dark and cold in the sea's depths, and

I was so small and afraid. My chest would grow tight, like it is now, and I'd have to tell myself to breathe. But back then, Mama and Simi would be by my side; they would reassure me. Of my place, of my purpose, of my role among our people. But there is no one to help me now.

I try to hold the thoughts back, but every memory feeds into another. My breathing grows labored. I take quicker, shorter, shallower breaths. It's like the very air I breathe is suffocating me.

I close my eyes, trying to block everything out. I tell myself it'll be okay. But the tears come anyway. I struggle to breathe.

A cool hand takes mine. Slipping into my own, fitting perfectly. She gives my hand a squeeze.

"I'm here," she says. "Whatever it is, I'm here."

"I'm sorry," I say, quickly wiping away the tears. Struggling with the words to explain something I've never told anyone.

"It's okay," she says. "It's going to be all right." And instead of leaving, she moves her hand to my back, applying gentle pressure. She moves her hand in circles as shivers rush up my spine. "Breathe," she says. Her eyes search my face, taking everything in. Finally, they lock onto mine.

Her cool gaze steadies me. "Breathe," she repeats. This time she takes in a deep breath and exhales. I follow suit and do the same. She rubs my back, still saying *breathe*—her voice coming out soft yet strong. Her hand never leaving. "It's going to be all right," she says, so confidently I start to believe it. Her gaze leaves mine to search around me. She finds my canteen in the pocket of my bag and hands it to me. She nods. I take a sip of water and then another. My shoulders relax. I exhale deeply once more. She moves her hand away, leaving a chill where her touch was.

When I look up, I'm on the ground, back resting against a small tree. Leyla sits still beside me.

"I'm sorry," I say. "We should go—"

"We've been traveling half the night. We might as well stop and rest."

I take another sip of water. Then I look up to the stars, eventually finding the Star of the Sea.

And that's when the panic returns. We can't stop, not with all of the spirits everywhere. "Please," I whisper, to the gods, to the spirits, and to myself. "Please, let me be." I think of home. I think of peace.

The woods quiet around me. Everything is suddenly still. Filled with a quiet, a peace that wasn't previously there. I raise my head, and that's when I notice: they're gone. Not hiding in the shadows. I can't feel them anymore. They're truly gone.

Somehow, they are gone. They listened.

After I am calm, I decide focusing on a task will help. "I'll make a fire," I say, standing up. I gather twigs and dry grass, and then I make a bed for the fire the way Mama taught me. From one of my pockets, I pull out the flint that she made sure I always carried, and using my knife, I start the fire. Once I have a small flame, I add more twigs. Bit by bit, the fire grows. I break off some larger branches and add them to fuel the flames.

I stand back and look at the fire and smile. Its sparks flicker up into the sky, and its flames chase away the chilly air coating my skin. Mama taught me almost everything I know.

I look up to the stars again.

Leyla closes her canteen and comes to stand beside me. "My father called that one the North Star. He told me I could always find it by first finding the drinking gourd." She points to a larger constellation, then draws her hand across the sky until she lands at the Star of the Sea.

"I believe your North Star is my Star of the Sea. My mother told me that if I ever needed to find my way home, that I could follow it all the way to the Kutmenian Sea."

The princess smiles at me as if we share a secret. "I like the Star of the Sea better. It's beautiful."

Silence falls between us as we gaze at the stars. A sense of peace falls over me that I haven't felt in a while. Suddenly, I want to share more about me, I want her to know who I really am.

"I see spirits," I say softly.

The princess doesn't jump; she doesn't look at me with fear. She merely turns to face me, her face revealing nothing but a willingness to listen.

"That's what happened back there—I saw them. They were . . . everywhere."

The more I speak, the easier it is to continue. Telling her about how spirits affect me, how I can feel what they feel. By the end of it, we're both sitting on a log side by side.

"I'm sorry for earlier."

"For what?" she says, her brow furrowed.

"For crying. It's just that—"

"Najja. You are allowed to cry. That's a perfectly normal reaction. If I saw spirits everywhere, if anytime I brushed past them, I got pictures of their lives, and not just their happiest moments, but their sorrows, their grief, I would be in tears constantly."

I give her a small smile, for normalizing emotions I'm so used to pushing down.

"Did your family have any tools to help you? Anything to teach you to deal with the spirits?"

"They didn't know. I never told them," I say. "With my mother, I never had the chance to. I'd dreamed of death—had terrible nightmares for years, but at the time, I thought they were just that. It was with her death that I realized my abilities, my cure."

"How old were you when she died?"

"Thirteen."

"Oh, Najja, I'm so sorry," she says.

I shrug. "It was years ago."

Leyla shakes her head. "I lost my father when I was nine, and it still haunts me. I blamed myself for it. I can't imagine if I saw his death and it happened anyway, that would eat me up inside."

"It did. And later, when I saw the first spirit, I never told Simi. It seemed so insignificant, so small compared to what she had to deal with. My mother was high priestess of our people. Just as her mother was before her. Our bloodline traces back to the original yamaja, so even though we no longer had our temples, she felt it was our duty to carry our traditions on. She took the duty on after our mother passed. So, I tried to hide my feelings, I learned to push them away. I figured she didn't need anything else to deal with . . ." My voice cracks. "Certainly not me.

"My people weren't much better. I had friends, once. But when I was about fifteen, there was this terrible plague. I saw my best friend's death . . . I foresaw all of it. I tried to warn them about the plague, to prepare for it . . . but it was too late. We didn't have money for the medicine we needed. It wiped out so many of my people.

And when it was done and over, they blamed me. They never said it, but they didn't have to. I was so alone after that. Always alone. I thought I was the problem. That I didn't deserve to be there."

I rub my hand over my arm, over the scars etched there from the cuts I first made when my mother died, when I started blaming myself for the deaths I foresaw and yet couldn't stop. Leyla places her hand upon mine, stilling my hand. "You were a child," she says. "It wasn't your job to save them. Was there no one else . . . with your powers?"

I shake my head. "I was the first in generations—that's why it took me so long to realize that my nightmares were visions instead. I was alone in my abilities, and in my pain. Simi tried, though. Without her——" All the pain I've been holding back surges within me again. I let go of her hand to wipe away the tears running down my face.

"When my sister died, it all came rushing back. All the feelings I'd pushed down, all the things I'd tried not to feel. I told you that I came here for Simi, but the truth is, I needed something to do and to believe in. I could feel myself growing numb, like I did after Mama died." I close my eyes still trying to push it all back. "I don't ever want to feel that way again. There's so much I don't want to think about, so much I'm not ready to face. So I guess I feel like I owe you because, as silly as it sounds, this journey has given me purpose." I take a deep breath and my shoulders relax. "It's made me feel less alone."

Leyla pauses before speaking, as if choosing her words with care. "It's not silly," she finally says. "I feel the same. I couldn't just sit there and wait and pray, but I'd be lying if I didn't say I was scared to come all this way by myself. My brother would've come, but I couldn't let him. And I would be miserable if I were here alone."

She looks up to the stars, and as if whispering her truth to them, says, "I get it." She slips her hand on top of mine. "My mind isn't always the most pleasant place to be."

She gives me a small smile. "I'm glad you're here with me. We're here and we're surviving and maybe, for tonight, that's enough."

"It is enough." I release a shallow breath, feeling my heart rate slow and my muscles relax. Like there's a weight I've shuffled off.

We stay like that for a time, looking up at the sky, sharing stories of the gods and the stars, stories her father told her and ones my mother told me, while remembering those we've lost. Eventually, the fire dies and the embers fade. The princess finds a place to rest, her pack underneath her head, her legs tucked into her chest. She starts to shiver, so I cover her with my blanket. Still asleep, she pulls it closer, fingers tucking it underneath her neck.

I do not sleep beside her, though I would like to. Instead, I find a spot nearby where I can keep watch, so that if danger comes, we can escape. As the hours pass, as the stars begin to fade, I find myself wondering what it would be like to curl up in her arms instead.

CHAPTER TWENTY-FIVE

Leyla

I wake the next morning. The grass is wet with dew and the morning is light and bright. The sky is perfectly clear. In the quiet of the morning, I'm at ease. My nerve pain is way more manageable. My head isn't spinning with thoughts all while struggling to fall asleep. I sit up and yawn, only to find two blankets atop me. I glance over to where Najja still sleeps, body curled up against a tree, and realize it must be hers. Those first few nights when we had to sleep outside, I always woke up shivering. She must've noticed that I was cold.

Warmth rushes through me at the thought, and I hold the blanket close. Her scent lingers there, earthy and laced with saltwater. I fold the blanket neatly and place it beside me.

Quietly, so as not to wake her, I pull Valdis's journal from my pack and flip through its ancient pages until I find the part of her journey detailing the Wastelands.

Lands lush and plentiful. When it rains, gold can be plucked from the ground, it begins.

But they weren't called the Wastelands then—they were nameless and belonged to no one, claimed by Thana during her reign. From everything I've heard, the stories full of monsters and decay, they are nothing like the place they once were.

"Sleep well?"

I jump. I was so immersed that I didn't hear Najja stir. Her face holds a small smile, and I can't help but feel that rush of warmth again that her smile is for me.

"I did, actually," I say. "For once."

"That's good," she says, smiling at me still.

I pull out the blanket from where I folded it up beside me. "I believe this is yours. Please tell me I didn't steal it off you in the middle of the night."

She laughs. "Sleepwalking and stealing blankets—you truly are the most dangerous creature of all." She looks down before I can read the expression across her face. "I gave it to you. You were shivering."

"Thank you." I don't know what else to say at the thought of her caring about me in this way. "Like I told you, my kind don't hold heat well. I should've known to pack two."

"That's all right." Her words are soft. "I have enough heat for us both. I mean, I'm a hot sleeper. Not that I'm hot when I sleep but that I—" She takes a deep breath. "Why don't you keep it? You'll probably need it before I do."

I laugh as she fumbles over her words, having never seen her so nervous. "You sure?"

She nods. I fold the blanket into my pack, still inhaling her saltwater scent as we begin the day's journey.

It's midday now. We've been walking for hours. Here, there are few trees, and so the sun beats down upon us. It adds to the exhaustion I feel, to the pain coursing through me. I look around at this desolate land where nothing seems to thrive.

"Do you think this land will ever go back to the way it was?" I ask. We have been silently walking, with a few conversations here and there. I feel the need to start another, to have anything distract me from the way my feet ache, the tingling up my spine, and my burning legs.

Najja stops, as if thinking deeply, then nods and continues again. "The land is much like its people—it needs time to heal."

I understand what she means; it's the same sentiment that many vampires voice. "*Peace will take time*, people like to say. There are many who even now still don't believe that the peace treaty will last."

"Makes sense," Najja says. "The peace treaty is only a year old. All they've known before is war. We're the first generation in a long time to even have the chance to come of age in peace. But can you really be at peace with those whose very life force you feed off of? It's not really a fair trade, your gold—something you don't actually need to survive—for their blood?" She smiles but it doesn't light up her eyes.

"You sound like Danai," I say, trying to hide my wince. "She'd often say the same. That we'd been at war so long that most of us never remember peace. That's changing now. If we devote half as many of the resources that have been devoted to training an army and becoming better soldiers, who knows what we can figure out. Maybe there is a way for us to survive without it."

"Animal blood?"

I shake my head. "For some reason it doesn't work the same.

But that's what I mean. The humans have studied us, and what they've studied is how to defeat us in war. What if we were part of that research? How many of our great scholars have instead died in battle? We don't know until we try, and if we don't try, I fear that peace will only be temporary. Before we know it, we'll be at war again."

I take another step, and I inhale sharply. This time it's spasms in my lower back. I'm pushing myself too much. But we are so close, I can't give up now. I have to save Danai. And so, I sweep aside the thought of taking a break and remind myself that a queen must be a pillar of strength for her people. That weakness is a condition a queen cannot afford to have.

I'm focused so much on being strong, on not showing Najja my pain, that I stumble over a rock and go plunging down.

"Leyla," she calls, catching me just before I hit the ground. Her hands grip me and she slowly pulls me up.

Everything spins and I latch onto her.

"Let's sit down," she says.

"I'm fine," I snap.

She keeps her hand on me, steadying me, and yet leans back ever so slightly and lifts an eyebrow.

"I'm sorry," I say. "I don't know what overcame me." But I do know. It's all this walking. It's the sun beating down on me.

Najja looks around and then takes my hand and leads me through the bushes and high grass until we reach a log in a shadier part. She motions toward it. "Why don't we sit awhile."

I want to protest, but she comes closer to me and starts to rub her hand across my back. It's so warm, so strong, so soothing. I feel . . . safe.

I am safe with her.

I think of what she has told me, of the truths she's trusted me with. And yet all I've done on this journey is try to hide parts of myself, parts that for better or worse make me who I am.

I lift my head up and turn to her. Her hand is still on my back, giving me the strength to proceed.

"Remember how at the Vurness protest Raina spoke about me not fighting in the war?"

Najja scoffs. "It was misplaced anger. The war is what they should've been mad about, not you not fighting in it."

"Fair," I say, "but war is an intangible thing. Whereas I am not. I am supposed to become their queen. I get the frustration. If I've never experienced it, if I haven't seen it, how can they even begin to get me to understand their pleas?" I take a deep sigh, steeling myself to tell her a thing Mama had me promise not to tell a soul. Much like her own illness, very few know of mine. *How would it look to have a queen ill?*

"The thing is, I wanted to go. I thought it was some great honor and I was honored to fulfill my duty—to follow the footsteps of many queens before me. I had trained to do so for years."

Najja grimaces as I say this, as pride infiltrates my voice.

"I know how it sounds, but you have to understand this was how I was raised. They had taken so much from us, *from me*, I wanted to take from them, too. It wasn't until Danai came back, until I witnessed the tremors she had in her sleep, the light she never seemed to fully get back, that I realized it wasn't an honor, it was a curse, and that my feelings about the humans aside, I'd do anything as queen to prevent another war. But back then, that's how I felt and I was counting down until we were deployed. There was only a week left."

I take another deep breath as the memories resurface. As if I'm there and not here, so helpless, so scared.

Najja moves toward me until our knees are touching. Then she places a hand on my knee and squeezes it as if saying, *I'm here*.

Imperceptibly, I lean into her. "One day, I was fine. The next, I woke up and felt like something was in my left eye. I went through half the day before I realized it, that part of my vision was gone. It was as if a bar was there and above it, I could see fine. But below, nothing. And my eye hurt as well. It was the scariest thing. My mother hasn't been the comforting sort in some time, but in that moment—"

"You needed her," Najja finishes, and when I look into her eyes, filled with sorrow, I know that she understands. That she craves the same thing. That feeling, that pull, that need to be with a mother you can't truly be with.

"It was a mistake. She took me back to my bedchambers, where she locked me in until the physicians came. She told me no one was to know about this. Thank the gods for Danai, who apparently kept coming by, sleeping at my door, until Mama—worried someone would see her—allowed her to be at my side. It was then that I realized I'd been feeling all sorts of pain all along. Tingling and numbness. A burning sensation in my legs. Painful headaches that got worse in the sun. I'd pushed it all aside, kept it to myself. But apparently, altogether, it's signs of an illness that cannot be cured. An illness that apparently my aunt had, but similarly told very few about.

"My mother had always thought I was lacking—too sensitive, too weak, too everything, and it was as if this only confirmed it. My brother . . ." A sadness creeps into my heart just thinking of

Malike and how worried he always was and must be. "I love him, but it's like I couldn't do anything myself. *Rest up, let me carry that, do you need a better chair?* I couldn't even hold a glass for too long without him offering to take it from me." I sigh. "Danai was the only one who knew who didn't treat me differently. She sparred with me, kicking my ass as per usual. She believed I could live a normal life—not that being a princess is anything normal. But soon after she was sent to war. With her gone, with Malike gone, it was just me, my pain, and my mother reminding me that I was a failure." That I am weak.

"Leyla," Najja says, calling my name with such force it compels me to meet her blue-gray eyes. Suddenly, I become aware of how little space there is between us. And from the way Najja looks at me, a second longer than usual, she does, too. It's so quiet I can hear her heartbeat quickening, just like it did yesterday when we were walking through the woods, side by side.

My eyes trail down to her lips as her smell fills my nose. Will she taste the same—will I taste saltwater on her lips?

"Leyla," she says again, my name barely a whisper.

My eyes trail up from her lips to meet her eyes. But it's not hers that catch my attention. Two pairs of yellow eyes, hidden in the bushes behind Najja, stare back at me. I blink rapidly and they're gone.

Concern draws upon Najja's face. "Leyla, are you okay?"

"I'm fine," I say as the hairs on the nape of my neck rise. I turn my attention back to her, but I hear it. A predator's growl. I can't see it yet, but it's close. Stalking us from a distance.

"Najja." I lean in close to her, my lips brush her ear. "Don't move."

Slowly, I trail my hand down her side. Reaching for the knife she keeps in her left boot—much lighter and easier to throw than my sword. I grip hold of the knife and tug it free.

Her eyes widen. "What are yo—" She cuts off when she hears a howl.

Slowly, the creature steps out from the bushes, looking straight at us. Then it snarls, baring its sharp teeth. Without thinking, I push Najja to the side. The creature leaps at me.

CHAPTER TWENTY-SIX

Najja

Beware, beware, she who happens upon garoux.

I rise from the ground, my face hot from adrenaline and our near kiss. A tune pops into my head like it's my own thoughts I'm hearing.

I shake my head, trying to get the tune to go away.

Leyla lies on the ground. I rush over to her. "Are you okay?"

She nods, and then her eyes widen at the creature dead beside her. My knife sticks out of its side. It has bright yellow eyes and a snout full of sharp teeth.

Beware, beware, she who happens upon garoux.
Beware, beware their bite.

I spin around, looking for the source of the song. It's so loud, like someone is singing to me.

The land is flat, full of dry brown grass, save for a large thicket in front of us so full of trees and bushes that I can't see through it. That must be where the creature came from.

Bumps spread across my arms. Dread burns through my gut.

Beware, beware, she who happens upon garoux.

Simi used to sing that song to me, teasing me with it when we were little. *Beware, beware,* she'd singsong, warning about the garoux. Mythical, wolflike creatures who only ever come out at night. But she hasn't sung that song for years, not to mention—she's dead. And yet the tune continues, on a loop. Each time louder and stronger than before.

That's when I see her. A woman cradling a baby, singing her to sleep. She sings the song of the garoux, large beasts who stalk these parts, whose bite is deadly.

"Najja, are you okay?" Leyla asks, doubt creeping into her voice.

And I realize I've started walking toward the woman. Leyla looks at me, not seeing what I do, and that's when I know that she's a spirit and I'm the only one aware of her.

Never ignore a sign from the dead, I've learned.

I turn back to Leyla. "We need to get out of here. It's a garoux."

I point at the thicket behind us, then look up to the darkening sky. Soon, it'll be night-time, and we don't want to be here. "We need to find shelter. Garoux only travel in packs. There are definitely more."

A howl and a high-pitched cackle rattle my ears. Much louder and stronger than the last time. "Tell me you heard that, too." I look to my left. A large shadow moves. It flits back and forth and then it's gone, disappearing into the thicket that casts even more shadows on the ground before us.

"I heard it," she says, trembling.

The cackling and howling increases and the ground beneath me blurs. Once again, dizziness creeps over me. *Cover your ears when you hear a garoux.* The tune slips into my head, and I snap my hands over my ears.

"Cover your ears," I say. "The noise confuses you!" I sink to my knees as the sounds crescendo over me. I hum to myself, trying to think of a tune, anything to distract me.

After a while, the cackling and howling subside.

But when I open my eyes, Leyla's gone.

The princess is gone but her pack remains. I scoop it up, placing both packs on my back.

Behind me, the thicket of trees sways in the wind. It's dense and dark. Each tree rubs against another. Some have branches that fan out. Some are rotted trunks. Most are dead or dying. It's hard to make out what or who is there. What if the garoux attacked Leyla? A lump lodges in my throat, tears pricking the corners of my eyes. What if—no. I can't think about that, not if I'm going to find her. I take a deep breath and enter, parting the scraggly branches with my knife and stepping over broken limbs. Deeper and deeper into the grove I go. I look up to where a patch of sky is; the Star of the Sea hovers above me. If I get lost, I can find my way out. *Just breathe*, I tell myself. *You can do this.*

Cackling echoes from my left. I spin around, sword in front of me. Slowly, I back up until something scratches me. I scream, then quickly cover my mouth. A corpse is tangled in the tree. Its hands are covered with strips of flesh that reach out as if crying for help. It must've been what scratched me. Its face is unrecognizable from it having been chewed off. Foam fizzles out of its mouth. From the garoux bite.

Even the tiniest scratch is poisonous . . .

"Najja!" Leyla leaps out of the darkness.

I sweep her into my arms. "You're okay." Her chest beats rapidly against mine as happiness surges through me, relief that she is fine. I don't want to let go but I do.

She motions to her ears—balled-up strips of linen stick out of them. "I can still hear their laughs, but it dulls them—it helps." She rips off two pieces from the hem of her dress and hands them to me. I ball them up and stick them in my ears.

"What happened?"

"I don't know. I got turned around. I ended up here." She motions to the grove and I look. A shudder goes through me. There are corpses all around. Some have been here so long they've already decayed. I can't tell where they end and the trees begin. Plants are already growing out of the bodies, from their mouths, their stomachs, roots pushing through their legs. People who came here, for one reason or another, and ended up dead—killed by garoux.

I swallow my fear; it won't serve me here. "Okay," I say, psyching myself up. "Okay," I repeat once more. "We can do this." *Think.* "What do we do?" And then it hits me. "How does the tale about the garoux go? About how they were around long before most people were?" I snap my fingers, trying to remember the rest and hoping that we were both told the same version.

"They used to plague villages until a young boy found a way to climb to the Heavenly Realms and ask the gods for their help," says Leyla.

"Yes! But their help did not come easily," I finish as the story comes to me. "The goddess Pyra issued a challenge. If the boy could contain her, she would give him a solution to his people's garoux problem."

Leyla grips my hand and continues, "She thought she could trick him, but the boy was no fool. He had watched before approaching her. He knew she was a shifter and he found ways to hold her, through all her phases, including—"

"Fire!" we both say, with a little jump.

"Which is what she then taught him how to make as a reward, because the garoux are afraid of fire." I smile, beaming at Leyla. We did it, together. "We just need fire," I say. The thought of getting out fills me with hope.

"Hold on." I crouch on the ground, looking for two dry sticks. Then I place my pack down and pull out a jar. Within the jar is a large piece of linen, wet with alcohol that can be easily used to start a larger flame. I rip off two pieces and wrap the first around the stick, and then repeat with another.

Laughter crescendos. "Najja," Leyla prompts.

I fumble for the flint in my bag. I strike it once. Nothing.

More laughter. And the snapping of jaws. Sweat builds on my forehead. We are going to die here and it will have all been for nothing. Simi will have died in vain.

"I'm so sorry," I whisper.

I strike the flint again.

Slowly the garoux appear. First their yellow eyes, piercing through the darkness. Then their snouts, dripping wet. And their teeth, pearly white and gleaming in the moonlight. All of them slinking out from the shadows. Nearly as high as our chests.

"If you've got a plan, now would be a good time for it," Leyla says.

I strike once more. The flames catch. The fire blazes. I point the lit torches in front of me, handing one to Leyla. A garoux lunges, but I sidestep it and wave the flame in its direction. It runs away.

Leyla moves behind me. I trace a line of fire on the ground and as we walk, it laps up the dry grass and burns, creating a semicircle around us. The garoux cower.

The trees begin to catch fire and as branches fall, a path is cleared—just ahead of us, outside of the grove, is an enclosed rocky area. A cavern.

"Run!" I say. We take off, legs pumping, adrenaline coursing through us. We barrel into the cavern and turn, torches held in front of us like weapons. But there's nothing. Nothing at all.

"They're not following us," I say. "It worked!"

"Now, we just have to wait it out. They're nocturnal, so they'll be gone in the morning."

We make a fire by the entrance, so they won't cross it.

"Now I know why my father said he always left a fire burning at night on his travels," Leyla says.

"We made it." I smile. "We're safe."

My smile drops as a tingling sensation rushes through my body. I feel hot, like I'm burning up, even though it's cool outside. I double over on the ground, thinking it's a vision, but this is something else. My entire body shakes like it's seizing up.

Leyla rushes over to me. "What's happening? Is it a vision? What's wrong?"

I try to speak but the words don't come out. I bring my hands to my neck and gasp.

Leyla touches my forehead, where sweat is building. "You're burning up."

I shake my head. I don't understand.

Leyla tilts her head up and sniffs. She lifts my jacket—nothing. Her eyes sweep across my chest, my neck, my shoulders, stopping on my left upper arm. My breath catches in my throat. Blood oozes out from a small bite mark, just enough to break the skin.

"You were bitten." Her voice trembles, not wanting to speak the truth we already know.

By this time tomorrow, I'll be dead.

They fell swiftly from the heavens one night, appearing in streaks of light.
They towered over us.
So beautiful, so strange. We could not look away.
One stepped forward in a gown of shimmering gold. Teeth sharp and piercing, eyes as red as blood.
She called herself the princess of the gods, said she could've been their queen. But on her coronation, she came here instead. To discover new lands, to be free.
Now, this princess is our queen and we must build her a throne.

—FROM *SHE WHO CROWNED HERSELF QUEEN:*
THE RISE AND FALL OF THE FIRST VAMPIRE, CHAPTER TWO
FIRST EDITION, 901 AD
MERKESH ROYAL ARCHIVES

CHAPTER TWENTY-SEVEN

Favre

1,201 Years Ago: The Lands of the Living

FAVRE'S DIARY

Day One

When we arrived in the lands of the living, we feasted. Drawn, I assumed, by the same hunger growing within me, we devoured the humans we saw.

It's important for me to note here that I tried—should I ever revisit these words.

I <u>tried</u> to hold myself back. I <u>tried</u> to be repulsed. To not be swayed as Thana fed from a human no older than I.

She sank her fangs into his neck. But then she pulled back, holding out his still body to me. She didn't have to say a thing; blood oozed from the wound smelling like the answer to my deepest desires.

I fed. Thana pierced one side of his neck and I sank into the other. I heard his heartbeat slow. I smelled his fear. And yet, none of that scared me. It delighted me instead.

What am I? I asked myself, as we moved from one villager to the other. The faster they ran, the louder they screamed, the more I enjoyed the taste.

By the time the sun's rays started to sink into the sky, the entire village was dead.

I let go of the body in my arms, cold and drained of its blood. I wept as my fangs retracted. At the lives I'd stolen, at the lives I'd steal.

Day Two

Malichora, they called us.

Taking the name from demons featured in their stories. The kind they told at bedtime, warning young children about.

"Don't stay out too late, the malichora will come. They appear human, but they are anything but. Sometimes their victims die. Sometimes they become malichora themselves."

A monster, that's what I am.

Thana disagreed. Vampires, she named us.

Then, she took a human—one who said he would not bow, who dared to call her malichora to her face—and impaled his body on a stake driven through his heart. He died, slowly, screams ringing throughout the courtyard. Only then did she sever his head and place it in front of the village she'd claimed as our home.

"Why?" I asked her when we were alone in our quarters together. "He was one man."

She held me in her arms as I spoke. "They already feared us," I said again.

"A reminder," she said, "that we are still gods and the right to name us—to call us demons—belongs only to ourselves." With that, she lowered herself in between my legs and trailed kisses down my stomach, giving me the pleasure I craved.

Day Six

With Thana's permission, some of the other gods created more in our image. Fledgling vampires, days old.

They drank the humans until their hearts beat faint. Then, they buried them deep underground. A graveyard of our own making—a graveyard whose inhabitants, a few hours later, were clawing out of the ground. An unsettling sight to see.

Unnecessary, yes. But a ritual Thana created to make a rather simple process seem much more complex, like we six were the few who could take away life and give it anew.

The huntress Neferain's vampires shared her giant, black wings. Vzira's, whose family built the castles of the Heavenly Realms, developed her same retractable iron nails that could dig into anything. And so, it continued like this, with the gods making vampires in their image.

All except for Thana, who had already made us, and myself.

I would not subject anyone to this.

Day Twenty-Three

Earlier today, we found the second vampire Neferain made, head severed and body impaled on a stake that was driven through his heart.

He was left for all to see in the center of the same village where Thana had done the same to a human weeks ago. The very village that was once theirs that we now claim is our home.

"Poison," said Suty, who was able to sense it at once. The healer deity's eyes were full of fear as he turned to Thana. "He was dead long before they staked him. It was poison that stole his last breath."

Soon Suty discovered the source. A flower that blooms upside down, its pink petals dangling to the ground. One of our newly made vampires explained that flower appeared several days before we arrived, when the sky opened up and started to cry.

Thana glanced at me, sharing a look I, at once, understood. For that was around the time when Kovnu died. They thought nothing of the new flowers at the time. But it seems that Kovnu had the last laugh.

To the humans, it is merely beautiful.

For us, ingesting its sap leads to death.

As the stake was taken down and the funeral pyre built, Thana ordered Neferain to take her new vampires, who were swift and strong like her, and punish those responsible.

"How?" I'd asked. "How will she know which ones? We have encountered dozens of villages and towns in the past several days."

But a wicked glint appeared in Thana's eyes—one that chilled me to my core. "If they are innocent," she'd said, "let their precious Kovnu save them now."

Day Forty-Two

Neferain is gone every night, sparking terror in humans everywhere. Teaching them a lesson, she told us. "Soon," she'd said, "they will never mess with us again."

Each time she returns, her own vampires increase. Of the places she visits, she offers the fiercest, the bravest humans a chance to join her. To have eternal life.

Now, there are hundreds of them. Oorvain, she calls them. After her family name. A family she can never return to, so a new one she creates.

An army of vampires loyal to her.

At first, Thana praised her. Like a well-behaved pet. But by the third trip, by the fourth, I saw something in Thana's eyes. A look I had seen before that I couldn't quite place.

"We've got to keep an eye on her," she'd said. Then she repeated it, more to herself than me.

I sit alone in our chambers. Ever since she expressed concern about Neferain, I've seen Thana less and less. And when I have seen her, she's been distant, going through the motions but not really here. Not to mention, her moods.

I tap my fingers against the leather-bound book in my hand, trying not to think of what's building within. Of the resemblances to Mother, I can't quite shake. By the time she died I'd grown so good at anticipating her, at molding myself to fit her every mood, it was as if I'd become her shadow. I barely knew where she stopped, and I began.

Footsteps approach. Quickly, I hide the diary. I barely adjust the floorboards and take a quick breath, smoothing my features, making myself appear pleasant, unaffected by anything, before she bursts into the room.

Blood drips down her arm, down to the sword *my* blood had borne in her hand.

Suddenly, worry is the only emotion coming to me now. I rush to her. "Are you okay?" My hands cup her face, searching for signs she's hurt.

She places the sword in the corner and, calmly, wipes her hands on a towel. It's only then that she speaks.

"I had to do it," she says softly, as if in a trance, still numb to whatever it is she thought she had to do. She drops to the ground, burying her head in between my legs. To protect—to protect us all. But still that look is in her eyes, the one I recognize but haven't been able to place.

What is she talking about? I cradle her, nonetheless, letting myself cling onto the intimacy I've missed so much.

Screams burst through the air. I start to leave, to follow the sounds. But Thana holds me back.

"Change." She points at my gown, now stained with blood. She begins to bathe herself, washing the blood out.

And then I know. And then I remember where I've seen that look before. She wore it when she came to me, to take me to the Heavenly Realms, just after killing her father.

Without a doubt, I know what has transpired.

Neferain, the once great war goddess, is dead.

FAVRE'S DIARY

Day Forty-Nine

> *Soon after burying Neferain, the Oorvain pledged their loyalty to Thana.*
>
> *I asked her for the truth. I berated her with questions. I was afraid. To kill someone so loyal to her just like that didn't make sense.*

"Neferain and I grew up together," she told me. "I learned to read her so well. She was building that army for a reason. I am certain of it. She was to overthrow me, and crown herself queen."

Thana pulled me into her lap, she cradled me there. She reminded me that I had sacrificed my wings to give her that sword, but she had made sacrifices, too. She took no joy in it, the killings. But it was what she had to do.

"Do you love me?" Thana asked me. But before I could answer, she kissed me. "I love you," she said to me. Her kisses grew more urgent then. "Do you love me?" she asked again.

She was right. We both had made sacrifices to be together, and it was first my idea to come here, to make this place our home. Besides, I didn't know Neferain. Not like Thana did.

Who am I to question her, after all she's done for us—after all she's done for me.

"I love you, too." I grabbed hold of her chin and pulled her down to me in a kiss. As I kissed her, I locked my fears away. When we pulled apart, my frown and the furrow of my brow was gone. I smiled up at her, unaffected, and I stored my fears away—just like I used to do when Mother was around.

CHAPTER TWENTY-EIGHT

Leyla

Present Day: The Wastelands

Using our torches, I make a fire. Then I drag her body beside it.

If we were back home, our physicians would have an antivenom. But we are here and not there. I must do what I have only seen happen once, years ago when Danai was bitten by a snake far from the castle. Most vampires are immune to all poisons and venoms, except the sap of the Deianira plant, but Danai is Zamiri, making her more susceptible than the rest of us.

How hot and sweltering it was. How we'd snuck out, using the tunnels, to watch the moon in its full glory. The grass was high where we were, and we didn't see the snake slithering by.

She fell to the ground, screaming out. It took a few seconds for me to even see the snake slipping away. I cried for help, and the guards came. But she was already swelling up, reacting badly to the bite. They put a blanket down on the earth and laid her on top.

After, they cleaned the wound and then bit her, using their fangs to draw the venom out of her body and into theirs.

It took her a couple days to regain strength, but she survived.

Mama felt Danai's near death was punishment enough.

I look back at Najja, shaking her gently once more. "I have to suck the venom out. But to do so, I have to bite you."

This time, she opens her eyes. Just enough for me to know that she's listening.

"I've never done this before. It could . . . end badly."

Her eyes scan my face, looking for the words I can't bring myself to say. Weakly, she draws in a sharp breath. "I trust you."

Her words hit me hard, stoking a flame that's barely there. I'd spent most of my life being reminded and thinking about what I lacked, and how short I always fell. Only Danai truly trusted me, knew I'd always have her back.

I grab Najja's hand, holding on tight as I steady myself, tears prickling my eyes. *I trust you*, her voice echoes through my head. I can do this. I must.

"It won't hurt." I pause. "It shouldn't." But I've never exactly been bitten myself.

I take a deep breath. I mutter a quick prayer to Morowa. Then I sink my fangs into her arm and her eyes flutter closed.

CHAPTER TWENTY-NINE

Najja

I open my eyes, but there is only darkness.

"Hello?" I call, but my voice is muffled and reverberates back toward me as if I'm inside a bubble. I can hear someone calling my name, but I can't see them, and it doesn't seem like they can hear me here. Slowly, then all at once, the darkness fades, giving way to the sea.

Yamaja become sea foam when we die. Am I already dead?

I stand on the shore, sand slipping between my toes. Before me, the sea stretches as far as I can see. It's so vast, so blue, that I can barely tell where it ends and the sky begins. If this is our afterlife, it's not a bad place to go.

Water floods across my feet, and I walk from the shore into the sea, tugged forward by invisible threads. Slowly, the water reaches my shins. Soon, I am submerged.

I swim for what feels like hours, until I come upon a rock in the sea. On it sits a woman, her back facing me. Her hair is long, knitted into two braids that are tied together, with a blue ribbon, behind her back.

Simi? I want to rush toward her, but waves rise, separating us.

"Simi," I scream.

When she turns, she's as she was before. Like nothing ever happened, like the Reapers never attacked. "Took you long enough." She frowns, as if disapproving, but her eyes twinkle and the corners of her lips slightly curl, as if there is a secret we share.

"Took me long enough?" I furrow my brows. "What do you mean?" I try to swim toward her, but I cannot. Eventually, I give up and tread water as she looks down at me from the rock on which she rests.

"Well, this is your head, isn't it? It certainly isn't mine." She laughs. "You always did favor this spot."

My head? I look around. This rock in the sea does look familiar, like I've been here before. Then I remember. It's several miles away from where we lived. If I left in the morning, I could get back before sunset. It was where I would go to be alone when I was younger—before the visions came—to sit, to think, to dream.

"But you're dead," I stammer. "How is this possible?"

Simi smiles again. "You made it so. I suspect you are in a state where you're not fighting so hard, so this happened."

"What do you mean?" I say, still not understanding how I could've created all of this, how this isn't real.

"You're not fighting *yourself*," she says, as if that explains everything.

I have always been able to see the dead, to see spirits lingering somewhere. But had I known I could talk to anyone I wanted, I would've done so sooner. How could Mama not tell me? I could've talked to her, she could've given me comfort when I had none, when I didn't believe in anything anymore—especially not myself.

"Don't look that way," Simi says. That's when I realize that the twinkle is not from joy but from tears pooling in her eyes. "It's what I've been telling you. What Mama always told you. Your powers are a gift, Naj. A gift you must explore. Not a curse. They're only a curse because you resist them, because you have hate for them."

"You'd resist, too, if they only brought death," I say.

She shrugs. "Death is inevitable. But this isn't so bad, is it?" She slips into the sea, and at once, she's before me. She takes my hand and squeezes it. We're together, like we're supposed to be.

My hand trembles in hers as I let out a low breath. "I just—I feel so alone without you. Without Mama. I did what you said. I found the princess. She's . . . not what I expected. She's not so bad." As I think of her, of how she makes me feel, warmth, comfort, and peace surge within me.

Simi smiles, giving me a look that tells me she knows everything.

"How do you know?"

"Because it was written. There were multiple paths, remember? Like I said, in one of those I saw you with her. Don't fret. You are exactly where you're supposed to be."

She places her hand on the back of my head and brings me closer to her. I rest my head on the crook of her shoulder, like I used to when I was younger. Simi resting her head on Mama, me resting mine on hers.

"Najja," a young woman calls. "Najja," she says louder.

Warmth washes over me at the sound.

"Leyla?" I look up, but I can only see the crisp blue sky beaming down at me.

Gently, Simi separates herself from me. "It's time for you to return."

"Come with me." I look up at her, begging her with my eyes.

"You know that I cannot," she replies, blinking away tears.

I stay like that, feeling all my emotions, the heartache, and the pain. "It's not—"

"Fair," she finishes. "You're right, it's not. But the gods never promised it would be. And these are the cards we've been dealt. You deserve to live and thrive, Naj." She places a hand on my heart. "I wish that for you."

I swallow slowly, as if something is caught in my throat, the pain of what really weighs me down lodged there. The guilt. The truth. Not just of how I survived when they did not, but that I want to live, I want to thrive. I feel like I shouldn't be allowed happiness, but I want it and I'm terrified of it.

I take a deep breath, and Leyla's voice grows louder. The sea and sky sway as if an illusion is breaking.

Simi pulls me close into a deep hug. "Before you go," she says, her mouth hovering beside my ear, "there is one thing you must know: in some of the outcomes I've seen, if the princess dies, Thana will rise and start a war bloodier than the last thousand years—a war over the dominion of the Heavenly Realms, the lands of the living, and all afterlives. A war over the dominion of all worlds."

CHAPTER THIRTY

Favre

Nekros

I wake in the middle of the night haunted by a song I sang to my daughter years ago. A song I barely got to finish before I thrust her into Lexa's arms, and the goddess snuck her away. It's distant and discordant, as if played by an instrument that hasn't been tuned or is meant to be in a different key. But it could just be that the voice singing it is wrong. It's not the person it should be: *me*.

The tune slides across my skin and makes me shiver. It makes me want to tuck myself into bed. Mother used to sing this same song to lull me to sleep, to ward off demons who might come in my sleep. Back before I learned the real monster was already in my home. Back before I learned to fear her.

Compelled to know why I hear it now, I follow the notes through the manor house.

It's after midnight, and the house is asleep. There are no Reapers

stalking the halls, no spirits wandering about. The sound takes me past the judgment hall and to another room whose door is slightly cracked.

I peek my head inside. At first, I see no one. But on a hunch, I slip inside the door, and that's when I see her. She dances alone in a white, tattered dress—a chemise, I notice on second look. Her hair fans about her shoulders, wild. She faces away from me.

Mother? I start to ask. But I stop myself; it's not her. Not because my mother couldn't be here. But because she glides more gracefully than my mother ever could. My mother had barely any toes left at the end; she gave them up long before I was born for one of her many spells. A love potion to win over a god. But instead of gaining the status she thought she would by becoming his wife, he died soon after she gave birth to me.

"Sometimes spirits don't want to move on," Asha says, popping up beside me.

I jump despite myself, and Asha smiles. "You all right?" she asks. "You hardly seem like the being who so fiercely murdered me not so many nights ago." She raises an eyebrow.

I ignore her and press my hands down to my sides, clutching my dress so as not to give anything away. "Do you just leave her here, dancing alone in this room?"

"The best thing we can do is give spirits a place to live out their days where they will be at peace, at least as much as they can be."

But I remember being trapped, being shoved into that bottle tree. Stuck. With no place to go, with no one to hear my weeps and screams. "Being stuck like that is not peace. That's torture," I say, my voice taking on an edge.

Asha lifts her head slightly, meeting my eyes. "Not all of us are meant for happily ever afters."

She's gone before I can say anything else, back to haunt the manor house and the woods surrounding it. Stuck, bound to this place, like this spirit and I seem to be.

When I return to my room, my hands still shake. I think of that spirit spending an eternity trapped in the same loop, in the same motions, in the same thoughts. Alone.

Loneliness sneaks up on me, presses against me—suffocating me.

I am so tired of being alone. I try to shake off my fears. I never thought I had anything to fear. In the Heavenly Realms, I had seen it all—I had seen the worst the world had to offer. Until they locked me up here, until they took the last freedoms I had. Until they made me feel like I did as a little girl, after Mother died.

Thana was always there for me. Thana understood who I am.

My own daughter hunted me down in the end—even though I saved her life. If I hadn't, none of this would've happened. It was all my fault.

I owe Thana her life once more.

Soon, I will free her. We will rule together. We won't make the same mistakes. This time, I'll make sure of it. I'll ensure I'm never forgotten. Never locked away and left to become that lonely, frightened girl again.

CHAPTER THIRTY-ONE

Najja

The Wastelands

I open my eyes, unsure of if I'm dreaming or awake.

"*And so, I succeeded, subduing the many-headed serpent who had stolen Morowa's crown.*"

Awake, I think, as I see the princess sitting beside me, reading from Valdis's journal. She holds the journal close to her face, blocking her view of me. Her voice has a slight rasp to it, like she's been reading for hours, like she hasn't stopped, and hasn't left my side.

The Wastelands. I take in the setting around me as, slowly, I remember. The princess sucking the venom from my arm, crafting makeshift bandages from her clothes to stop the bleeding, the princess—*Leyla, sweet Leyla*—saving my life.

She turns the page and continues reading, "*Wanting to prove to the gods that I could best any challenge, that no task was too great for the chance to have my beloved return to the lands of the living, I brought to the queen of the gods not only her crown but each of the serpent's heads as well."*

I clear my throat.

She stops mid-sentence and lowers the journal. "You're awake." Her lips curl into a wide smile. She starts to reach for me, as if to give me a hug, but stops and places her hand in her lap instead.

"What story was that?"

"One of Valdis's trials. She wrote about it." Leyla closes the journal. "The trials were tasks the gods set for her to accomplish before they'd show her how to get her beloved back from the island of the dead. This was the final one. And as she says, she meant to prove to them that no task was too great to have the woman she loved back by her side." Her gaze on me is intense when she says that, as if there's something more she wants to say. But she doesn't, and an awkward silence falls between us.

"I feel rested," I say, breaking the silence.

"Well, sleeping for two days will do that."

"Two days?" The gravity of her words hits me. "But your friend. You didn't have to—"

"Stay? No, I couldn't leave you." She shakes her head. "I could no more leave you than I could not go on this journey for her." She gives me a small smile. "Besides"—she points at the Typhian mountain range that's much closer now—"it can't be more than a day's walk from here." Relief fills her voice and I'm overcome with a mix of emotions. Guilt, for delaying her, and others I can't quite place. A want, a desire, a need. I push the blankets off me and bring myself to standing. I close my eyes for a second, feeling dizzy.

Leyla reaches for me, an arm steadying my legs. "Be careful," she says.

The sounds of the night rise around us, humming and buzzing, all coming together like a band of insects playing just for us. "Do you hear it?" I begin to hum the tune.

I bend down, holding out a hand. "What are you doing?" She laughs, as she lets me pull her up.

"I read somewhere about these things called balls . . . Have you ever been to one?"

She shakes her head. "I've only read about them, too. Supposedly, Thana and the other fallen gods used to have them all the time."

At the mention of Thana, Simi's warning echoes in my ears.

"What is it?" Leyla looks up at me, concern etched across her face. "You"—she reaches out to lightly touch the middle of my forehead—"always get this little furrow right here whenever you're worried about something."

"It's nothing," I say, smiling down at her, something bittersweet filling me even as I do. After we reach the mountains, after we get to Nekros and find her friend, we'll return to our lives. Simi's warning made no sense anyway. There's no need for me to pass it along, not yet. "May I have this dance?" I hold my hand out to her.

She chuckles and takes my hand.

Giving in to the want—the *need*—to be closer to her, I slide my arm around her waist and pull her toward me. I let her nearness give me strength. It's not just that she saved my life—I've done the same for her, after all—or that I still feel weak from the bite, but that she makes me feel steady. There's a calm I feel when I'm with her. A quiet, an ease I haven't felt in years—since before Mama died, since my powers came to me.

A blush creeps up her cheeks and she looks away. "Where did you learn to dance?" she says as I pull her close to me.

"Only at the finest schools, of course," I say. Laughter reaches her eyes, and they twinkle.

Leyla slides her hand behind my waist, resting it there, a soft pressure at my back. It fits perfectly, like it's supposed to be there, like she's connected to me.

"I was wrong about you. I thought you were—"

"Conceited? Spoiled . . . bloodthirsty?"

"All of the above." I laugh, shaking my head at the memory of our first meeting, at how much has changed between us during this journey. "Although, there is that one time you stole my blanket. I would say that's pretty ruthless, stealing a poor girl's blanket out here in the cold."

She rolls her eyes. "Sure, sure. *Now* I've stolen it. I distinctly remember you giving it to me." She laughs. "Speaking of which, I was completely right about you."

I raise an eyebrow. "Well, I *am* older."

Leyla shakes her head. "I mean how determined you are, unwavering in your loyalty, and deeply caring."

My heart swells at that—she sees who I am at my core. I trail my hand up and down her back and feel her shiver as I do.

She holds my gaze for a moment and then she looks down and smiles. "But also, yes—at first I thought you'd be an old woman. That you'd tell me my fate and be off."

"No one can tell you your fate," I say. "I'd like to see someone try. You're your own person, Leyla. Multiple paths. And only you are going to decide the right one to take. You followed after Danai even though everyone told you not to. You made your own choice. That's what I . . . like about you."

We fall silent again. We continue dancing as the sun, slowly, begins to rise.

Leyla looks up at the sky, rays of orange and red bursting through the starlit sky. "This reminds me of a story."

"Tell me," I whisper, wanting to hear anything she wants to say, anything she needs to share.

"It's about these two lovers." My ears perk up at that. "There's a song that sometimes accompanies it." Leyla begins to hum a beautiful tune that sets the stage for the story she weaves of two women from very different backgrounds who fell in love.

"Then one day, a plague fell," she says. "The tavern owner's mother had died when she was young. She got very sick and couldn't afford to see a doctor, because her money had all been devoted to her daughter. So the poor falling ill hit very close to home for her. Thus, the tavern owner turned her business instead into a public hospital for the sick. She tended them day and night."

"She felt guilty," I say softly, knowing full well the burden of such guilt. Leyla adjusts her hand to squeeze my side.

"Yes," Leyla says. "She was consumed with guilt. Always had been; now even more so. She was determined to do for others what she couldn't do for her mama: save them."

"And, of course, she grew sick."

"Yes," she says again. "Her wife had heard of a witch who could aid those desperate enough. The tavern owner begged her wife to stay; she wanted to spend her last hours together. But the seamstress was determined to find a cure, so she left home—she left her love's side—and searched far and wide until, finally, she found the witch. But what she didn't know was this witch wasn't a witch at all, she was Lexa, goddess of discord and strife, who so loved to play tricks on others. Lexa gave the seamstress a potion to save her beloved. In return, she merely asked her what time she liked best: day or night. The seamstress replied, 'Day, of course,' and returned home. But the potion was no ordinary potion. To make it, Lexa had captured the seamstress's shadow—the reflection of her soul. Just as the wife drank the potion, the sun set."

"And then?" I ask.

"The seamstress died," she says, meeting my gaze. "Right there. She died and her wife woke and cried and cried and cried upon seeing her body. The next day the seamstress woke as her wife died. But neither was really dead. They soon realized they could meet for fleeting moments, before the other fell into a deep sleep as night gave way to day—"

"And day to night," I finish. "Blessed to survive, yet cursed to rarely see each other, for only one could exist in day and only one at night. What a sad story."

Leyla shrugs. "I think it's kind of beautiful, actually. Romantic."

I lift an eyebrow. "Death is your idea of romance?"

She shakes her head. "No. Definitely not. I don't want anyone dying for me."

"Me either," I say quietly.

"But the story isn't about that," Leyla continues. "It's about the lengths people will go to for one another. And I know the irony, I'm here because of my best friend, but still I never understood how you could care so much for someone—someone you've just met—why you'd be willing to . . ." Her voice trails off.

"Why what, Leyla?" I say, desperate for the rest.

Slowly, she meets my eyes. "Why you could want, need someone enough—need to have them in your life so badly that a fleeting moment would be enough."

She looks up at me, eyes searching . . . waiting . . . until I can't wait anymore. Our lips meet simultaneously. At first, the kiss is slow. Hesitant. Like we are waiting for someone to give us permission to do so. And then, deeper, breathing the other in—as if my very survival depends on kissing her.

"Wait," she whispers. Her chest heaves in sync with mine. She puts a hand on my chest that's heaving in sync with hers and gently pushes me back, putting space between us.

I furrow my brows, searching her face for an answer. Did I do something wrong? Did she not like it? She bites her lip, like she does when she's anxious about something. Her eyes study the ground. "I know most times I seem fine, and I'm not trying to assume. I mean, it's just kissing. I just want to know—I need to know that . . ."

Her words barrel into one another, and it takes me too long to realize what she's speaking of—the conversation she began right before the garoux attack. The words I didn't say to her, the words I should've said to her. The words I should've realized she needed to hear. After all, I know what it's like to not be what others expect you to be, to have how they see you change overnight. That, for me, made it so much worse than it had to be when I got my powers. If my once friends feared me, shouldn't I also fear myself?

I step closer to her. Her lips are trembling now. "I'm not going anywhere." I cup my hand under her chin and lift her head. After a moment, her eyes trace upward until they meet mine. "Thank you for trusting me enough to tell me. I know it wasn't easy. You are not weak, Leyla. It takes strength to go through what you have and stay true to who you are." She smiles at me and, as she does, her eyes fill with warmth and with a softness that I would've perceived just weeks ago as a vulnerability. I would've pushed away anyone who made me feel like this.

Thoughts begin to swirl in my head of how different we are. Of how, of all people, we never should've met. I push them away. I want her. I need her. In this moment, that has to be enough.

"Leyla," I say from that place of need. "I want you," I say aloud. "I want you exactly as you are."

This time, she's the one who grabs me. She pulls me close to her, kissing me feverishly. Standing on her toes, she clings to me, intertwining her hands in my hair, pulling me toward her, her mouth hard on mine as her heart beats rapidly, hammering against my chest.

Suddenly, kissing is not enough. Kissing doesn't quiet the ache within me. I pull back and she whimpers.

"May I—"

"Please," she says.

I forget about the pain I'm still dealing with.

I forget everything but her.

In one motion, I scoop Leyla up, carrying her back to the cavern, laying her down upon the blankets. She's beautiful in the light of the torches that surround them. I take a step back, looking down at her like that, sprawled out in the middle of this cavern in the middle of this desolate, haunted place.

"Are you going to join me or just stand there?" she says, a grin on her face that makes me wish I had the time to stand here, to slowly explore every part of her, to memorize her.

The mountains. The entrance to Nekros. And Simi's warning that didn't quite make sense. And our lives, our duty to our people that would make whatever this is . . . impossible.

I lie down beside her, setting aside my worries, my fears, for just one night. One night to memorize all of her, to never forget.

Our legs intertwine. Slowly, she takes off my shirt, lifting it over my head.

She pushes up my sleeve, sees the scars carved there.

She looks up at me, her gaze soft.

Somehow, without me saying it, she knows. She kisses my scars. Trails kisses across each and every one. And then I cup her chin, pulling her back up until we're face-to-face. She tucks a loc behind my ear and leans in for another kiss. Hungrier than the last. We kiss and we touch, desperate to orient ourselves to each other. Every scar, every birthmark, every curve. We stay like that, each memorizing the other, as the sun rises, and eventually, we fall asleep intertwined.

CHAPTER THIRTY-TWO

Favre

1,020 Years Ago: The Lands of the Living

FAVRE'S DIARY

Early Evening

The castle is decorated perfectly for the winter ball, an evening that kicks off a week of festivities to celebrate the year's end, Thana's birthday, and the completion of this castle, our home. Yet, even as I look around, only seeing perfection, I can't quiet the feeling that something will go wrong.

The newly built castle towers into the sky. Built on

the bones of the numerous humans killed by Thana, deaths that I've become numb to, that I've done nothing to stop.

Not just the humans we feed off of, but other vampires, other gods, too.

Neferain, who was building an army of her own to attack.
Vzira, whom Thana said was planning a coup.
Suty, who had supposedly been eyeing her throne.
Over the years, they've all turned up dead. Only myself, Thana, Anae, and Lexa are left.

Sometimes, I think of the girl I was, a girl who would give anything for ~~love~~ revenge, for that's what it really was. I wanted Kovnu killed and for that I would've paid any price.

Was it all worth it in the end?

Earlier this evening, Lexa told me she has a plan, that there's someplace safe the three of us can go, where Thana would never find us. A place deep in the desert, created by Suty, before his untimely death. Lexa plans to leave with Anae this week, hoping this season's festivities will provide the distraction they need. "Please come with us," she said.

But before she asked, I already knew that my answer would be no. If I go with them, I'm sealing their deaths. Thana might let them go. Me, she never will.

She needs me.
She loves me.
In her own way.
The ball is soon to begin. I must go.

Late That Evening

The party was not a success.

Vampires came far and wide to celebrate my wife, their queen. They brought gifts, each more elaborate than the next. Nearly two hundred years ago, when we first arrived, I would've never imagined it: a nation to rival that of the Heavenly Realms. Of course, I also would've never imagined what would happen next.

Just as the last gift was presented, the doors to the great hall burst open wide and two women stepped forth.

Not vampires.

Not humans either.

But beings I'd never seen before.

Anae went pale as they walked in. Lexa and I shared a look, both of us confused. Who would arrive uninvited at a ball like this? Who would dare to face Thana's wrath and risk their lives?

Thana, of course, demanded to know who or what they were.

"Yamaja," they said in unison. One of the original beings of this world. Created by the goddess Anae when she was still only that. Before Thana changed her. Before she left the Heavenly Realms. The yamaja sneered when they looked upon their creator. They sneered at Thana, too.

At that, Anae tried to escort them out. Her eyes seemed to plead with them.

But Thana gripped her arm, drawing blood, until Anae sat.

"Continue," Thana said.

The first yamaja stepped forward but didn't deign to bow, claiming knowledge of a prophecy. "A gift for our queen," the other called it, but her tone made it clear she didn't see Thana as their queen at all.

"You have already become a great queen," they said in unison, "but you will become the most well-known." They claimed Thana's name would be spoken in places she had never been and will never be. But that one day she will meet her end. Like her father and his before him: at the hand of her own child.

The room fell so silent, I could hear the beating of my own heart, and everyone else's, too. Anae's skin was absent of its warm tones and was now a yellow brown. Beads of sweat formed on her brow. She looked like she was going to be sick.

Then, the strangest thing happened. Thana threw her head back and laughed. "A child?" she cried out. Her laughter echoed throughout the room as she said, "In that case, I have nothing to be worried about. Favre and I alone cannot make a child."

That did not quiet the dread within me. Gods are born in mysterious ways. Neferain from the ashes of her father's funeral pyre. Anae from her mother's brain.

"As you say, your majesty," said the yamaja in a mocking tone. They exited the room undeterred, leaving as quietly as they had arrived.

The celebration was set to last long into the night with dinner following the gift exchange. My sense of unease only amplified with each course. One bloody delicacy after another, until the final was brought: a sweetened wine infused with blood.

Anae started to choke before she could even finish the glass. Lexa went to help her, but it was too late. She fell to the ground, dead before us.

Thana tossed back her own wine and then asked me to dance.

Three Nights Later

I'm sick to my stomach. I have been for the past few days.

I tell myself it's just Anae's death, fresh on my mind. The death of almost all the gods. The very gods who left behind their own lives to follow her here. Gods Thana supposedly held dear.

Aside, of course, from Thana, there are only two of us now.

But even then, I know that's not it.

I know it's something else.

Ever since that evening, I haven't been able to keep anything down.

In the early mornings, while everyone else was asleep, I'd taken to wandering the halls. It's the only time I have to myself—when I can write in this diary, when my thoughts can be free.

This morning Lexa found me, appearing from the shadows of a corridor. When we first met, we were strangers. Over the years we've become friends. A friendship built upon a shared need: to survive.

My hand kept moving to my stomach. I could feel it again. That same motion.

The reason I rushed from bed, before my movement woke Thana, and came here.

A kick.

Lexa saw my hand drift to my stomach. She immediately placed hers there. Her eyes widened with fear when she felt the kick, too.

Lexa once again begged me. "Leave with me," she said. "She'll kill you."

I was confident in my own safety. Thana loves me. Thana needs me. The power flowing through my blood. Power that over the last years has kept us from harm. But the child? Even if she has my powers, Thana would never risk it. The yamaja might've been strangers, but they spoke of the truth. Thana's father had killed his father and she had killed hers. Who is to say the pattern would suddenly stop here?

I never dreamed of being a mother; I never wanted that life. But then I felt that kick and vowed to do what my mother never did. I will put my child's needs first.

Lexa had listened to me speak about my mother. She understood. She felt the same about hers. Together we made a plan, to give my daughter the life—the love— we never had.

Nine Months Later

I demanded a private birth. That was the only way. We swapped the babies just as mine was born. I barely got to hold her, to name her, to sing to her a lullaby. On my orders, Lexa whisked my daughter away.

Thana entered the room while I was asleep. I wasn't really, but I pretended to be.

When Thana saw the child, she didn't smile or coo. She merely plucked the child out of the crib, and I never saw that babe again.

CHAPTER THIRTY-THREE

Leyla

Present Day: The Wastelands

I wake in Najja's arms and don't want to separate from the moment just yet. I want to savor this for as long as it can last. I snuggle closer and close my eyes, but after a few minutes, she wakes. "Good morning," she says softly. She kisses me, slowly pulling away. I'm tempted to pull her back to me, deeper into my embrace. But the shadow of the mountain looms over us, an ever-present reminder of why I'm really here: to save my friend.

Over the next day, we make our way up the Typhian Mountains, the very ones where Valdis entered Nekros in search of the woman she loved. Unexpectedly, there's a path, but the hike is brutal. The grass is all but nonexistent, almost as if others have been here before.

The discovery reassures me—though we see no entrance, we must be heading the right way. Still, many small rocks line the path, making it difficult to walk. A few minutes feels like an hour; an hour feels like days.

Najja keeps track of the time and every so often makes us stop for a break. I resist, wanting to push through, but she insists, reminding me that I won't be helpful to Danai dead.

"We don't know what, or who, is waiting for us in Nekros. We need our energy," she tells me. She says it breathlessly, and I realize she must be struggling still. I give her hand a squeeze and nod.

Finally, the sun sinks lower in the sky, giving us a break from its harsh rays, and I look up. The top of the mountain is in sight. I exhale as a surge of energy bursts through me. I can make it. We're almost there.

Soon enough, we reach the peak. Only, no matter how hard we search, we can't find an entrance anywhere—or a path that might lead anyplace but here.

Najja points at the journal in my hand. "It doesn't happen to say how she entered, does it?" Sweat drips down the side of her face.

I shake my head and show her the blank pages. After Valdis writes about reaching the top of the mountain, the handwriting stops. "It just ends," I say, my voice heavy with despair. As if her story ends there as well. What if that's all this is, a story? What if there's no way to reach Danai after all?

"Hey," Najja says, moving closer. She rubs her hand on my back, and I relax, leaning into her. "Don't let your mind imagine scenarios that aren't true. Until we get there, until we find her, don't give up."

I look up at her and feel myself swelling with hope, with determination. I won't give up. But there's also something else—feelings for her, that no matter how I've tried, I can't push down.

"Najja——" I start.

The ground rumbles. Najja stumbles backward. She looks behind her shoulder and her eyes widen with fear. In one quick motion, she pushes me back. I fall but catch myself before I hit the ground. And all at once, the ground underneath her crumbles and disappears entirely.

And her with it.

CHAPTER THIRTY-FOUR

Najja

I scream as I hurl toward the ground. I close my eyes, fearing the worst, but then I notice the air around me is slowing down. *I'm* slowing down. I'm not plummeting hundreds of feet to my death; I'm descending, as if I'm tied onto a rope and someone is lowering me to the ground.

Eventually, I stop screaming. And land perfectly on my feet.

"Leyla?" I call, but there's no answer. My voice echoes around me. I look up from where I fell. It's too far for me to see clearly, to make out much up there at all. Water drips onto my head. I look for the source. Is it raining down here? Then I realize it's from stalactites hanging over my head, like hundreds of knives, all pointing at me.

I shiver.

The floor isn't uneven. It's smooth, eroded rock, as if water once was here. Then I hear it: rushing water. I press my ear to the rocky walls; the sound is loud and sure and strong. Could it be the Sea of Sorrows? The very sea that leads to Nekros?

"Najja?" Leyla calls. Her voice is filled with panic. "Are you okay?"

I look up and the piece of sky above me is darkened by a figure. "Leyla!" I call again, my voice surging with joy. "I'm all right."

She lets out a strangled laugh, relief puncturing the worry that had crept into her voice. "Good. I'm going to look for a way down."

"No need. Just jump," I say, before realizing how unreasonable I must sound. "You'll be fine," I add. "Trust me," I say, knowing that she does. I've never given her a reason not to.

Except you haven't told her what Simi said. How if she dies, Thana rises; how there's something larger at play. I brush aside the thoughts. What good would that do her? It would only make her more afraid. It would only make her doubt herself more than she already does.

"How do I know you're really you? What if you're a shade?" she says, referencing the mythical creatures that appear first as shadows and then take your very form.

"Come kiss me and you'll find out." The words leave me before I've realized I've said them. Heat rises to my cheeks, and I look down, blushing, even though there's no one else here to see.

She says nothing and I smile, imagining her cheeks reddening. "Just for that, I won't." She laughs and positions herself in front of the hole. "This one's for you, Danai." This, she whispers, but it echoes all the way down. Then she jumps.

Moments later, she lands. She stumbles but I catch her, pulling her close to my chest. She looks at me, her eyes meeting mine. Her smile flashes before she quickly looks away, as if shy. "We should continue on."

I nod. This isn't the time for that. Later. Slowly, I let her go. I swallow when I release her, suddenly wondering if there will be a later.

"Which one first?" she asks, not sensing my trepidation.

Before us are three tunnels, three paths we could take. Three paths that could go anywhere, that could go to Nekros.

They're nearly identical. Just three dark openings.

"I guess let's start with this one." I point to the tunnel to my right. "After you, your highness," I say with a slight smirk, trying to hide my nerves.

Quietly, she slips her hand into mine, giving me a light squeeze. "Together," she says, and we walk into the dark.

CHAPTER THIRTY-FIVE

Leyla

The first tunnel is a dead end. The second, too. We head down the last one, hoping it'll finally lead somewhere.

Water drips from stalactites. They grow longer and sharper until they graze just over our heads. We have to duck and weave between them to avoid being scratched. The farther we walk, the more the space tightens around us.

Sweat beads build on my forehead. My hands are clammy and warm, even though it's chilly here. *Breathe, Leyla*, I think as I shiver. I pinch my arm to keep myself focused. But as we go farther and farther in, as the walls enclose around us, my breaths grow thin and I'm gasping, as if there's less and less air around us.

"Najja?" I reach for her, but stumble.

"I'm right here, Leyla. Right in front of you."

I know. I can see her. And yet my heart still quickens as the space grows smaller and smaller, until we can only walk one in front of the other, until we're hunched over, nearly crawling on the ground.

"I need air." I gasp for breath. What are the chances this leads to Nekros? What if there's no way out? What if we get trapped down here? Does Nekros even really exist? My anxiety sends me into a panic. I close my eyes briefly. *Drip. Drip. Drip.* Every sound is heightened. I rub at my face. Then I feel a hand in mine.

"Take a deep breath with me." Najja grazes her thumb over my hand. She starts counting down. *Ten. Nine. Eight. Seven . . .* All the way to one and then back up to ten again. All the while, holding my hand as we walk within the mountain. Soon, the space eases up. I let out a sigh of relief. "Thank you."

She grazes her thumb over my hand again. Heat ripples through me. Her hand tightens, then she lets go. The absence of her warmth is immediate.

"I used to train the littlest yamaja how to swim and dive. They're often scared when they first begin. But the thing about being a yamaja is you have to. It's our whole purpose. If we don't dive deep into the sea for the threads of fate, who will? It's dark down there, so dark we can barely see. And it's cold. Freezing cold. The nooks where the threads are found are so small, only one of us can pass through at a time. I would teach them in the same way my mother taught me. I would take them, one by one, and hold their hand, counting down from ten while we swam."

My heart fills as she speaks, as she strips away her barriers, revealing this side of herself. "You were gentle with them. You assuaged their fears," I say.

"It was my duty," she says.

"You loved it." I recall the pride in her voice.

Her voice gains a wistful air. "I did. I've spent so much of my life hating who I am that I forget it wasn't all bad." She draws in a deep breath. "But, Leyla, what if—what if, after this, there's no one left? What if my home is gone?" She exhales as if the question is a weight she's been carrying, plaguing her thoughts and keeping her awake at night.

"Then you'll find a way to rebuild." I take her hand. "Remember, you're not alone now. You said your sister foresaw the attack—do you really think she'd allow everyone to die?"

"No," says Najja. "She wouldn't. She would've saved some of them, somehow."

I squeeze her hand. "It's like you told me, have faith—don't let your mind imagine what you don't know is true."

We continue on, deeper and deeper through the mountain. We wade through large puddles of water where rain has collected. We climb over walls to get to the next passage. We walk, we crawl, we jump from ledge to ledge. One tunnel leads to another, and we just have to trust that this will lead us where we hope, we have to trust in each other, until finally, we find a hole in the wall. A massive one, like a boulder ran through it. The chamber we are in is bright, illuminated by the sun shining through. Which is odd, because when we entered the mountain, the sun was setting. We might've walked for hours, but not so many that it's a new day.

I look up at Najja; she's confused as well.

It's so bright that we can clearly see the walls covered in images carved deep into the limestone. A vampire. Drained of her blood. Buried in a tomb. And then reawakened—by the gift of blood.

Chills creep up my arms at the thought, of being trapped, hanging between life and death. Waiting to be freed.

What could someone have done to deserve such a fate? What story—what warning is this?

I motion to Najja. "Do you know what this is? I've never heard this tale before."

Najja stares at the wall, taking it all in. "She wears a crown." She points at the vampire, at a detail I didn't pick up. "Is she one of your queens?"

I shake my head. "I don't know of any queens who were buried alive." I look at the chamber floor that's scattered with bones and ash. "Maybe this is a story that wasn't passed down." I fall silent, not putting voice to the question that comes next—*why would they do that?*

Najja inches closer to me and slips her hand through mine. "Many have come this way and died." She points along the ground to where there are grooves, as if someone, or some creature, dragged something along this way. "This chamber was once inhabited." Her voice is low and uneven.

My eyes search along the chamber. They land on something coiled up, on what appears to be animal skin. I motion to Najja. She pokes it with her sword, scraping up some of the skin. She holds it up to the light; it's snakeskin. From a really, *really* big snake.

"I don't see anything here, though." I press my back against the wall, looking high and low.

"I don't think it's here anymore. We haven't been that quiet." She grabs more of the skin, spreading it out. It's several times as long as her. "If there was a snake this big here, it would've found us by now."

"Thank the gods," I say. My shoulders relax. I nod at the hole in the wall. "Looks like there's only one way forward, then."

I walk closer to the hole. There, the sun is so bright we can't see what's on the other side. Najja comes up beside me, her shoulder brushing against mine. Fear catches in my throat, and the hairs on the back of my neck rise.

The sun blinds me as I step through the mountainside. It takes my eyes a few seconds to adjust, but when they do my fear dissipates.

Before me is a river. And a boat.

CHAPTER THIRTY-SIX

Najja

"This is it!" Leyla exclaims. "This must be it." She points at the river. "The river all souls journey down to reach Nekros." Her voice is light with relief.

She starts to climb into the boat. The boat is so ancient, surely it might sink before it ever gets her safely to Nekros. But that's the least of my concerns right now. The reliefs on the walls within the mountain about blood awakening an ancient queen. Simi's prophecy and her warning about Thana waking if Leyla should die. It all swirls together in my head.

"Najja?" Leyla calls as I stand frozen in place as the truth reveals itself to me.

"Leyla." I inhale sharply. "There's something I need to tell you."

"Come on." She waves me toward her, to where she stands by the boat. "You can tell me on the way there. The sun's still out; we should leave now. I'd rather not be out on a river in the dark."

"Leyla," I say, softer this time, pleading for her to hear me. As

I walk slowly toward her, Simi's words push to the forefront of my mind. It all makes sense. Her prophecy about Leyla being at the center of it all, about us being at the precipice of a great war.

If the princess dies, Thana rises.

Leyla's blood must somehow be the key.

My words come out in one breath. "It's a trap. It's always been a trap. Leyla . . . I have something I need to tell you." And everything I've been keeping secret spills out of me.

Her eyes widen as I repeat what Simi told me. "You've kept this to yourself all this time?"

"I was unconscious, sick, how was I supposed to know it was real? And what was I supposed to say? 'Hey, I think you might awaken an evil queen and lead us all to war'?"

Leyla throws her hands up, waving them as she speaks. "Yes, exactly that. You *lied* to me. You *hid* things from me. What was it, did you think that I was too *weak* to handle it?"

"No, I just wanted to . . . protect you. If I was wrong, I didn't want to worry you. I wasn't sure what was real and what wasn't. But then . . . then I saw those reliefs." I point to the mountain. "What if it's all trying to tell us something? What if it's trying to warn us? What if by going there, you set into motion something that was supposed to be forgotten?" *I don't want to lose you.* "It's too dangerous," I say aloud instead.

"I don't need your protection, and this entire trip has been dangerous. The only thing that changed as of late was what I told you . . . right before we . . ." She looks away from me but not before I catch tears sliding down her face. "So now, because of that, I need protection?"

I swallow, silencing myself. With every word I dig myself into a deeper hole. How do I even begin to tell her that yes, I do see her differently, but not in the way she thinks. What's changed is how I feel about her. I can't lose anyone else.

"Leyla, please." I reach for her. But she slips away.

"Thana is dead," she says. "My ancestress killed her. But Danai—Danai is alive." Her voice cracks. "She has to be. I came here to save her. I have to save my friend." With that, she climbs into the boat.

"Leyla," I plead.

"Don't." She holds up a hand. "I trusted you."

I'm forced to watch as she rows away, toward the island where souls go at their end, to the place where shadows meet.

CHAPTER THIRTY-SEVEN

Favre

1,001 Years Ago: Nekros

FAVRE'S DIARY

Leave Thana or die with her. Lexa's warning echoed through my head.

On my daughter's eighteenth birthday, like Lexa had promised me, she told Clea the truth. Where she came from, who her mothers were, the prophecy that made me send her away.

Clea was horrified. To be the daughter of the queen who was causing her world so much pain.

So, she rallied a hunting party, to make that prophecy come true.

An attack was coming. But Clea wanted to give me a chance to escape—a life for a life, she'd said.

But I am just as responsible for the bloodshed as Thana. I kept her secrets and protected her.

And so, we raced on horseback, as fast as we could go. Trying to put as much distance as possible between us and them.

Finally, right when I began to give up hope, we reached a sea. A wide, crisp, and limitless sea.

The magic that lived within me spoke. It told me what to do.

I gave the sea my blood.

I gave until my breath grew faint; until I was so weak that I could not stand. At first, I thought: this is my end. But again, just as I began to give up hope, the sea shook awake. Waves crashed, like it was angry. The water parted and spat up a single rowboat with just enough room for us two.

Thana climbed in first and I after her. We rowed and rowed and rowed. All the while not saying a word. After all, what was to be said? How could I make up for this? For betraying her and sealing her fate in the way I did.

In silence, we reached this island in the middle of the sea, as the sun was beginning to rise and our flesh beginning to burn.

A wood stood before us; we walked into it to hide from the sun.

A house was in the middle of it.

A tree was in front of the house.

A peculiar tree, hanging with glass bottles instead of leaves. A tree Mother once told me about. In one of her rare stories about her life <u>before</u>—before she met Kovnu, before she moved to the Heavenly Realms.

But Thana entered the house while I was trying to recall the full story, the warning in its words.

And so, I followed. And as I did, I caught sight of the house's foundation—of its rotting wood.

What is done is done, Mother used to say. What has been set in motion shall pass.

CHAPTER THIRTY-EIGHT

Leyla

Present Day: The Sea of Sorrows

Love makes you weak. Mama's words ring in my ears, as I push back the tears threatening to spill. Tears over someone who I could never be with, who is from another place, who lives another life, who things wouldn't work out with in the end.

You don't know that. But I push away that hope, too. I focus, instead, on the journey before me. On what I came here for: to save Danai.

The sun rises before fading once more, giving way to the dark slowly, then all at once. The boat parts through the reeds and soon they give way to a great, limitless sea.

I row, trying not to let the thunking of the water against the boat lull me to sleep. The boat does most of the work, correcting course as if it knows where it needs to go and merely needs me to usher it along. Which is fine; my thoughts are loud enough, my memories cramped. With those who are not here and should be.

With the blue-gray sky of the day and the green-blue sea. With eyes that match its waters, the girl those eyes belong to, who quiets my storms. With the vastness of it all.

"The Sea of Sorrows," I say aloud. And yet a worse name couldn't have been chosen—how can so much beauty be within such pain?

I gaze at the sea. What if by leaving, I rushed Mama's death? What if I've caused her heart to break? Consumed her with worry, thus weakening her strength and quickening the disease's spread? *A queen must put her people before herself.* And yet I did the opposite. I deserted my people. I left my nation without an heir. Najja's worries echo through my head on a loop. I told myself that I was coming here to save my friend, but at what cost?

Najja would also say that I worry too much about my mother, that I need to focus more on me. Danai would echo the same. But Najja isn't here. Danai isn't either. One I left; one was taken from me.

I am all alone.

My heart aches from the very thought of it, from the guilt I've tried to brush away. I know I shouldn't blame myself—it's not my fault. But the thoughts swarm in my head, and I can't seem to outrun them. What if this and what if that. They make me sick, every bit of me questioning myself. My anxieties are shredding me apart inside, one strip of me at a time. Tears prick the corners of my eyes; one blossoms into several; several into many. They run over.

I failed them all. I failed my nation. I can never win. In pleasing one person, in saving one person, I'm abandoning another. I try to snap myself out of my spiral, to remember Najja's soothing touch, but it's like some other force is here, causing me to feel too deeply, causing me to only think about the pain.

I am ruled by my emotions and limited by my pain—*weak*, Mama always says. I am unfit to be queen.

And if I am unfit to be queen, what has all of this been for? Suffering her endless insults, braving her day after day. If I am unfit to be queen, what's the point of trying?

My arms shiver, and my teeth chatter. I am alone. One person—one girl—trying her best to bail out a sinking ship. Only I'm not in a small pond; I don't just have one failure or regret. I am a sea full of them.

I cry, and the water ripples. I cry, and something slinks beneath the surface. A voice, many voices break through. *Leyla*, they whisper. *Come near.*

Their voices are so sure, so full of comfort. What harm would it be if I stop rowing? My arms are exhausted anyway. My muscles are burning and sore. I need a break. A quick, *cool* dip. The waters will relax me and ease my pain. The sorrows I can't let go. The sea will take it all away.

I sway to the rhythm of the boat, the waves thunking against its sides.

Slowly, hands reach up and out of the water, like there are people in the sea dancing, swaying, too. These hands wrap around my own. They are cool and soft to the touch. The hands circle my arms. They brush my shoulders. Caress my cheeks and stroke at my hair.

Suddenly, their grip turns firm, and they jerk me toward the water.

My eyes flicker open as the hands from the sea tighten around my neck. Hands as white as snow coursing with veins that pulse without blood. My eyes trail up and meet their featureless faces, as if they are but figurines molded with clay.

I scream. It is too late. They tug harder and I fall, splashing into the sea.

Leyla. Come closer. They are not gentle now.

I push back, but their pull is sharper. Water-wrinkled fingers push into my flesh. Thin, brittle nails scratch at my skin. I cry out and I kick. But as one falls off, another latches on. The souls clamp onto me like weights. It hurts to fight back. I'm so tired. Of trying to do all the things. Trying to be the perfect daughter. Living up to expectations I never stood a chance against. Blaming myself for things I can't control. Caring deeply. Acting as if I'm okay, as if the pain I feel all the time doesn't affect me. Failing yet again.

Saltwater fills my mouth and runs down my throat. My hummingbird pendant slips from my neck. It floats just above my head. I reach for it as water floods my lungs. I try to clasp my fingers around its chain. But it hovers out of reach, too far away.

Papa. I think of how I grabbed the pendant, floating in that river red with blood. I should've tried harder. I could've saved him. I shouldn't have demanded that trip to begin with. Had I not, he would still be here. My aunt, my cousins would still be here. Everything would not have changed for the worse, had I not—

STOP IT! My head screams. *Stop doing this to yourself.*

I'm tearing myself apart bit by bit, fraying at the hems like a too-worn dress.

Maybe I could have saved him. Maybe some of it was my fault. I was the one who wanted to take the trip. But I was only a child, barely nine. I can't base my entire life on maybes.

Yes, Danai would've been far away had we not gotten into that terrible fight, had I not been too selfish to let her leave. But I am doing everything I can to make up for that, I am trying to save my friend. And when I do, when I have her back with me, she is free to go where she pleases. A relationship in which one has to ask permission to follow their dreams isn't a healthy relationship at all.

I have always done the best that I can. That has to be enough.

I kick at one of the souls, freeing my left leg. I fight against them as they try to pull me back down. Back, into the sea's depths. Down, into the darkness that reminds me of the dark corners of my own soul. I *must* save Danai. I *must* return home. I am not Mama. I will never be my mother. But I am her heir.

Danai needs me. My people need a queen.

I think of Najja, and Malike as well.

I am not alone. I never have been.

I swim and I swim, kicking the souls away from me. I fight. I don't stop until I reach the surface and see the boat once more. I pull myself up into the boat and cough up water.

My heart beats wildly. I gasp for air.

I look around, expecting to see the creatures, but the sea is calm.

I reach into my bag and pull out a blanket to wrap myself with. But the blanket I pull out isn't mine, it's Najja's, and I'm sad all over again.

Before I know it, I'm crying and wishing I could go back. Back to her. To have her here with me, soothing me. But I can't. I can only go forward, and I must learn to soothe myself. So, I row and row and row, until I see the outline of an island.

An island shrouded in shadows.

The boat inches toward the land. As soon as I can, I jump out and pull the boat to the shore. Along the shoreline are other such boats, remnants and pieces, vessels long forgotten. Remembrances of people who made it here but didn't make it out.

Where Shadows Meet

A dark wood stands before me.

I step out the boat and my sandals meet the sand. My breath slows, my wet clothes cling onto me as I try to take it all in: the island, the wreckage, the towering trees. "I've made it," I say hesitantly, as if I'm not sure this isn't just a dream. Except it feels real. I've made it to the place we say is our world's end.

I stand just before the wood, head tilted up toward the highest branches.

The wind howls, the trees sway as if bowing and whispering, *welcome.*

Welcome to Nekros. Welcome to the island of the dead.

CHAPTER THIRTY-NINE

Najja

She's gone. She left me. Everyone always leaves me.

I kick at the ground, and dirt scatters everywhere, carried by the wind. *Why does everyone leave?* I think to cry out and curse at the gods, but what will that do? Bring her back? I laugh sourly. No, it won't. The gods won't bring Leyla back, just like they won't bring back Simi or Mama. Besides, it's not like she's dead—she's alive. She made her decision; she left without giving me the choice to be by her side.

I push down so many memories. I shove away her smile, the way her whole face changed when she laughed, how she listened to me, how she cared. The taste of her lips on mine, her chest heaving over mine. I try not to wonder if she'll be cold. If she'll be safe out there without me by her side.

Foolish. So foolish for her to leave. To run headfirst into danger. To not think about anything or anyone else. To save her friend at the cost of her own life.

I hoist my pack onto my shoulder, ready to give up and walk back the way we came. Back, through the mountainside; back, to the Wastelands; back, to Vurness—all the way home.

I don't make it five steps before a shooting pain pushes me to the ground, before a terrible vision overcomes me, making me clutch my head and scream.

Blood. Blood, everywhere. All across a stone chamber floor. Leyla sprawled out. Heartbeat fading. Gasping for air. It must be her blood. She's dying? *She reaches out in front of her. "Najja," she whispers before her eyes flutter closed.*

It takes me several minutes to recover, to pull myself, gasping, from the vision's depths, to reassure myself it can't be now. Leyla couldn't have left more than a few hours ago. There's no way this is happening yet. *It can't be*, I tell myself again and again, even though I don't know if that's true.

She called my name.

"She called my name!" She reached—she was reaching for me, as if I was right there.

Hope surges through me. I can make it. I have to save her. I can save someone this time. But uncertainty washes through me. *Why bother? If she wanted you there, she wouldn't have left. You're always too late. You'll only see her die.*

Just like I saw Mama and Simi die, just like how those visions came true. Ever since my visions started, they've always come true. If I see someone die, they always do. But I can't just sit here, I can't walk away. I can't give up on her without a fight.

I turn around and head toward the river that leads to Nekros. I drop my pack onto the ground, leaving behind anything that'll slow me down.

Najja, the river calls. *Come to me.*

And so, I do. I push through the reeds; I swim faster than I ever have. To find Leyla, to save her before my vision comes to pass and I lose the only person I have left—before I can tell her how happy she makes me and share the deep feelings I'm beginning to feel.

CHAPTER FORTY

Favre

Nekros

Once, long ago, I believed that my life would be like the stories Mother told me of girls who suffered but ultimately found happily ever afters. For suffer I did. But as I grew to learn, those tales were lies.

Power, Mother taught me, was the only way to gain anything in a gods' world. The only way to be seen as an equal. But the power running through my veins, the power Mother passed down, required sacrifice. To achieve the greatest things, such power demanded the only sacrifice worthy enough: *yourself*.

My mother gave so many parts of herself throughout the years, until the last thing she had left was her life. This she gave attempting to make Kovnu a sword, one that could kill any god. Kovnu gave my mother many promises. And so, when he asked this of her, Mother believed he'd save her from her fate, from the price her powers asked for to create such, and reward her by bringing her back from the dead.

I watched her drain herself of every ounce of her magical blood to create the sword, but she died before she could complete the spell.

The king never brought her back.

Never trust a god, I learned then.

But Thana isn't just a god. Thana rebuked that king—her father—and the very gods she came from. Thana is the only person who accepted not just my powers, but who I really am.

And so, I would give what it takes for us to be together again. Surely, Thana, if she was in my place, would do the same.

When the princess enters the wood, I rip out my hair—much like I did with my wings all those years ago, to complete my mother's spell, to create the sword that started everything, the sword that set Thana free.

I rip out the hair that Thana loved so much. I pull out every strand. Blood cakes under my nails. It runs down my face. As I pull, memories slip away, too. Our first kiss. Our first time making love. Thana's first promise, broken.

I give until I have nothing left to give, much like I did the first time we met.

Before me, an iridescent pool forms. Right in front of the bed on which I sit.

A mist rises from the pool, made from my pain and sorrow and tears. Thick and shapeless. Of and controlled by me.

"Go, my love," I command it, softly, the way I might my own child if I hadn't given her up, too. Without saying anything more, the mist knows what it must do.

After the mist is gone, I lie upon the bed. My hands tremble as a cool sea breeze comes in from the window, rippling through my bedchamber. My scalp tingles. I shiver. But I don't mind. My hair had always been too unruly, too thick. Reminding me, even when I didn't want to remember, of when Thana and I met.

I swallow slowly, inhaling the fresh air to cool my nerves.

Maybe I *am* like my mother, but that doesn't mean I'll repeat the past.

Love, as I learned from Mother, requires sacrifice, too.

CHAPTER FORTY-ONE

Leyla

A gloomy wood stands before me, with wild and rough and stubborn trees. Branches sway in the darkness, rustling against one another and casting shadows onto the beach. The shadows inch onto my body, my skin, making dark patterns like the ones Mama bears.

I take a deep breath, steeling myself, and walk into the woods.

The woods bow and sway more the farther in I walk, as if expanding, tightening, and then closing in on me. I count down from ten and then back up, like Najja taught me, keeping my breath steady as each step leads me deeper into the darkness, scraggly branches scratching my arms and legs.

I shudder as a sharp howl echoes. It pierces through the trees, coiling around me and pushing bumps onto my arms and the back of my neck. I shiver.

I freeze. "Reapers."

Shaking my head, I continue on. *They aren't here for me.*

I expect the woods to be loud, for a cacophony of sounds to

rise up. To be like the forest Danai and I fled to when we were only ten, attempting to follow Valdis's path to Nekros, to ask the woman I believed to be a goddess why she took our family away.

We'd barely entered the forest when Mama found us and taught me one of her many sayings that now live in my head. *A queen must—*

"*—put her people before herself,*" Mama finishes my thought, just like she did the last time I saw her, when we were together in my chambers. But Mama is not here. She can't be, and yet I heard her, swear I saw her—dressed in her nightgown, shivering with cold, standing in this very wood with me.

I shake my head and blink several times.

I think of how I let the souls pull me down. How at the last moment I changed my mind. How I thought of those I wanted to see again, how I craved finding Danai. I was so close, so near to death, and yet at the last minute I fought back. I resisted. But if I am resolved, determined to save Danai, to become the queen my people need, why do I feel so lost and tired? So hopeless, like the worst is yet to come.

An hour passes and I'm still walking; the fog grows thicker and thicker. First hovering over my ankles, then my shins, and soon over my knees and to my hip. A tingling sensation rushes through me. I am unusually light.

Calm down, I tell myself. *It's only an afternoon dew.* But the mist continues to rise, as if it has a mind of its own. I shake my head. Blinking as if dirt got into my eyes. Sleep crud, more likely. I'm probably just tired. That must be it, why I feel this way, why my brain is still swimming with so many doubts. This journey has finally taken its toll, and I need to rest. I rub my eyes and yawn, covering my mouth with my hands. And then mist is all around me.

I can't see anything but the mist. A wall of shimmery white covering everything.

Suddenly, a voice that I'd recognize anywhere calls out. "Leyla!" Danai yells, and at once, I know she's afraid.

Danai? I spin around. But no one is there.

"Danai?" I call and then I see her, beckoning me forward. "Run," she says, brown eyes wide. "She's coming. We have to get out of here."

"She?" I ask, as a shudder rips through me. "The goddess of the dead?"

But before Danai gets the chance to answer, a Reaper appears. It grabs Danai in its hands and then it's happening all over again, the terrible moment she was taken.

"No!" I scream, falling to the ground to beg. "Please," I say. "Take me instead!" But the Reaper has her in its mouth. It clamps down on her neck and blood oozes out.

"Leyla!" She reaches for me.

"NO!" Pain goes through me as my heart rips in two. I came all this way, I was so close, this can't be happening again. Abruptly, when I think it, the moment disappears all together. There are no more screams.

"Danai?" I spin around, but I don't see her. The Reaper has vanished.

I hear another scream. *Najja?*

I shake my head. This is a dream. She's not here. I left her behind. I will not have her death on my hands.

My feet grow heavy as I trudge through the dirt, trying to run back and forth through the mist, searching for my friends. Dirt clings to the tears on my face; it cakes on my sweaty hands.

A voice rumbles through the forest floor. Soft at first, then louder. It whispers my name, and when I look up, a dirt path has cleared before me. It's lined with trees that curve into an arch; its floor is dusted with fallen leaves.

At the end of the path is a house. It calls to me.

CHAPTER FORTY-TWO

Leyla

The house stands like a remnant of a past long forgotten. I walk up to its wrought-iron gate, tug it open, and step through. Grass grows before the house, so overrun, it scratches at my knees. Shattered windows with jagged teeth peer down at me. There are vines that have climbed up and around the once-white columns that decorate the house's front, choking them and pushing their way through the windows. The walls are charred, the paint peeling.

Next to me is a tree. Blue glass bottles hang from its branches; they clank loudly as if warning me to stay away, do not disturb. Just then, rain starts to pour. The clouds turn an ominous gray.

Danai. She is here. Something beckons me near.

Gripping my knife, I push the front door open and step into the darkness. A cool breeze prickles my skin.

Before me is a once grand staircase. The metal rail is broken off in pieces, the marble steps crumbled. Carefully, I make my way up. All the while, the mist follows me. Deep down, I know this is where I'm supposed to be. Once I reach the top, there's an even darker hallway waiting. It's lined with candles like the halls back home, yet not like those at all. Pearly-white hands float along the walls, attached to nothing and no one. Each hand holds within it a candelabra.

The inside of the house is stale and humid; the dank, thick, sweaty air catches in the back of my throat and refuses to leave. I push down the fear building inside my chest and walk over the dust-swept floorboards until I reach a door at the hall's end.

My hands grab the knob. A jolt zaps through me. The door springs open as if my touch is the key.

In the middle of the room is a single spindle. I run my hand over it slowly.

"Ouch." I draw back sharply. Blood wells on my finger from where I've just pricked myself. When I look up, a middle-aged woman is before me. A cloak shrouds her almost completely. All I can see is her stormy-blue eyes, the same color as the darkening sky.

The woman splits into three.

A younger woman, the woman she is, and an older version of herself.

The past, the present, and the future. Three women. Different and yet the same. They speak to me as one.

"What is it you most want?" they say.

"Stop these tricks," I command. "Where is my friend?"

"What is it you most want?" they repeat, voice hollow, rumbling under my skin.

"I just told you. I want to save Danai." What sort of twisted game is this?

"And so, you shall have that chance, but what do you truly want, princess—what is it you wish to know? You have tried before to find us and find one of us you did. But she could not tell you what you wanted, what it is you so desire."

"You're yamaja?" I stumble back. "I thought your kind disappeared, turned to sea foam when you died. Why are you here, on Nekros?"

The older one breaks into a toothy grin. "We do, but remember, this isle is not as it seems. It was shaped by the gods. Much is possible here." They step toward me, eyes staring me down. "What is it you—"

"I want to know my fate," I interrupt. "I want what I've always wanted, to know who I'm meant to become." As soon as I say it, I clamp my hand over my mouth. "No, I didn't mean that. I don't want to be here. I just want to save my friend."

But the women merely shake their head. "You cannot go back. You can only go forward. It is time for you to know the truth."

The room disappears. *Was I ever in a room to begin with?* It shifts to the castle, and I know I must be asleep, passed out in the forest somewhere. *Wake up, Leyla*, I say. *I can't be here. Wake up.* But no matter how many pinches and little slaps I give myself, the scene does not change. I'm forced to watch and listen as a young woman about my height appears and runs through the castle halls.

"Wait," I say, but she keeps going. I run to keep up with her. She makes a sharp turn and enters a room. I know this room, it's my room, but instead of paintings of heroes and myths, the walls are bare—an off-white color. The young woman stands just within the doorway. A yamaja sits on the edge of her bed.

The young woman turns around, as if confused, then steps farther into the room.

"Mama?" I call when I recognize who she is. But she pays me no mind.

"Did you lead me here, yamaja?" she says. It's the same tone Mama uses when she has no time for any of my failures.

The yamaja shakes her head. "No, your highness. You led yourself."

Mama ignores her and begins to pace. "I have many questions, but none I need a yamaja for," she says, dismissive even then. "Fate is for the gods—"

"And we are their messengers," finishes the yamaja.

"No, thank you," she says; her voice grows solemn. "I already know what my end is to be."

"How long have the signs been there?" The yamaja motions at the floor. I follow her gaze to where black veins encircle Mama's legs.

But that doesn't make any sense. Mama always said that her illness came on recently, that a yamaja told her about her future illness. And yet, here she is, eighteen and already sick. Mama knew how she would die since she was my age, so why did the yamaja upset her so? I turn back to the scene unfolding before me.

"You are dying," the yamaja says.

Mama laughs. "Tell me something I don't know."

"You do not fear death?"

"We all must die," Mama says. "I am already luckier than most—I know that which shall bring it forth."

"Ah, but you do not know when."

Mama sighs. "I do not care to." Her lips are thinly pursed. "Fate is for the gods to know and for us to accept."

"You will be a great queen," the yamaja offers, as if that would provide comfort.

"Impossible." Mama shakes her head. "That will be my sister's role."

The yamaja shrugs. "You will be a great queen," she repeats, "but the same cannot be said about your daughter."

"My daughter?" Mama furrows her brows.

The yamaja nods. "You will end this great war, but your daughter will undo your legacy and bring destruction to this world again."

Mama stumbles back. Her face warps with rage. "How dare you." Her voice is a knife's edge.

"Think what you think you must," says the yamaja. "Ignoring this matter shall not stop fate. In fact, the only way to change things is to stop your daughter yourself. You mustn't allow her to take the throne."

Mama approaches the yamaja, red eyes burning. "If you don't wish to regret this, choose your next words carefully," she says.

But the yamaja doesn't even flinch. She stays exactly where she is. "A queen must put her people before herself. Kill your daughter." She stares directly at Mama. "She must never become queen."

CHAPTER FORTY-THREE

Leyla

Kill your daughter. She must never become queen.

When I become conscious, the yamaja is gone, and I'm within an empty room. A chill has settled in my heart. My memory, slowly, returns to me. The prophecy the yamaja gave Mama that her daughter would reverse it all.

Me.

I *am* that daughter.

Mama's constant chides. Her warnings that fate is only for the gods to know. Her outlawing of the yamaja. Was it all some sort of misplaced attempt to stop me from knowing my fate? To protect me? I look around the room for a sign—any sign—but it's as if none of it ever happened. There's no yamaja. No Mama. No spindle. Was it a dream? Playing with my worst fears, that I will always fall short of her every expectation, that I will fail and undo everything that she and my ancestresses have all worked so hard for.

That's when I see the door before me. When I entered, there

was only one, the door behind me. I shake my head; it was likely always there. My memory is still foggy.

I feel like I'm supposed to be somewhere else. As if there's something I'm supposed to be doing. But it's like there are moments missing from my past. *You cannot go back, only forward.* So, I walk toward the door.

The door is made of solid bronze. The edges glow as I come near. I raise my hand and touch the surface. As my palm settles on top, it creaks opens, revealing yet another hallway lit with burning flames.

I take a step and then I stop. I turn to look back. A single drop of blood is splattered on the floor, exactly where I thought I saw a spindle. I wrinkle my brow in confusion and shake my head. I have to continue.

I step into the darkness.

With each step, more candles flicker on. Held again by suspended hands. They come from the wall but this time they seem even more alive. A pinky twitching here, a thumb's movement there. Wax runs down them, dripping and forming puddles, slowly solidifying—congealing on the earthen floors.

Stairs descend before me. Little steps, leading into the darkness. Each one is more and more eroded, until eventually I am gripping the walls themselves to steady myself.

Left foot, right foot. Step. Step.

The stairs lead to a large chamber covered in bronze panels mapping out a story—someone's life.

A childhood in the Heavenly Realms.

The drinking of a king's blood, becoming the first vampire.

I take it all in. I've seen these before, in the castle's library. It is Thana's story. But the farther I walk, the more the panels change, the more they diverge from what I know. Not a story of how knights killed Thana, but of how they failed to do so. How they trapped her for eternity, locking the door with a god's spell. A door that can only be accessed by one from Thana's bloodline. A curse that can only be reversed with more blood.

At once, the room brightens. In the center is a tomb much like the ones the humans bury their dead in, giant structures with a relief of the dead person atop. This one is finely carved, inlayed with gold. I shudder when I see the words engraved on the side:

Here, even gods weep.

Leyla. A voice calls to me, thousands of years old, gravelly, and more ancient than anything I know.

Thana.

I turn and run for the door.

We have traveled as far as we can. Past a treacherous sea and through a wood with a life of its own. To a house, this house, where we wait. Thana stands by a window, gazing at the crisp blue sky.

I think of my wings. Of the many things I shed to be with her. Wings that could've taken me—us—far away from here.

Their ships have hit the shore and soon the hunting party will reach us. We can run no farther; there is nowhere else to hide. I made my choice a millennium ago.

My fate and Thana's are forever bound.

—FROM THE DIARY OF FAVRE
CIRCA 200 AD
MERKESH ROYAL ARCHIVES

CHAPTER FORTY-FOUR

Favre

I trace my fingers along the door's gilded frame. A door that like so much else was created by the gods. To punish me. To taunt me.

The words along its frame are in a language so old it has no name. I run my hand over them, following along: the story of how an angel came to be, the gift my mother was granted by the gods, and how Thana and I met.

Here, and only here, lies the truth. The full account of Thana's rise and demise. It was through this very door that the princess went. My heart swells—how easily the girl followed my carefully laid plans. How foolishly she opened the door to my beloved's tomb.

Tomb. Too nice a word for what it really is. A lavish prison, a secluded hole. A place where Thana was supposed to reside for all eternity, drained of her blood—forever among the dead. And to think that the final thing this required was the hair off my head. Hair I don't need anyway.

A shiver runs through me when I unconsciously rub my back,

where my wings, beautiful and powerful, once were. Both brutally ripped off to give Thana a sword to kill a king, an act that would allow us to be together undeterred.

Tears fall down my face, wetting my cheeks and blurring my vision. This is what I wanted, right?

Thana.

The only person who truly loved me—at least that is what Thana said. Loved me in a way no one else did, understood me like my mother could not. *True love requires sacrifice*, I remind myself. I brush away my tears and take a deep breath before I walk down the winding steps. My hope to be reunited with Thana is what has kept me alive all these years. Who would I be without her?

With each step, I relive memories of how they chained me. The hunting party—gods, humans, yamaja, vampires—that came for us. They dragged me here to watch them drain Thana of her blood and bury her alive.

With each memory, I grow stronger. Stronger and more determined. To get back at them for everything. The yamaja, who I've already dealt a grave blow, who played a role, too. The vampires who turned their back on their queen, the humans who foolishly went along, and the gods who cared not who they hurt in their eternal quest to keep themselves in power.

We will rule the world.

As I walk, I run my hands along reliefs carved into bronze telling Thana's story. It looks like a temple honoring her, but in actuality, it is a warning: *Turn back, now. Leave.*

That's when I see her. Thana. They couldn't kill her, so they locked her away in a casket made of gold in the shape of her body. It lies flat on the marble floor, illuminated by the same candelabras that decorate the hall, with more bronze panels circling the room. It is like a throne. The casket holds court in the center of the room, and the gold shines as bright as ever. Here, she could reign—but only over her own memories, for here, she is alone.

At least she used to be. The princess stands before Thana's casket, her face horror-stricken. I feel my lips curve up. She must've realized her mistake. That she's in Thana's tomb. That she has gone where she was never supposed to go, to a place that shouldn't have existed.

But it is too late. Too late for the girl, just as it is too late for me to turn back and choose another life. The princess can't undo her role in this present any more than I can change my past.

The girl spins around. She tries to leave, but runs right into me, where I wait in the shadows. She stumbles back but slips on the eroded stairs. With a wicked smile, I pick her up.

The beginning of the end.

CHAPTER FORTY-FIVE

Najja

The Sea of Sorrows

The winding river gives way to a limitless sea. It reminds me of home. At first, the sea is calm and clear. But as time passes, so do the tides misbehave. It takes more effort for me to push against them, for me to not be dragged away.

When I was younger, I'd dream of going on such adventures. Of slipping into our sea and letting it take me where it willed. Sometimes, in those dreams, Simi would join me. No matter how far we traveled, Mama would always be waiting for us, back at home. But I am not a little girl anymore; this is nothing like those dreams.

The more I swim, the sharper the saltwater burns, hurting my mouth, nose, and throat. With every stroke, my shoulders ache even more. I jolt to the side as a sharp sting spreads across my side. A pink jellyfish bobs away, its tentacles brushing across me, leaving their mark on my skin.

I grit my teeth, trying to shake it all away, the dreams I no longer have, the pain I constantly feel. *Focus*, I tell myself. *Focus on where you are and on what lies ahead.*

Najja, the sea calls. Much like the sea did on the day Simi died. Simi, who should be here, not me, much like Mama, who died saving me.

Najja, it sings. I swim deeper underwater to avoid the sun's overbearing rays. When I do, that's when I see them: the near-translucent, shapeless things swirling below me. Spirits. As I near them, I feel their memories popping into my head as if they're my own.

An old man whose daughter died of a disease—without the medicine he could not afford to buy. A girl who forever blamed herself for her mother's death, the mother who died giving birth to her. A soldier who lost his best friend in the Thousand Years' War, the friend who died to save him.

But they are not my memories, they are not me, I am merely on the outside looking in. And from here I can see the truth: terrible, unfortunate things happened to them. Things for which they feel they were to blame, denying themselves the forgiveness they deserved.

Like Mama and me. She was out in the ocean with me, diving for silks, when the hurricane began. She got me to safety atop a boulder when she slipped and hit her head, the waves pulled her under, and she died. The hurricane was too strong, even for us. We both would've died had she not saved me.

Or Simi, who sacrificed herself for me. A decision I, too, would've made in her place.

I have blamed myself, I have cursed at the gods, I have told myself I didn't deserve to live, to be happy, to thrive. But their deaths were not my fault; I couldn't have changed things. I think back to the conversations Leyla and I had, to the many times I told her to be kind to herself, to stop blaming herself for things she didn't do. So why do I still blame myself? Why do I mistreat myself in ways I wouldn't her?

I swim faster, trying to keep the rising voices out my head. I fight against their painful memories. *I am not Simi*, I tell myself. *I will never be her.* And I might never understand my powers in the way Mama did either. But I came here for a reason: to save our world from great danger, to be the yamaja I was raised to be. To save Leyla, who has become the friend I never had. And, if she can forgive me, maybe something more.

As I swim, I count slowly in my head. Calming myself, slowing my heart. I swim through this sea so full of sorrows that every stroke makes me ache. I swim even though my muscles burn, even though they beg me to rest. I swim and swim until I hit the shore, until my fingers touch the sand.

I gasp, coughing up water. When I look up, a towering forest is before me. To my right is a boat. *Leyla's.* I have reached the island of the dead.

CHAPTER FORTY-SIX

Leyla

Nekros

I awake in a cold room, so chilly that bumps appear on my skin and my teeth chatter. Slowly, my vision comes back to me, my eyes adjust to the dark. A story is engraved upon the wall, a continuation of the one I saw as I walked down the hallway, before I saw Thana's tomb and knew at once that I had somehow opened a door that was intended to be forever forgotten.

I'm tied to a large pillar, my hands behind my back just barely touching someone else. I turn my head as much as I can until I make out the person's features, the Zamiri mark on the back of her neck, a spider—the creature their founder, the goddess Lexa, favored so much—and the now-tattered dress she wore when I last saw her as the Reapers swept her away.

"Danai," I say, overcome with relief. But she doesn't move, doesn't say anything. I am too late. I push against the ropes binding me, tied tight around the pillar and across my chest. Ropes restricting my hands as well. With every inch I move, they only tighten more. Finally, I'm able to just barely latch onto her wrist, where I feel her steady heartbeat. I let out a deep sigh. She's merely asleep.

"I'm going to get us out of this," I say.

A booming laugh fills the silence. A woman steps through the dark until she's mere feet away from us. She's been there the entire time, watching and waiting.

"I'd like to know just how you're planning on accomplishing that." Her gown is so dark it's as if it's made of a starless night. She looks at me straight on in a way that unnerves me, that makes me want to scream.

"If you're thinking I'm the goddess of the dead, you're wrong," she says, just as I was drawing that very conclusion. "I killed her." She laughs as if it's nothing to kill a god. "Her spirit's probably around here somewhere. She's been moping about ever since she died."

She steps closer and I catch the glint of my knife that she holds in her right hand. I tense up.

"Why are we here? Why take my best friend and now me? What purpose does this solve? Who even are you?"

In an instant she's before me. She moves so fast I barely saw her leave one spot and appear in another. My eyes widen with realization: she must be a vampire. An ancient one.

"I'm Favre," she says, as if that explains everything. "Some have called me a goddess, some a witch, but most importantly, I'm Thana's wife, and you're going to help me bring her back to life."

I'm still trying to process what I just heard when Favre crouches down in front of me. She plays with the knife in her hand, releasing it and then catching it, toying with me.

As my mind swirls, Favre speaks of her origins. Her life in the Heavenly Realms with Thana and how they actually came to be here. I try to make sense of everything. How much has been erased from our history texts, how many lies have been passed down.

"The gods were content to let Thana come down here. To rule the humans, Kovnu's 'little pets' that Morowa never cared for because he spent more time with them than her. They let her rule unchecked. Only descending when *they* felt threatened—when Thana began to kill those who'd originally sided with her, when *they* feared that she sought to rule *them*, too. And so, a hunting party captured us both and put a spell on Thana's tomb. Only a direct descendant, a queen's blood, can begin to undo it and bring her fully back to life.

"Your mother is dying; her blood is of no use. It had to be you. It doesn't matter what you have and haven't done, where you were and weren't. This is inevitable, my dear." With that, she looks at me, her red eyes stare me down. "You can't escape your fate, princess. It was written long before you were born."

You can't escape your fate. Her words echo throughout me. Is it my fate that I'll die here and so give way to the greatest evil our world has ever known? My fate to bring destruction to our world, just like that yamaja told Mama all those years ago? What's the point in fighting, then, of surviving—if, ultimately, it's all inevitable? Does fate really choose for us without giving us power over our own lives?

Danai shifts behind me, waking up in a panic. She struggles in her ropes. She tries to speak, tries to scream, but her words are muffled.

Forget fate. I have to fight for those I love. If I give up now, what happens to Danai? I might not know how much is real, how much is predetermined, but I do know she's depending on me.

"Please," I say, looking up at Favre. "Let her go."

Favre laughs. "Why should I do that? I intend to take your blood and discard her when I'm done. She is of no use to me." She laughs again but it sounds almost forced. I frown. If she only needs me, then why hasn't she killed me already?

"Fine," I say, on a hunch. "Let's get this over with. Kill me."

Favre's laugh turns into a frown. She silences altogether.

I find myself smiling at the thought. It's not a win, but it's something. "You can't, can you? You need something else." What if Favre never meant to take me, what if she always meant to take Danai, to lure me here? She said the tomb was spelled but if the answer was just that they needed the blood of a direct descendant, that would've been too easy. There must be something more to it. I look up at her—it suddenly makes sense. "You need me to sacrifice myself."

Favre smiles as if proud. "Not just any sacrifice but one to save someone you love. Just as my daughter, a thousand years ago, to save the people she loved so much, gave her own life to bring down their queen."

"Your daughter?" My eyes widen. "But . . . Clea . . ." I think back to what I know: that Clea gave her life to bring down Thana, to save all vampires from their bloodthirsty queen. "If Clea was your daughter, then—"

Favre gives a small shrug. "Then you are also descended from me."

"How could you do this to your own family?"

"Family?" she scoffs. "Family is what you make it, and Thana is the only family I have left. Enough of this," she snaps. "If you want to save your friend, your life is forfeit. After all, that's only fair. You're the reason she's here."

You have no idea what I've done for love. Just as you have no idea what you may one day do. Mama's words ring in my ear. She was right, but not in the way she wanted to be. Danai wouldn't be here if not for me. If not for my inability to let go, my fear at being alone once more, she would've been training with the Merkesh instead of in the capital with me.

It has to be this way. Danai will go free. I ball my hand into a fist, determined that she has to live. But as I do, metal digs into my palm. My ring. My scorpion ring. The one with the poison inside of it. But who is to say if the poison still works, who is to say that this poison from the Deianira plant that can kill a vampire can kill one who is also a fallen angel, a sorceress, and a god?

"Untie her," I say. "Let her go. And you can have it—my blood." A plan brews within me. If this doesn't work, at least Danai will have a fighting chance. She will warn the others.

Favre shrugs as if in agreeance, then claps her hands. "I'll give her a head start." The ropes around Danai's mouth and hands disappear. For a moment, Danai looks as if she wants to attack her, but instead she crouches down beside me. Her anger, her frustration dissipate into sorrow.

"Take this." I press my ring into her hand. "Find the yamaja, her name is Najja. She'll help you get back safely. Show it to Malike and Mama, so they know I found you. Tell them that Thana is coming."

Favre huffs with amusement. "Yes, please tell your little friends. As if warning them will do any good."

I press the ring into Danai's hand again, digging it into her palm. She clenches her hand around mine, then furrows her brows. She opens her hand, looking again at the ring. I lower my voice. "You'll be risking your life, too."

She slips her arms around me. "I wouldn't have it any other way."

"I'm sorry," I say, "for everything. I—"

But she shakes her head. "Later," she says, just like she did in the marketplace before she was taken and everything I knew changed. I tighten my grip around her, hugging her for what may be the last time. If I survive this, I will do better—I'll be a better friend.

Favre pulls Danai off me and shoves her to the ground.

"Go, now," she says. "Or I'll kill you, too."

Danai scrambles up, looking back at me just once before running out of view.

"Any last words?" Favre smiles at me, twirling the knife in her hands.

I shake my head. "None for *you*." I close my eyes, steeling myself for what's to come. When I left the capital, I told myself that Mama would've never made such a mistake—would've never taken this journey to begin with. But now, knowing the full truth, maybe as much as we are different, in some ways we are the same. I think of Najja in that mountain, pleading with me to stay. Maybe what we do—what we'll go through to save those we love— is what matters in the end.

Favre approaches, bending down in front of me. Before I can get in another breath, she plunges the knife into my chest.

CHAPTER FORTY-SEVEN

Najja

Leyla's screams pierce my ears moments after I land upon the island.

"Leyla?" I call. I run toward the shrill sounds, heart racking against my chest. Branches scratch my side, my hand, my face, my legs. I run, following the sound until I reach a clearing in the middle of the woods. Leyla's screams echo around me, but she's nowhere to be found.

Giant trees surround me, their branches arching up high into the sky. Reminding me of how small I am. How powerless I have been to save those I love. Is she even here? Were those screams hers? Or is this wood merely playing tricks on me, making me believe my worst fears?

I fall to the ground. This can't be happening. I am a fool. This is my fault. I should've trusted her in the way she did me. I should've told her earlier the truth. I didn't have to carry that burden alone, I didn't have to work through it by myself. By trying to protect her,

I pushed her away. We could've come here together; we could've made a plan. She'd still be alive.

Stop that, I tell myself. *You don't know if it's too late.*

If Simi were here, she would pray to the gods; when she prayed, they always answered. Mama, she had her ways, too. But I am not them; I never will be.

Nor have I had to be. I reached Leyla on my own, I helped her—we helped each other—make it this far. Maybe I just need to trust myself, the same way Leyla trusted me and Simi did, too.

I look up to the sky, the clouds swirling above. This place is full of the dead. I can feel them everywhere. I think back to the forest in the Wastelands when I made those spirits disappear. To when I spoke to Simi as well. The dead and I have always had an understanding. The only thing stopping me has been myself.

I take a deep breath and I listen. I have to find where Leyla is. Memories begin to surface of every moment I saw something I didn't want to, back to the first times, like when I told my best friend's mother that her daughter would die within a week. When I lost my friends, when they abandoned me, I saw my powers as a curse not a gift. I became afraid of them.

"I am still afraid, but she needs me." I pull myself up and stare right into the woods, into the trees all around me making me feel so very small. "Take me to her."

The wind picks up and whooshes past me. Something unlocks in my soul.

"Please," I whisper. "Where is Leyla? I know that you can hear me."

The wind snaps, and I stumble back. Standing before me is a spirit.

"Who are you?"

She wears a gown of velvet indigo that nearly blends into the dark night.

"My name is Asha," she says. "I was once the goddess of the dead. I know this place and these woods better than most. I can take you to your friend. She doesn't have much time."

CHAPTER FORTY-EIGHT

Leyla

Favre throws my knife aside. My voice is hoarse, nearly gone, from the screams pushing forth from my lungs. Blood gushes from me and onto the ground, flowing directly into the tomb. The tomb where Thana lies not dead but merely sleeping. All this time.

"Don't take it personally," she says. "It's not."

A shadow slinks in behind her, sneaking up as she's occupied with me. "This isn't either," yells Danai. She jumps onto Favre, piercing her neck with my ring, its sharp edges dig into her to release its poison. Favre falls to the ground, shaking.

Danai rushes toward me. "Watch out!" I croak.

Favre hits Danai off me with a strong backhand and swings her to the side. She grins as she hovers over me, teeth rattling, body heaving from the poison's spread. She places a foot on my stomach and presses down as blood gurgles up from my stomach and out of my mouth. "Nice try," she says. Then she shoves me into a corner.

Danai yanks her away from me. Favre raises her hands to her

neck, as if choking, then coughs up blood. She stumbles toward the tomb—slamming against it. The top cracks and falls away. The ground beneath us violently trembles, as if something was triggered and the house is now destroying itself.

CHAPTER FORTY-NINE

Najja

Asha leads me into a house in the woods, up a winding staircase, and down a hallway with floating hands—until we reach a door at the end of the hall that's wide open. All the while I hear Leyla's screams urging me to save her.

I rush down the darkened corridor, down the eroded steps, until I reach a room with a single tomb.

A young woman who must be Danai is fending off another woman. The woman falls, writhing, onto the floor. But Leyla is not there.

I search all over for her, then find her in a dark corner. It's just as it was in my vision. Her hands clutch her stomach, and she's bleeding out onto the floor. Her blood flows into the passageways carved into the ground that lead into what must be Thana's tomb.

No. I run to her. There must still be time.

I fall to the ground, kneeling before her. "Leyla," I yell. "Leyla," I say again.

Danai rushes over and places her head on Leyla's chest. "Her heartbeat's faint, but she's still alive." Her voice sighs with relief.

I start to scoop Leyla up, to carry her out of here. But she cries out in agony and so I stop.

"She's lost too much blood," says Danai. "She needs to feed first, so she can heal."

Just then, the ground shakes. Dust from the ceiling falls onto our heads. Asha appears right next to Danai. "You need to go," she says to me. "Entering this tomb must've set off something, the entire house is sinking to the ground."

Just then, the roof above the entryway crashes down, blocking the way out. Danai and I share a look, filled with dread.

"Don't worry," Asha quickly says. "I've found another way."

"Take her." I motion to Danai. "Get her to safety."

"Who are you talking to?" says Danai, and I realize she can't see her.

"I'm not leaving Leyla," Danai says, after I explain.

"You're just as stubborn as her," I mutter. Danai crosses her arms, glaring down at me. I say the one thing that might convince her to leave behind her friend.

"She came all this way to save you," I say, as I pull Leyla into my lap. "If you don't survive, and she does, regardless of it being your choice to stay, she'll blame herself."

She closes her eyes as if considering my words and, when she opens them, they're watery with tears.

"You will save her?" she asks, hesitating.

I meet her eyes and nod. "If it's the last thing I do."

Asha leads the way, her spirit stirring up dust for Danai to follow. Danai's footsteps echo as she exits, leaving me, the dying woman Danai attacked, and the princess behind.

I pull Leyla onto my lap. Her heartbeat is even fainter now. I sweep my locs to the side, baring my neck.

"Drink." I guide her mouth to my neck, to the veins pulsing there. But she doesn't move.

Tears well in my eyes as the ground shakes and more cracks appear in the walls. "Please, princess," I whisper. I squeeze her hand.

But just as I do, I feel her. Cold lips graze my skin. She sucks at my neck, caressing one spot. Then her fangs break through and pierce into my vein.

I cry out, the pain intense, but soon it dissipates. Leaving me with a warmth spreading all over me, warmth that sets my nerves ablaze.

As she drinks, she shifts ever so slightly atop me. She grinds into my lap, shooting pleasure through my body.

I exhale as the warmth builds and I lose myself in the sensation. I feel everything, her hunger, her will to live, and her desire. Her heartbeat quickens and syncs in time with mine.

Leyla

As I feed, I take Najja in. Her hand ever so softly cradling my head. Her skin that burns with warmth, warmth that quickly fills me. Her skin that as I licked, tasted of salt from the sea she swam to rescue me.

My body melts beneath her touch, beneath the hands that cup me, that I wish were exploring my body once more, like they did just a few nights ago under the stars. Once again, we are together in the darkness. Our bodies warming each other to our cores.

Can these feelings about her that continue to burn within me survive—can they thrive in the light? Feelings that after all this, I know she must share.

"Leyla," she calls to me. Her voice, aching and wanting, sends shivers down my spine.

I answer her by leaning into her, trying to close any gap between us. So that even if she moves her hands, her warmth never will.

As I feed, my wound begins to heal. As I feed, I feel her pleasure build from within.

She shudders beneath me, and I pull back, nipping at her collarbone and then kissing her neck wound so that it, too, will heal.

As the island rumbles, as the pillars fall, she scoops me into her arms and carries me out of here. And though I do not know what's to come next. I know that I am with her, safe in her arms.

CHAPTER FIFTY

Favre

As the house crumbles and the island falls, I push myself up from the stone floor beside Thana's tomb. "A gift to you, my love."

The princess's blood travels into the tomb as the ring's poison flows through my neck, paralyzing me and constricting my veins.

The greatest power requires the greatest sacrifice. Like Mother, I gave and gave. Maybe Thana was no different from those men—using the promise of love, instead of violence, to get what she wanted until there was nothing left to give.

My wings, for passage down to earth. A place I never wanted to live.

My child, to assuage Thana's fears. A daughter that might've made me laugh and smile.

Finally, my life, for Thana's. A life full of dreams I barely got to live, dreams I'll never get to see carried out.

"Once upon a time," I whisper, my voice raspy, as I recall how

Mother used to begin her tales. "Once upon a time there was a little girl who loved happily ever afters." My chest constricts as I inhale my last breath.

"Life is nothing like those tales."

EPILOGUE

Leyla

The Sea of Sorrows

I wake lying in the hull of the boat that brought me to Nekros. Najja rows, and Danai's beside me. I let out a sigh of relief.

"You're awake." Danai pulls me in to a hug. Her eyes are already watery. "I don't know what to say. You came all this way for me."

I pull her closer to me, hugging her deep as tears prickle my eyes. "You are the best friend I ever could've asked for—you are like a sister to me. I'd do it again, no hesitation. There is nothing you need to say."

"And I'd be by your side." Najja turns around and flashes me a smile so bright, I'm instantly warmed.

I look up to the sky, to the stars above, and whisper to them my thanks. For getting me here, for saving my friend, for saving me, for having us all together safe and sound.

Tears stream down my face; relief washes over me.

A strong gust of wind blows, knocking me to the side ever so slightly. The hairs on my neck stand up. Slowly, I turn around.

The island we left is in the distance.

Leyla.

A voice calls.

Ancient. Powerful. Hungry.

To my beloved:

I have just returned from the Isle of Nekros. I am hesitant to call us victorious.

We are to say that Clea, Thana's daughter, perished there, that she valiantly died killing her mother. When, in truth, she gave her life for a spell created by Lexa. Yes, the same fallen goddess who betrayed Thana and secretly raised Clea came to our aid. It is a spell that can only be reversed with the blood of a queen descended from Clea and thus Thana.

And so, people shall be told a lie. Until that lie becomes the truth. Passed down through the tales that make up our world.

We could not kill her. We could only trap her there.

My love, I hesitate to say this part, for my words may make it true. But Thana, she is too powerful. I fear she cannot be killed.

Valdis

—FROM THE LETTERS OF VALDIS
CIRCA 200 AD
MERKESH ROYAL ARCHIVES

The Mnaran Royal Family Tree

When Thana left the Heavenly Realms, she established a new era. Which is why we vampires notate time as Before Descent or BD (before she left the Heavenly Realms) and After Descent or AD (when she arrived here, the lands of the living). This family tree does not include royal family members who were humans turned into vampires by blood exchanges.*

KEY

italics = deceased

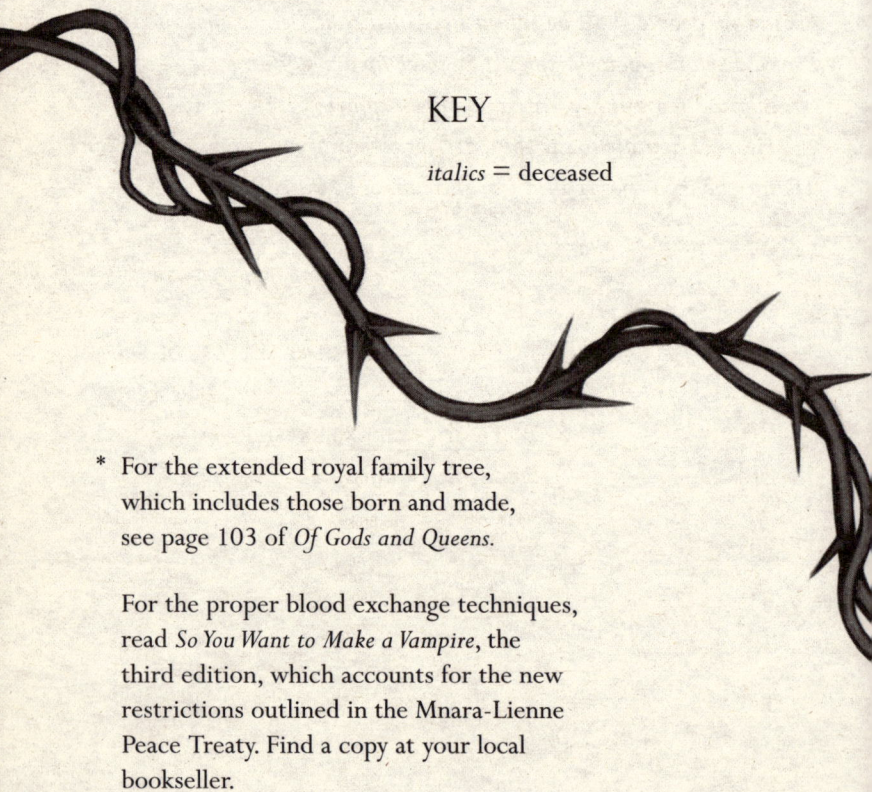

* For the extended royal family tree, which includes those born and made, see page 103 of *Of Gods and Queens*.

For the proper blood exchange techniques, read *So You Want to Make a Vampire*, the third edition, which accounts for the new restrictions outlined in the Mnara-Lienne Peace Treaty. Find a copy at your local bookseller.

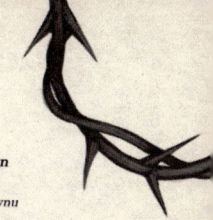

Name Unknown
God of Medicine
Physician to the Gods

Name Unknown
Earth Goddess
Goddess of Rebirth

Name Unknown
Sky God
slain by his son, Kovnu

Suty
God of Deserts, Healer Deity
slain by Thana

Name Unknown
Goddess of Deceit

Kovnu
King of the Gods
God of the Sun and Creation
slain by his daughter, Thana

Morowa
Queen of the Gods
Goddess of Spring and Fertility

Lexa
Goddess of
Strife and Discord

Thana Adaeze
Former Crown Princess of the Gods
Goddess of Night and Childbirth
First Vampire
Founder of the Adaeze Bloodline

Name Unknown
Prince of the Gods
God of the Harvest
and Death

Unknown Lover ── **Clea the Queenslayer**
Leader of the
Adaeze Bloodline
died killing her mother, Thana

Myla Adaeze*
Leader of the Adaeze Bloodline
died in battle
* conceived her daughter, Nandi, by donor

Nandi Adaeze ── **Callum Oorvain**
Leader of the Adaeze Bloodline   Lord Protector of
First Queen of Mnara   the Royal Military

Marii Adaeze
(formely Zamiri)
Queen Consort of Mnara
Eldest Daughter of the
Leader of the Zamiri

Lena Adaeze*
Queen of Mnara
Leader of the Adaeze
Bloodline
*killed by humans in
the Red River Massacre*
** conceived her children
by donor*

Karina Adaeze
The Ruthless
The Broker of Peace
The Lioness of Mnara
Queen of Mnara
Leader of the Adaeze
Bloodline

Raza Adaeze
(formely Merkesh)
King Consort of Mnara
Ambassador to Lienne
*killed by humans in the
Red River Massacre*

Zora Adaeze
Crown Princess of
the Adaeze
*killed by humans in the
Red River Massacre*

Zoran Adaeze
Prince of the Adaeze
*killed by humans in the
Red River Massacre*

Zara Adaeze
Princess of the Adaeze
*killed by humans in the
Red River Massacre*

Leyla Adaeze
Crown Princess
of the Adaeze

Malike Adaeze
Prince
of the Adaeze

The Bloodlines of Mnara

Of the five fallen gods—the gods who descended with Thana from the Heavenly Realms—four, in addition to Thana, created bloodlines that make up our Nation of Mnara. What follows is an account of these bloodlines, their role in our society, founders, current leaders, and how offspring are produced.

ADAEZE

ROLE(S): The Royal Family
FOUNDER: Thana Adaeze, Former Crown Princess of the Gods, Goddess of Night and Childbirth, First Vampire and Queen
LEADER: Queen Karina, the Lioness of Mnara, the Broker of Peace
OFFSPRING: Vampires born and made. All Adaeze are part of the royal family, but only Adaeze born a vampire (i.e. Thana's direct descendants) can birth a vampire through intercourse with another vampire or a donor and lay claim to the throne. All Adaeze, regardless of origin, can turn humans into vampires by blood exchange.

OORVAIN

ROLE(S): Military and Nobles
FOUNDER: Neferain, from a family of war gods, Goddess of the Hunt
LEADER: Lady Calli, Protector of the Royal Military, Member of the Queen's Council
OFFSPRING: When one Oorvain dies, another is born from their ashes.

ZAMIRI

ROLE(S): Nobles and Merchants
FOUNDER: Lexa, Goddess of Discord and Strife
LEADER: Lord Kaimen, Head of the Queen's Council
OFFSPRING: The Zamiri frequently reproduce with humans, and, in this way, they are able to have children. Because these children primarily subsist on human blood, they are vampires—even though many no longer have fangs.

MERKESH

ROLE(S): Scholars and Historians
FOUNDER: Anae, Goddess of Knowledge and the Sea
LEADER: Lord Mazero, Lord Chancellor of the Anaeum (an academy for prospective Merkesh), Member of the Queen's Council
OFFSPRING: Comprised of vampires originally from other bloodlines, who must first study to take the Merkesh test and then, upon acceptance, renounce who they were in order to enroll in the Anaeum.

SINTU

ROLE(S): Merchants, Tradespeople, and Unskilled Workers
FOUNDER: Vzira, Goddess of Beauty and Craftsmanship
LEADER: Lady Runessa, Member of the Queen's Council
OFFSPRING: Blood exchange, by turning a human into a vampire.

—OF GODS AND QUEENS: THE MNARAN ROYAL GENEALOGY
7TH EDITION, 1192 AD
MERKESH ROYAL ARCHIVES

ACKNOWLEDGMENTS

This book started with two images. A Black vampire princess. Snow streaked red with blood. The winter setting you'll see later. But the princess, she stayed and immediately started telling me about herself.

If only writing the book was that easy. It took seven years (and many revisions and rewrites) for this book to become what you have before you. The story I'd always imagined it could be. Of vampires born and made, the humans they've been fighting for centuries, and the gods that created them both. A story about a girl with dreams filled only of death, a princess who fears she'll never be good enough to wear her mother's crown, and a fallen angel who'd do anything for love—even if it costs her life. A story in many ways about the power of love (whether good or destructive) and if it's possible to change your fate. (Want to know the answer? Read Book Two.)

Writing can be a lonely task. Yes, these characters lived rent-free in my head, whispering to me at all hours, but the act of not just writing a novel—as I'd written a few unpublished manuscripts by the time I started *Where Shadows Meet*—but revising it and figuring out what feedback to keep and what to discard in favor of your

story, required so much from me. In many ways, I came into myself while writing this book. I figured out who I wanted to be and, in turn, this story showed me its final form.

To say it took a village is an understatement; all the love and thanks to mine.

First, my parents. I am the reader I am because of them. I grew up with shelves full of books featuring characters who looked like me. During a time in which publishing diverse stories wasn't as widely talked about as it is now, they went out of their way to ensure I knew the legends, myths, and folktales of my people, of Black Americans, of the American south. This gave me a very necessary foundation to become the writer I am now. These stories sparked my imagination and led me to seek out more stories and to, eventually, create worlds of my own. My parents are also the ones who introduced me to my first vampire films (*Blade*, *Underworld*, *Dracula* (1992), *Queen of the Damned*)—and I'm certain they did not expect those movies to have the impact they did, but thank you nevertheless.

Second, my siblings. I'm the oldest of five and for them, much like Leyla did for Danai, her sister of sorts, I'd go to the end of this world and back.

The rest of my family and friends, you of course know who you are. Thank you for talking to everyone, including people at the grocery store, about my first two books, the anthologies I edited—*A Phoenix First Must Burn* and *Eternally Yours*—and constantly asking me when I was finally going to write a novel myself. Especially my writer friends, I don't know if this book would exist without you—thank you so much for your encouragement, love, and support over these years. In particular, Arvin, Sara, and Akshaya for being early readers and Petty Timers because, well, every writer needs a group chat and you are mine <3

My cats... Quinn, Raven, and the newest member of the family (the one who officially made me a cat lady), Lucy. Your antics and cuddles have kept me sane throughout so much.

Finally, Jessica. Thank you for helping me to figure out what was missing from this story and, in many ways, my life. Love. You can forever be my travel princess.

As a former editor turned literary agent and author, I've seen first-hand how those working "behind the scenes" truly make books what they are. I couldn't have done it without my publishing teams, without every one of you who at some stage did something to make this book better and help launch my career.

Special shout-out to Pete Knapp, for being the first in the industry to encourage me to write this story—thank you so much for everything—Hillary for your edits that made this world that much stronger, Sara for selling it, and Paige for helping me believe in myself again.

On the editorial side, special thanks to Carla, this book's acquiring UK editor, and Ella, who came onboard after it was sold and whose enthusiasm—as well as compassion as life was lifing—has meant so much over the years. And finally, Vicki and Vanessa. Thank you for everything. The time I needed to make this book even stronger. For asking questions like, why are your vampires afraid of sun... questions that made this world even more unique. And for telling me it needed more romance. You were of course right.

To my readers, whether you've been with me since *A Phoenix First Must Burn* or this is your first purchase of mine, thanks to you I get to do what I love. Also, about the ending to this book, I promise to make it up to you and give you a happy ending to the series . . . well, depending on how you define that ;)

Finally, to my younger self. My twenties were . . . well, as you know, they were an . . . adventure. I used to wonder if I'd ever make you proud, if I'd ever overcome . . . well, you know. I don't wonder that anymore. You would've loved this book. You'd be so proud of me, the woman I've become. I'm so proud of us. Here's to many more stories, especially vampire ones. Thank you for always waiting until you finished the next book in a series. Thank you for fighting for us, for believing in us. Thank you for never giving up <3

Thank you for choosing a Hot Key book!

For all the latest bookish news, freebies and exclusive content, sign up to the Hot Key newsletter – scan the QR code or visit lnk.to/HotKeyBooks

Follow us on social media:

bonnierbooks.co.uk/HotKeyBooks